No One's Bride

Scandal Sheet Survivors
Book 4

ADELE CLEE

No One's Bride
Copyright © 2023 Adele Clee
All rights reserved.
ISBN-13: 978-1-915354-30-3

Cover by Dar Albert at Wicked Smart Designs

Chapter One

Chadwick's Auction House
Broad Street, Bloomsbury

Miss Ailsa MacTavish stood before the vast oak doors as if expecting to see an ancient Roman god standing guard. Janus was the keeper of keys, custodian of the metaphorical gateway between the present and the future. A symbol of beginnings and ends. His image was that of two faces. One gazing into the past. One staring towards one's destiny.

Change was on the horizon.

Ailsa felt it deep in the marrow of her bones.

Whatever happened behind these doors today would likely see the end of a friendship, albeit a strained and somewhat antagonistic one. Lord Denton meant to win the rare copy of Thomas More's *Utopia* and didn't care who he trampled over in the process.

A love of old books was the only thing they had in common, and perhaps a steely determination to succeed.

Indeed, while her parents had returned to the Highlands, Ailsa had remained in London for one purpose: to purchase *Utopia* for her private collection.

Like her Scottish forbears, she would need to hold steadfast against an English invasion. Few men tolerated a woman reading, let alone owning such a valuable antiquity.

Inhaling deeply to bolster her courage, Ailsa turned to her chaperones, Mr and Mrs Daventry. "We have five minutes until the auction begins. Hopefully, the men have taken their seats and I can sneak in unnoticed."

It shouldn't be difficult.

After a terrifying incident at her come-out ball five years ago, blending into the background had become an acquired skill.

"At least we know there'll be one man amongst them who will offer you a seat," Mrs Daventry said, the frustration of many browbeaten women evident in her tone. "They will answer to me if they attempt to throw you out."

Ailsa smiled to herself. When a lady had married the most intelligent, most dangerous man in London, she could afford to be bold.

"I dinnae care if they give me the cut direct as long as they permit me to bid on the book." Being a Scot and a spinster, insults rolled off her like rain on a new umbrella.

"I registered your name personally," Mr Daventry said, confident she would not encounter a problem. "Mr Murden raised no objection and is expecting you to place a bid."

He gestured for them to mount the stone steps and held the heavy door open before following them inside. With dark wood panels and paintings of dour men lining the walls, the large hallway was an inherently masculine space that smelled of musty coats, stale sweat and cheap cologne.

Ailsa could barely feel her legs as she climbed the stone

staircase to the first floor. Her heartbeat thumped loudly in her ears. Entering a room full of grouchy men was difficult enough. Knowing Lord Denton sat amongst them added to the growing tension.

The door hinges creaked as she entered. One man turned in her direction, the lively hum of conversation dying when thirty others followed suit.

The air proved stifling.

The groans and grumbles were audible.

"Doubtless she's suffering from a megrim and has lost her way," said a thickset gentleman with bushy white hair. "Someone should see her out before she swoons and delays the auction."

"It's the MacTavish chit," a well-groomed man sneered. "She bid on Lady Ingram's diary last month before Denton won the memoir."

"They'll not let the Scots own More's *Utopia*. It would be tantamount to treason. The devils will probably use it for kindling."

The exuberant Mrs Daventry placed a reassuring hand on Ailsa's arm. "Don't let them intimidate you. I met my husband at an auction and had to battle against the *ton*'s contempt. So you see, Miss MacTavish, we are similar in many ways."

Hardly. The lady's vibrant red curls enhanced her womanly appeal. Ailsa had fastened her copper locks in a tight knot hidden beneath a simple poke bonnet.

Mr Daventry met the gaze of the studious gentleman behind the lectern and gave a curt nod. "Find a seat, Miss MacTavish. We'll wait outside until the auction is over. Mr Murden won't tolerate distractions."

"What?" she whispered. "Ye're leaving?"

"We'll be within earshot," Mr Daventry assured her.

Mr Murden cleared his throat and peered at her through crooked spectacles. "Come forward, Miss MacTavish. Time is against us. We must begin the proceedings posthaste."

The Daventrys slipped out of the room, leaving Ailsa alone in the viper pit. With tentative steps, she approached the aisle separating the rows of crowded benches. The men spread out, making it clear there wasn't a spare seat in the house.

She spotted Viscount Denton sitting at the end of a row. The handsome lord met her gaze, tutted and raised his blue eyes heavenward. She would rather sit on the dusty parquet floor than beg for his assistance.

Tension cut through the air.

Tears threatened to fall, but she would not give these mean men the satisfaction of seeing her cry.

Ailsa raised her chin. "I shall stand, Mr Murden. I need only raise my hand to bid, and the auction should be over quickly."

Lord Denton muttered what sounded like an expletive and stood abruptly, straightening to a height of over six feet. "There's room for you here, Miss MacTavish." He must have sensed her resistance. One should not mistake his golden locks for a halo. "As you say, I doubt we'll be here long."

Since winning the Tudor lady's diary, since stealing it from under her nose, Ailsa had spent sleepless nights cursing him to the devil. The man had no interest in a woman's social plight from a bygone era and had bought the book out of spite.

Still, they were friends of a sort, and her knees would likely buckle once the bidding started. It would only antagonise him more if she refused, and this was hardly the place for a verbal spar.

"I thank ye for the kind gesture, my lord."

"Unlike some men, I've not forgotten my manners," he said, glaring at the fools seated behind him. He stepped into the aisle and motioned to the sturdy oak bench.

Ailsa leaned closer and whispered, "I would prefer to sit at the end of the row, my lord." She would not sit beside the gruff fellow who looked ready to bind her hands and prevent her from bidding.

Lord Denton bent his head, the smell of sandalwood cologne encompassing her. "Being so tall, I need to stretch my legs, madam." He lowered his voice and fixed her with a stony expression. "You're my main competitor. Be grateful I've not tossed you over my shoulder and deposited you in the broom cupboard."

She eyed him narrowly. "I'll warn ye to keep yer hands off my person, else I might stab ye with a hat pin."

"Do you want to sit down or not?" he said bluntly. "Perhaps you should leave. I'm confident you've had a wasted journey. Nothing will prevent me from winning that book today."

Oh, the man was beyond obstinate.

"Never underestimate a Scot." Ailsa possessed her father's stubbornness and was by no means afraid of this man. "Nothing would give me greater pleasure than wiping that smirk off yer face."

Aware they were the object of everyone's attention, Lord Denton conceded. "In a bid to ease your impending disappointment, Miss MacTavish, I shall let you take my seat."

Her heart leapt at the minor victory.

Until she sat down and realised the lord had no option but to sit at an odd angle. His knee touched hers, the sudden contact sending a jolt of awareness from her neck to her navel.

Lord Denton hissed a breath, his annoyance evident.

5

Eager to avoid further delays, Mr Murden demanded silence while he called the first lot. "Here we have an early eighteenth-century copy of Alexander Niccholes' self-help manual *The Discourse of Marriage and Wiving*. Who will start the bidding at fifty pounds?"

A man in the front row raised a wooden paddle.

Another hand shot up.

Lord Denton remained rigid in his seat.

"Are ye nae interested in seeking help to find a wife, my lord?" she mocked. The mere mention of wives and marriage usually brought the lord out in hives.

"I made a blood oath not to marry until I'm fifty," he uttered.

"One ye made with Mr St Clair, yet he married yer sister months ago." After secretly loving Helen for years, it came as no surprise when Nicholas St Clair broke his oath. "I'm told ladies are scrambling to be the diamond that makes ye break yer vow."

The man was an insufferable grouch, but even Ailsa could see he oozed an inherent masculinity that drew women in droves.

The lord tutted. "Then they'll have a twenty-year wait. And I came here to purchase a book, not discuss my personal affairs."

"Ye came to bid on a book," she corrected. She would sell her soul to the devil to prevent him from beating her again. "There's nae guarantee ye'll win."

He inhaled deeply before casting her a sidelong glance. "You're wearing perfume. Spirit of Luna. I recognise the floral notes. Interesting. I did not take you for a hypocrite."

Only two months ago, she had chided him for wearing an excessive amount of cologne. "I havenae changed my opinion. One's true mate is drawn to one's natural aroma.

But I hoped the cloying smell might choke my competition."

His piercing cobalt gaze drifted over her face. "Or maybe you're tired of looking like a spinster and seek to make a match while your parents are out of town."

An unladylike snort escaped her, drawing many a disapproving eye. Ailsa bent her head and lowered her voice. "I'd wager every book I own ye'll marry before I do."

He arched a curious brow. "You would?"

Drat! The words had left her lips without thought.

Pride persuaded her there was nothing to fear. Despite her father's insistence she find a husband, she had no desire to surrender her independence.

"Aye, if ye're willing to do the same."

"That's hardly fair. I have to marry eventually."

Ailsa smiled. "I understand. Ye're afraid ye'll lose."

"I'm not afraid, madam. I merely point out that the odds are in your favour. Only a fool would make such a wager."

The auctioneer hit the lectern with his gavel, the bang loud enough to wake the dead. "Sold to Mr Peterson for five hundred and thirty pounds. Though a wife will cost him considerably more."

Laughter erupted. A few men shared tales of their wives' lavish spending. The auctioneer flicked through a pile of papers while preparing for the next lot.

Keen to offer Lord Denton terms before the bidding began again, Ailsa said, "Shall we set the bar at ten years? Whoever marries first within that time frame must surrender their entire collection. Would ye consider that fair, my lord?"

The gentleman's mouth formed an arrogant grin. "As a man of my word, one keen to keep his oath, I'm willing to commit to ten years."

A frisson of panic coursed through her. Beneath Lord

Denton's fine coat was a spine of steel. His middle name should be Determination. Still, she held her resolve. If anything, the wager would be a shackle around her neck, a means of forcing her to follow her dreams and resist the pressure to marry.

"There must be one stipulation," the lord said. "Should we find ourselves victims of schemers and become honour-bound to marry, the wager would become void."

While Mr Murden presented a copy of *Fables* by Mr Gray, Ailsa considered the possibility of being duped by a rogue again. After the hurtful incident with Mr Ashbury five years ago, she took every care to present herself as plain and dull. One misstep and she might easily face ruin.

"Aye, if there's proof of villainy."

Lord Denton grinned like his horse had won the Derby. He offered his bare hand. "One shake and the oath stands."

Ailsa glanced down—and hesitated.

For no sensible reason, her breath caught in her throat.

The man wished to seal their bargain, yet there was something captivating about his broad palm and long fingers. Like most English lords, his manicured nails conveyed wealth and elegance. Bronzed skin and bulging veins spoke of a strong, muscular body to accompany an equally resilient mind.

Would his touch be as firm as his opinions?

Or was he gentle when holding a woman in his arms?

Good Lord! Why would she even care?

"Well?" he prompted. "Had a change of heart?"

Banishing her wayward thoughts, she slid her palm over his and clasped his hand. "I abide by my oath. I'll nae marry anyone during the term of our wager."

Lord Denton firmed his grip and repeated the vow, his gaze shifting between her gloved hand and her face. A few furrows marred his brow. For a confident man, he appeared strangely troubled.

Was he having second thoughts?

Perhaps the heat radiating from their palms shocked him.

Perhaps an odd tingle chased up his arm, too.

When it seemed like he might never relax his grip, Ailsa snatched back her hand. She stole one more glance at his long fingers before dismissing them from her mind for good.

They fell silent.

Both faced the auctioneer.

Both sat rigid.

Seconds passed, then they happened to look at each other at precisely the same time, both releasing a grumble of annoyance.

Mr Murden smacked the lectern with his gavel again and congratulated Lord Eccles on his purchase. "Next, we have a rather unusual offering dating back to the fifteen hundreds. A grimoire of sorts."

A grimoire?

The term made Ailsa sit bolt upright.

All thoughts turned to her visit to the mystic's tent at the Bartholomew Fair and the crone's cryptic prediction.

You'll marry a man who puts you under an ancient spell.
One found in a tome of old.
It is your fate, your destiny.

Ailsa gulped when the assistant presented the red leather-bound volume. It looked thick and heavy, like it held centuries-old secrets. The gold metal corners were tarnished, perhaps from the spillage of magical potions. Like firm hands, two intricate clasps bound the pages together. A message from an otherworldly force warning the fainthearted not to dabble.

Then the assistant did the most shocking thing possible—he opened the tome and read the first few lines from a love incantation.

Ailsa contemplated jumping to her feet and begging him to stop. But the bidding started at thirty pounds, and the devil closed the book.

Every fibre of her being urged her to raise her hand.

Was it not better to own the grimoire than let it loose amongst the men of the *ton*? Then a shocking thought took hold. What if Lord Denton decided to bid and learnt of a spell to make her subservient?

She thrust her hand in the air, much to the lord's surprise.

"I understood you to be an intelligent woman," he whispered, his strong hands gripping his solid thighs as if trying to stop himself from bidding. "What the devil do you want with a book of fake incantations?"

But Ailsa didn't answer.

A raw-boned gentleman in the front row, dressed from head to toe in black, turned and stared at her with some menace. His sharp, assessing gaze sent an icy shiver skating down her spine. In an emotionless voice, he offered forty pounds, almost defying her to bid against him.

In a room of thirty men, no one dared make a challenge.

Ailsa raised her hand again, though Lord Denton tugged the sleeve of her pelisse and whispered, "You don't want that book. Mark my words. It will bring nothing but trouble."

Despite feeling a little unsettled, she managed a weak smile. "Why? Do ye believe in bad omens and superstitions?" Had he visited the fortune-teller's tent, too?

"Only people of unsound mind delve into the realms of witchcraft." There was an urgency to his tone, a tinge of fear. "Withdraw your interest, madam. Don't make me intervene."

Saints and sinners!

The viscount was obstinate and often exercised his patriarchal dominance but was rarely so rude. He might be used to commanding English women but would not find a Scotswoman so biddable.

Ailsa frowned. "I can do as I please. Ye're nae my father nor my husband." She looked at the auctioneer and gave a curt nod. "I will pay a hundred pounds."

"Strike the lady's offer from the record," the lord shouted.

A few men in the room gasped.

The sinister fellow at the front gave a wolfish grin.

"Denton's right," the rotter behind her mocked. "The woman's head is full of nonsense. Heaven forbid we let her loose with a book of spells."

His minions laughed.

Affronted, Ailsa stood. "Lord Denton is nae my keeper. Unless anyone else cares to bid, the grimoire is mine for a hundred pounds." She would lock the tome in a chest and throw away the key. Then no man could subdue her with a spell.

Mr Murden consulted his papers before surprising them all by saying, "Let me settle this argument by revealing that an anonymous buyer is willing to pay a thousand pounds for the book."

Shocked whispers breezed through the room.

The devil in black looked ready to murder Mr Murden.

Ailsa grew instantly suspicious. She faced Lord Denton. "Are ye the mystery bidder? Is that why ye stopped me raising my offer?"

The viscount jerked his head. "Don't be ridiculous. I'm an educated man. Why would I want a book of drivel?"

"This is what happens when you let a woman attend an auction," said the bigoted oaf behind. "It causes nothing but chaos."

Ailsa swung around and met the tubby man's gaze. "Be quiet, else I might cast a spell and turn ye into a filthy hog. It willnae take much effort."

Lord Denton laughed.

The man rarely smiled, let alone showed signs of mirth.

Mr Murden struck the lectern with his gavel, so hard he would need a carpenter to smooth out the dents. "Silence! The bid stands at one hundred and fifty pounds. Are there any more offers?"

The shady fellow in black stormed from the room, muttering death would likely befall them all.

"Miss MacTavish?" Mr Murden said with a weary sigh. "Do I hear two hundred pounds, or might you sit down so we can continue with the sale?"

As Ailsa didn't have a thousand pounds to waste on a whim, she was forced to concede. Besides, she wasn't sure she wanted to own a book coveted by a man who threatened murder.

"Ye may continue, sir," she said, sitting down.

"This whole thing has turned into a farce," the lord grumbled.

"Aye, one of yer making," she snapped, watching with some trepidation as the assistant packed the grimoire into a small wooden casket. One would think it was a vicious animal desperate to escape.

Mr Murden attempted to settle those in the room by hastening to the next antiquity. "Lot four is the much antici-pated Thomas More's *Utopia*."

Ailsa's heart lurched. Her mind was still hazy after her interaction with Lord Denton. Suspicion flared. Had he meant to set her on edge? Had the handshake and the threats been part of a ploy to unnerve her?

Mr Murden gestured to the leather-bound book held carefully in his assistant's gloved hands. "Here we have a rare seventeenth-century edition of *Utopia*, one of the first printed in English. As one might expect, there's foxing on the pages, but the ...."

"Why do you want the book?" Lord Denton whispered.

Ailsa did not look at him. "Why do ye want the book?"

His silence stretched for a few seconds.

"Because my brother died in search of his utopia." Spoken in the lord's blunt tone, the sentiment carried no emotion. "I mean to donate it to Cambridge as a legacy in his name."

Possessing her mother's kind heart, Ailsa's resolve faltered. It was a touching gesture from someone who was always cold and cynical. Her reasons for wanting the book might seem silly to a man who occupied a powerful place in society.

"More's version of an ideal world is flawed. 'Tis a symbol of an unjust system. In a perfect place, men will nae dominate women. They'd be equals. The book is a reminder of the ongoing fight."

The lord huffed. "You cannot afford to beat my price."

He was probably right. "We shall see."

Five other men wanted More's book. The frantic bids came from all corners of the room. Before Ailsa could catch her breath, the price reached six hundred pounds.

Lord Denton would win again. The wicked glint in his eyes said he meant to own the prized volume. Doubtless, pride was a factor.

"Eight hundred and twenty pounds," he said, the words

like the lash of a whip, punishing the lowly fools who thought to best him.

One by one, his competitors withdrew.

Ailsa made a quick calculation. She could afford an extortionate twelve hundred pounds but questioned whether vengeance was her only motive for wanting the book.

"Well, Miss MacTavish?" Mr Murden prompted.

The room fell deathly silent.

Then the door creaked open, and a colleague waved Mr Murden to the back of the room. The auctioneer's cheeks turned the colour of his burgundy waistcoat.

"You've a moment to consider your next move, Miss MacTavish," he said before giving a bumbling apology and leaving his lectern to attend to the interruption.

"I'll pay two thousand pounds," Lord Denton said with a hint of compassion. "Three thousand if I must. I suggest you withdraw and let us bring this matter to a swift conclusion."

Having heard his reason for wanting this rare edition of *Utopia* and accepting she did not have the funds to win, she conceded.

"Did ye speak the truth? Do ye mean to donate the book in yer brother's memory?" His brother had died years ago after contracting a tropical fever abroad. Surely he wouldn't be so callous as to play to her emotions.

He inhaled sharply. "I have many faults, madam, but I never lie."

Gripping a letter in his hand, Mr Murden returned to his lectern. He shuffled on the spot, his cheeks still flaming. "Erm, forgive me, but the clerk forgot to hand me the written bid. An anonymous collector is also keen to purchase *Utopia*."

Lord Denton shot to his feet. "I shall pay two thousand

pounds. Call proceedings to a close and declare me the lot's winner."

Mr Murden started shaking. "My lord, the collector agrees to pay up to ten thousand to secure the copy."

"Ten thousand?" the lord spat. "This better be a joke, Murden."

Ailsa had never seen the viscount so angry.

To bring an element of calm to the situation, she tugged his coat sleeve. "'Tis more than ten times its worth. Dinnae fret. There will be other copies. I'm told there's a similar edition at a sale in Oxford next month."

A muscle in the lord's jaw twitched. With a murderous glint in his blue eyes, he looked every bit a fallen angel. "I demand to know the name of the bidder."

"The information is c-confidential," Mr Murden stuttered. "If you mean to continue, you must place your next bid, my lord. It currently stands at eight-hundred and seventy pounds."

"This is outrageous. I'll not drive up the price and increase your commission. Know this shoddy approach will leave a stain on your reputation."

"Can we just get on with it?" one person called.

"I've an appointment across town in an hour," another said.

Mr Murden raised his gavel. "This is your last chance, my lord."

Lord Denton cursed under his breath while Ailsa gave a relieved sigh. Feeling the sharp sting of disappointment would serve the viscount well. The man couldn't have everything his own way.

The gavel came crashing down on the lectern.

Ailsa stood, keen to leave the oppressive den and gather

her wits. But then Mr Murden called her name, and the room descended into silence once again.

"We will deliver More's *Utopia* to your father's address in Pall Mall, Miss MacTavish. Expect delivery later today."

Deliver the book to her father's address?

"I beg yer pardon, sir, but ye've made a mistake." Was the man so addled he couldn't recall who'd bid? "The anonymous buyer won the auction."

Lord Denton clenched his fists at his sides. "Isn't it obvious? Your father is the anonymous bidder."

Mr Murden cleared his throat. "That I cannot say. Whoever placed the written bid added a stipulation and wished to gift the book to you, Miss MacTavish. Consequently, you own the rare copy of *Utopia,* madam."

Chapter Two

"Congratulations, Miss MacTavish." While a gentleman might silently seethe, Sebastian let his anger show. "I'm not sure whether to commend you on your devious tactics or berate you for cheating."

Being so sure he would win, he'd had a plaque made in his brother's memory. A shiny tribute to celebrate a life that had ended abruptly. Something so opposed to the cold, empty crypt.

"My lord, I assure ye, this is as much a surprise to me." Miss MacTavish met his gaze, her jade-green eyes softening in a bid to disarm him. "My father made nae mention of bidding on the auction. On my oath, he keeps his purse strings fastened tighter than yer clenched fists."

"Who else would spend a ludicrous sum to ensure you won the book?" He had marked her as intelligent, even interesting in an annoying sort of way, a bluestocking, but never naive.

She frowned and shrugged and gave a convincing performance as someone completely clueless. "Certainly nae my friends. They advised I spend nae more than a few hundred pounds on the tome."

Perhaps they had all whipped together.

Four ladies who wished to test his resolve—including his own damn sister.

Sebastian tried to rein in his temper. Seeing the grimoire had raised a flurry of old doubts and fears, a plague of unwanted memories.

He had sat in the auction room, staring at the wooden casket as the assistant removed the sinister red book, recalling the day he received Michael's belongings from *The Perseus*. Amongst the grooming implements, snuffboxes and mountain of books, he found a small grimoire containing a list of spells and herbal remedies, the pages foxed and well-thumbed.

Had Michael died from a tropical fever?

Or was he consumed by a strange wickedness?

Was he considered a bad omen amongst a superstitious crew?

"Forgive me, my lord." Murden's croaky voice dragged Sebastian from his morbid musings. "I have three more lots to get through today, and beg you to continue this conversation outside."

"Oh, I'm leaving. Even if you produced a copy of Shake-speare's *First Folio*, I would not frequent this house again." This was the third time he had failed his brother. And by God, it would be the last.

Resentment firming every muscle, he stormed past a dumbstruck Miss MacTavish. Instinct said she was not party to the deception. Why would a woman who spoke with such candour deliberately mislead him?

All eyes were upon them.

No doubt the story would appear in tomorrow's *Scandal Sheet*. The writer would ridicule the woman, draw her as a grotesque caricature, a creature from myth. Anything to show her behaviour was not what society expected of a lady.

Sebastian's conscience pricked him, forcing him to pause and face her. "Allow me to escort you to your chaperones, Miss MacTavish. There'll be documents you need to sign."

He expected her to curse him to Hades. The lady's tongue was as sharp as her intellect, but her mouth curled into a weak smile, and she merely nodded.

He didn't offer his arm.

Theirs was an odd friendship.

They sniped at each other, sparred and crossed swords. They tested each other's logic and wit, but they never touched.

Never.

Not until today.

He was still trying to determine what had happened. The merest brush of her hand had made his heart lurch. Perhaps his reaction stemmed from confusion. A lady with firm opinions should not have dainty fingers and a gentle grip. A confirmed bachelor should not consider it his duty to protect her.

The whole thing proved confounding.

The Daventrys were not waiting on the landing.

Before reaching the stairs, Sebastian brought Miss MacTavish to an abrupt halt, the brittle silence forcing him to say, "Might I have a moment of your time?" They often locked horns but never chastised each other publicly. "I spoke out of turn earlier."

"I swear, I knew nothing about the written bid," she said.

Sebastian focused on the only logical explanation. "Perhaps your father failed to mention it because he knew you would object. I know you like to think of yourself as independent, but—"

"It's nae my father's doing. Now my friends are married he wants me to abandon my hobby and focus on finding a husband."

Based on their wager, Lord MacTavish had a long wait.

Based on her outspoken manner, it would take ten years to find a man willing to tolerate such strong views.

The lady leaned closer. "That's the only reason he agreed to let me remain in London. He doesnae care about books but thinks I have a better chance of making a match here. 'Tis why yer sister agreed to play escort, why the Daventrys accompanied me today."

Knowing they battled like bears over a scrap of meat, Helen had quickly informed him Miss MacTavish would be their companion at Lady Winfield's ball.

"Your benefactor will make himself known at some point." He sighed to release a wave of disappointment. "I would rather you have More's *Utopia* than see it go to a buffoon who lacks a basic knowledge of the text."

She jerked in surprise.

They never exchanged compliments.

Seeing the grimoire had muddled his mind.

Evidently, the same spell had taken control of her senses because she said, "If it means that much to you, you may have the book."

Sebastian froze.

The kind gesture threw him off kilter.

"Have it? Have More's *Utopia*?" He braced himself while battling a storm of emotions. Perhaps he'd nodded off during the auction, and this was all an absurd dream.

Miss MacTavish frowned. "What's wrong? Ye look like ye've missed the last rowboat to Skye and been forced to make camp on the shore."

He was floundering and needed to find safe ground.

"Madam, I pride myself on being a fair man. I don't steal sticks from children, and I don't browbeat women into submission."

Relief coursed through him upon witnessing a flash of thunder in her eyes. "Trust me. I've my own mind. Ye couldnae bend me to yer will nae matter how hard ye tried."

No, and he wondered if that's why he liked her.

He was safe with Miss MacTavish.

They could argue, debate most subjects and she wanted nothing in return. Not his wealth or title. Not his undivided attention. Not to writhe rampantly in bed.

Still, suspicion flared.

"What would you want in return? Not marriage, surely?"

In marrying him, she would please her father and get to keep her precious books. Is that why she had been so keen to make the wager?

Miss MacTavish laughed. "Marriage? Good heavens! We'd kill each other within a week. And dinnae take this as an insult, but I'd need a passionate man. One who lights an inner fire, nae one who gives me cold shivers."

Cold shivers?

So, she hadn't felt a sudden burst of warmth when they touched.

Offended, it was Sebastian's turn to scoff. "Trust me. If I so desired, I could heat your blood. You wouldn't want to kill me, Miss MacTavish. Within a week, you'd beg me to bed you thoroughly."

"Thoroughly? Is there any other way to bed a woman?" She narrowed her gaze as if struggling to picture the scene. "Besides, I doubt ye could raise the enthusiasm."

Had he been willing to prove his point, he might have openly assessed her figure. Her breasts were more than ample, and he had caught the dainty turn of her ankles when she'd taught Helen a Highland reel. Her lips were plump and ripe for the taking. Heaven knows what her hair looked like when it wasn't scraped back in a severe knot. He might find the notion intriguing if he was of a mind to bed her.

"You're probably right." He smiled as he recalled her comment about a male penguin giving his mate a perfect pebble. He'd be damned if he'd scour the foreshore searching for the prettiest stone. "Lust is an important factor when seeking pleasure, and we're barely civil."

Why was that?

He had a good relationship with Helen's other friends.

"Exactly my point," she quickly agreed. "Talking is as important as kissing when two people decide to indulge their whims."

"I disagree." Sebastian wondered how she'd come to that conclusion. His mind turned to Lissette, a widow whose company he kept periodically. She spoke. He never listened. Rarely contributed to the tedious conversation.

"As I've nae desire to prove ye wrong, let's return to the matter of Thomas More's book. Once I've discovered the identity of my secret benefactor, I shall seek permission to swap it for Mrs Ingram's diary. I cannae see what ye'd want with the musings of a Tudor housewife."

"Ah, you want to make a trade."

He should have known she had an ulterior motive.

The niceties were a facade.

"Aye, it seems like the perfect solution."

They might have agreed terms had the effervescent Mrs Daventry not called to them as she climbed the stairs. "There you are. Which one of you won the rare copy of *Utopia*?"

Annoyed at the intrusion, Sebastian grumbled silently to himself. He wished to continue his private conversation but could not be rude. "I shall let Miss MacTavish explain."

The lady did not mention the grimoire and spoke only of the written bid placed by an anonymous benefactor. "Lord Denton believes my father may be responsible."

"Who else would part with such an extortionate sum to make a woman happy?" Only someone who cared for her well-being. But then another thought struck him. Did Miss MacTavish have a secret admirer? And if so, why did the idea prove vexing?

"I agree one cannot put a price on love," Mrs Daventry mused, "but Lord MacTavish believes books are the reason his daughter remains unwed."

A blush touched Miss MacTavish's cheeks. "I remain unwed by choice. Men want to own women like they do horses."

Yes, to keep a tight grip on the reins and ride them at their pleasure, though he doubted Miss MacTavish had considered the latter.

"Not all men." With tenderness in her gaze, Mrs Daventry glanced at her husband as he mounted the stairs. "Strong men see marriage as a partnership."

Daventry came to stand beside his wife. "Well, you've not murdered each other. That's a good sign. Though you both appear deflated."

Sebastian had no choice but to repeat the damn story again. "I can understand a private collector paying over the odds, but I'd like to know who gifted the copy to Miss MacTavish."

Daventry shrugged. "In the scheme of problems, it's hardly important. There'll be other copies for sale."

No, winning the auction was not as important as catching thieves and murderers, but when a man felt like he'd failed his kin, he'd shed blood to restore the balance.

Miss MacTavish understood. "Unless ye've walked in a person's shoes, ye cannae judge what's important, sir."

Daventry held up his hands in mock surrender. "Has the wind changed? It almost sounds like you're defending Denton."

Everyone knew Sebastian riled her temper.

That he made a habit of sounding like an arrogant arse.

Miss MacTavish's assessing gaze drifted over Sebastian's face. Like the natural world, her intelligent green eyes reflected an independent spirit. "Let's just say I understand his reason for wanting the book."

Sebastian forced a smile. He should not have mentioned his brother. "Come tomorrow, I expect we'll be snapping and snarling at each other like frustrated terriers."

Anger was his permanent companion.

Like a comfortable coat, he felt naked and cold without it.

Indeed, the need to leave the auction house and put some distance between himself and the Scotswoman led him to bring the conversation to a swift end.

"Well, I have a pressing appointment across town and shall leave you to deal with matters here." Perhaps he would visit Lissette, though the thought left him equally flaccid. Indeed, it was time to sever all ties.

"Once I've discovered the identity of the mystery bidder, I shall contact ye about making the exchange. Assuming ye're willing to trade the lady's diary."

"I'll give the matter some thought," he said, aware the Daventrys were watching them with curious fascination. "And we can discuss it on Friday when we attend Lady Winfield's ball."

She merely nodded, yet he wanted her to berate him. To strip the shirt from his back and whip him with her sharp tongue.

Bantering with Miss MacTavish helped to chase away the ghosts.

These polite exchanges left him unsettled.

So unsettled, unease slithered across his shoulders as he left the auction house and stepped out on Broad Street. He stood still for a moment, settling into his armour. This damn restlessness had nothing to do with losing the book and everything to do with a comment made by Miss MacTavish.

I'd need a passionate man, and you give me cold shivers.

He should be relieved she had no romantic interest in him.

And he was. The thought of bedding the termagant was preposterous.

Still, masculine pride left him desperate to prove a point.

It's the grimoire! his inner voice warned.

Since seeing the ancient spell book, his world had shifted. Miss MacTavish had shown her caring side, and there'd been that strange energy buzzing between them. A sensual hum in the air.

Hellfire!

He had offered her a grovelling apology for his rudeness.

Was that not evidence the stars were misaligned?

Thank heavens the grimoire remained in the casket, destined for some other crazed fool. Thank heavens he'd never have to gaze upon the book again, else he might be compelled to show the lady he could rouse more than cold shivers.

"A little dog would be the perfect companion." In the candlelit bedchamber, Lissette sat at her dressing table, brushing out her golden hair, staring at Sebastian through the looking glass. "Something small, like a pug or a fluffy white Pomeranian."

Doubtless the animal would yap endlessly.

Much like its mistress.

Lissette's lips made a perfect pout, and her tone turned childlike. "I would be his mama and buy him a pretty cradle with silk hangings so he might sleep next to the bed."

On the scale of boring conversations, this one topped the list, along with talk of Miss Turford's bunion and the maid's hacking cough.

"I failed to purchase More's *Utopia* at auction today," he said before his voice seized from lack of use. He omitted to mention he'd been cheated out of winning the rare tome.

"Never mind. There'll be other paintings."

"It's not a painting. It's a book about a fictional society."

Miss MacTavish would press him for a detailed explanation before questioning his ideas. Lissette said, "Perhaps it's a good thing. It sounds rather dull."

Not as dull as watching this woman admire her reflection.

Fully clothed, he sat on the end of the bed, wondering what Lissette would look like with her hair scraped back in a severe knot and minus the rouge. Then he pictured Miss MacTavish sitting there, her red hair like a wild burst of flames, her eyes bright, wearing that sheer silk negligee, not a tartan day dress.

For the first time since walking through Lissette's door, he felt a warm stirring in his loins. A flicker of desire for a woman who'd give him fifty lashes with her tongue if she knew his current train of thought.

Damnation!

That blasted spell book had wrought havoc with his senses.

He was having visions, conjuring imagined scenarios.

Is this what happened to Michael? Like an addict in an opium den, had he lost all grasp of reality? Had he thrown himself overboard, and that's why there was no body to bury?

For fear of contamination, we had to have a sea burial.

"Are you not undressing?" Lissette shot him a questioning glance through the looking glass.

When had she ever stared deeply into his eyes?

As many times as she lost her temper. Not once.

"I came merely to talk." Perhaps Miss MacTavish was right, and talking made kissing better.

Her nose wrinkled. "Talk? Whatever for?"

He laughed to himself, all illusions slipping away to reveal the bare bones of this meaningless relationship. As if to prove he was wasting his time here, Miss MacTavish's bewitching words drifted into his mind again.

If it means that much to you, you may have the book.

Without doubt, it was the kindest thing anyone had said to him.

He was at a loss to know why she cared.

Maybe she didn't care and merely viewed it as an opportunity to own the Tudor diary. Either way, their verbal tussles hardened his cock more than anything that happened beneath Lissette's bedsheets.

Sebastian stood and straightened his coat.

"You're not leaving?" Lissette's voice grated like grinding metal. "You've been here half an hour, and it's only ten o'clock."

He shrugged. "There's no easy way to say this. We're unsuited, and we've both grown tired of using each other." And he would not bed one woman while thinking about another. Not that he wanted to think about frolicking with Miss MacTavish. "You need someone who visits more frequently."

And he needed to find a different pursuit.

A new venture to occupy his time.

One that did not involve annoying women.

"Yes." Lissette's sad sigh sounded hollow. "Often, you're like an empty shell. It's like you're lost in the wilderness far from home."

Unable to argue, he took a few seconds to study Lissette's silky skin and pouting lips, yet it did nothing to spark a fire in his blood.

"I need someone who's excited to see me," said the woman who had no interest in talking. "Not someone who mopes like they're at a funeral. You're miserable most of the time."

Perhaps because he spent sleepless nights consumed with morbid thoughts. Because his life was one long funeral while he waited in limbo for a body that had never arrived.

He closed the gap between them, placed his hand on Lissette's shoulder and met her gaze through the looking glass. "You deserve better."

Lissette patted his hand as if keen to be rid of him. "And you need to find a way to enjoy life instead of being constantly in the doldrums. When did you last laugh at something amusing?"

The answer came amid a vision of wild green eyes and fiery locks. One involving Miss MacTavish threatening to turn Sir Henry into a filthy hog. Only last week, Sebastian's reserve had crumbled when she accused him of padding the shoulders of his frock coat to look more manly. Though that had been more a snort than a chuckle.

He bid Lissette farewell, left the house and marched along King Street to where his coachman had parked the carriage.

Jenkins appeared shocked to see him and was likely annoyed he would miss his nap. "Where to, milord?"

Sebastian glanced at his palm. Touching Lissette was akin to touching cold marble. He'd not felt the sudden surge of excitement. Had not experienced the warm tingling racing up his arm. There had been no need to prolong the time spent in her company. No regrets about leaving, only relief.

"Home." Sebastian hesitated. "But take a detour via Pall Mall." Miss MacTavish lived a stone's throw from King Street. "Drive slowly and stop near Schomberg House. I mean to ensure all is well at the MacTavish household."

He should be relieved he had ended things with Lissette. So why was every muscle tense? Why was his withered heart gripped by a strange foreboding? Why was he keen to sit alone in a dark carriage, hoping to glimpse the most annoying woman in London?

Chapter Three

"I'll need you to sign the note, miss. To confirm you've received the casket." The young man from Chadwick's handed the ebony box to Monroe, Ailsa's butler, and scrubbed his hand over his unkempt side whiskers. "If it weren't so cold, you might want to open it and check the contents. Make sure there's no damage done."

What could happen to a book in transit?

"That willnae be necessary." It was ten o'clock, and he seemed in a hurry. Having grown tired of waiting, she had instructed Monroe to lock the doors and go to bed. Stifling a yawn, she signed the note and gave the delivery man a crown for his trouble. "Best be on yer way before the fog settles."

He doffed his hat. "Thank you kindly, ma'am."

As he left, something made Ailsa poke her head around the jamb and glance out onto the dimly lit street. Through the haze of white mist, she expected to see a cart, the Chadwick name emblazoned on the side. But the fellow climbed into a waiting hackney, and the vehicle charged off into the night.

There should be nothing odd about that, yet receiving the stranger's gift had the hairs on her nape prickling to attention.

"Place it on my father's desk." Ailsa motioned to the study. "Then ye may lock the doors and retire for the evening. And take a dram of brandy. There's a chill in the air tonight, and I dinnae want yer bad chest getting worse."

Monroe carried the small box as if it were filled with lead. He shuffled his feet, the walk to the study leaving him breathless.

"Ye'll stay in bed tomorrow."

"Ma'am, I cannot—"

"'Tis an order, nae a request."

Gratitude filled the man's tired eyes. He left the box in the middle of the uncluttered desk, bowed and plodded away to lock the front door.

Amid the dark confines of the masculine room, Ailsa stared at the package, unsure why her heart pounded loud like a death knell. All she need do was lift the lid and examine the old volume. Perhaps when her father wrote to confirm he was the mystery bidder she would not feel so ill at ease.

"Good night, ma'am." Monroe coughed as he passed the door.

"Good night."

Don't leave me alone.

The words shot into her mind. A warning from somewhere deep in her soul, though there was nothing to fear from an old book. Perhaps Thomas More's aggrieved spirit clung to the pages. Maybe the ghost of the man who'd lost his head haunted those who owned a copy.

"Och, now ye're being ridiculous," she said aloud before leaving the room and closing the door.

A frisson of fear in her chest made her turn the key in the lock and take it with her upstairs. A story in last week's *Times*, mentioned thieves scouting auctions with the intention of stealing valuable antiquities.

Once in her chamber, she warmed her hands on the dying embers, then rang for her maid. Ivy helped her undress, but it was late, and the girl had been awake since dawn.

"Get to bed. I can plait my own hair, and I mean to read for a while." Only half an hour ago, Ailsa had struggled to keep her eyes open. Now, a sickening sensation in her gut said she wouldn't sleep a wink.

Ivy curtsied. "Very well, ma'am. Will you be staying with the St Clairs tomorrow? I don't mean to pry or speak out of turn. Your father would be angry if he knew you were here alone."

She wasn't alone. She had the servants for company.

But Ivy was right. Having vowed to spend time with her friends, she should stay with Helen. But Lord Denton was a regular caller at his sister's abode. And the St Clairs were so in love, it might persuade the most determined spinster to marry.

"Aye, I shall stay with Mrs St Clair tomorrow night."

Ivy's smile spoke of relief. No maid wanted to lie to their employer, and Scots were known for their fiery tempers.

It took Ailsa half an hour to comb all the knots from her hair. By the time she'd finished, tears trickled down her cheeks. Perhaps cutting it to her shoulders would help to tame the unruly locks. Overcome with an odd urge to do something drastic, she rooted around in the drawer, found the scissors and contemplated snipping off a strand.

But the rattle of a doorknob downstairs stole her attention.

It was probably Monroe raiding the brandy decanter.

Since taking delivery of the book, a knot of unease had tightened in her belly. A chill had penetrated her bones. Perhaps Monroe was abed, and the odd fellow in the hackney had returned to prowl through the house and steal the antiquity.

Was that why he had asked for the master?

Why he called so late and peered over her shoulder?

Ailsa gripped the scissors and crept towards the bedchamber door. Ivy had left it ajar, so she pricked her ears, praying Monroe would cough to settle her fears.

The confident clip of footsteps in the hall spoke of a fit and healthy man, not an ageing butler struggling to breathe.

'Tis just a footman, Ailsa told herself.

Still, she daren't call out.

The rickety board at the bottom of the stairs creaked, and a masculine voice whispered a curse. The servants knew not to step on it until Mr Brown came with a replacement.

Her blood chilled.

Her heart almost stopped beating when she peered into the gloom and saw a dark figure slowly mounting the stairs.

Should she hide?

Was it not better to burst onto the landing and confront the devil?

Would Monroe find her lying in a pool of blood in the morning?

Logic said she should raise a hue and cry, make enough noise to scare the villain. Send him fleeing into the night.

Gathering every ounce of courage she possessed, Ailsa burst onto the landing, only to come face-to-face with a giant.

A giant who smelled of women's perfume.

A giant who looked remarkably like Lord Denton.

She would know the twist of that arrogant mouth anywhere. "Merciful Lord! Ye scared me half to death. What the devil are ye doing in—"

In a move one might see in a pugilist's den, he spun her around, hauled her against his chest and carried her into the bedchamber.

She would have cried out, but he smothered her mouth

with his hand. The attractive hand she had admired hours earlier. She might have jabbed him with the scissors, but they fell from her grasp as she tried to wriggle free.

The man had lost his mind.

Losing the auction had left him deranged.

Had he noticed she wore nothing but a cotton nightgown? At the auction house, he'd mentioned throwing her over his shoulder and locking her in the broom cupboard. Surely he'd been joking.

Drawing her behind the door, he held her tight against his chest. Her loose breasts were mere inches from his forearm. Her bottom was squashed against his groin.

She should be mortified, crippled with embarrassment, scared to the marrow of her bones, but a more shocking sensation took hold. One she knew to be the stirrings of arousal.

Good grief!

"There's a thief in the house," he whispered against her ear. His breath came quickly, but he took the time to inhale the scent of her hair. "If I release you, you mustn't make a sound. I need to find him."

Ailsa nodded. When fearing for one's life, there was something comforting about being held in a man's strong embrace. Then she remembered the man in question was the dreaded Lord Denton and quickly prised herself from his grasp.

"A thief?" she whispered, whirling round to face him. "How do ye know?"

His gaze slid over her hair, lingered on her mouth, dipped to the open neck of her nightgown. "I was passing on my way home and saw a suspicious fellow waiting by the railings. He entered via the basement door."

"Then why are we hiding in my bedchamber?" She had

never entertained a gentleman at home, let alone in her private sanctuary.

The viscount scanned the dark room, a smile touching his lips when he noticed the bookcase crammed with old volumes. "I wanted to ensure you were safe before brawling with a mindless villain in your basement."

"How did ye get in?" Ailsa grabbed the scissors from the floor. He was sober and by no means a reprobate, but one had to take precautions. "Monroe locked the door."

The lord shrugged. "It was open."

"Oh!" The poor butler's head had been in the clouds for days. "I'm coming with ye. I'll nae wait here wondering what's happened."

Lord Denton knew better than to argue. That didn't stop his curious gaze roving over her white nightgown. Doubtless he found the dowdy garment unflattering. Hence why he grumbled and tutted to himself before leading the way downstairs.

They crept through the house and eased the basement door open though the hinges creaked like an alley cat's whine.

Ailsa stared into the gloom, her knees almost buckling when she realised his lordship was right.

The shadows shifted like a malevolent spirit, a strange ghostly form lingering at the foot of the stairs. The mass moved, morphing into the dark figure of a man who turned quickly and darted along the corridor.

A stream of obscenities left Lord Denton's lips as he took to his heels and gave chase.

Hearing the commotion, Monroe rushed out of his room, lost his footing and crashed into the viscount.

"Cursed saints!" Lord Denton yelled.

Monroe collapsed into a heap on the floor, his tired muscles giving out.

"Go! I shall see to Monroe," she panted, giving the lord her scissors and urging him to continue his pursuit. "Hurry, before the villain escapes."

Lord Denton brooked no argument. He jumped over Monroe's body and disappeared down the dark corridor while Ailsa called for the head footman's assistance.

They managed to lug Monroe into his room.

After sending the other nosy servants back to bed and tucking the blankets around the dazed butler, Ailsa drew John into the corridor. "Ye'll resume the role of butler until Monroe is well. I'll send for Dr Mackenzie in the morning and will reside here until there's a notable sign of improvement."

Perhaps it was a blessing in disguise.

Her parents would understand why she had not stayed with the St Clairs. Monroe had served her father faithfully for twenty years, and his health was a priority.

A dishevelled Lord Denton returned, his blonde hair mussed, his breath coming in shallow pants. "I lost the blighter." He braced his hands on his knees, hauled air deep into his lungs. "I lost him on Cleveland Row. He must have entered St James' Park."

Splatters of mud clung to his trousers. A sheen of perspiration coated his brow. The muscles in his shoulders bulged with tension, and his jaw was as firm as Kilt Rock. For a reason unbeknown, the sight caused an odd fluttering in Ailsa's chest.

"Did ye say ye were passing and saw the thief enter?" she said for the footman's sake. Heaven forbid John thought she was entertaining the lord upstairs while the servants were abed.

"I fear he may have been trying to steal More's book."

The footman stood in his nightshirt and breeches, his gaze moving from Ailsa's nightgown to the strapping figure radiating a potent masculinity.

"My lord, we should decide whether to call a constable." They would not call a soul. The fewer people who knew they were alone together in the house, the better. "And ye look in need of a brandy." She faced the footman, ignoring the flash of intrigue in his eyes. "Keep a watchful eye on Monroe. I shall ring if we're to expect visitors."

The man bowed and returned to the butler's room.

"We shall talk upstairs," Ailsa whispered, giving a series of hand gestures to inform Lord Denton the walls in the basement had ears.

When a woman spent a few months of the year roaming freely over the wild Highland hills, wading barefoot through babbling brooks, she often forgot social etiquettes.

Ailsa climbed the dimly lit stairs first—as any gentleman would insist—but not while wearing nothing but a nightgown.

The lord's sharp intake of breath brought a hot flush to her cheeks. She could almost feel his searing gaze roaming over her back, dipping to linger in forbidden places. Reaching the top stair was as painstaking as climbing Creag Mhor's summit.

Ailsa closed the servants' door and returned to the hall. "Help yerself to brandy, my lord, while I hurry upstairs and dress." Forced to face the indomitable peer, she gestured to the drawing room. "There's port if ye prefer. Then ye might explain how ye came to be in the area."

She should thank him, escort him out and bar the door, but thoughts of the intruder returning had her shivering to her toes.

"I lied. I wasn't passing the house." He winced like she had torn the confession from his lips. "I asked Jenkins to park across the street because I sensed something was amiss."

He had come to spy?

She was surprised he'd given her a second thought.

"Ye mean ye had a premonition?"

"I had a bad feeling, not a supernatural experience," he scoffed.

"That something terrible would occur?"

"No, that there might be a problem after the auction." He dragged his hand through his hair and huffed. "I don't know. Perhaps the mysterious benefactor couldn't bid on the book and used you to obtain the copy. Who else would steal into your home mere hours after you received a rare antiquity?"

He had a point.

It could not be a coincidence.

"The man from Chadwick's brought the book an hour ago. He came in a hackney and was in a hurry to leave."

Lord Denton muttered a curse. "Then whoever broke into the house must have been waiting until you took delivery."

Her pulse raced. That meant the fellow would return.

She wasn't safe at home.

Not as long as she owned that book.

But she couldn't just give it away. What if her father had bought it as a gift? She should write to him and ask but it would take weeks to receive a reply.

"There were thirty men at the auction," the lord contin-ued, the usual hot undercurrent of anger marring his tone. "It will be impossible to find the culprit."

"Aye, but only a handful made a bid."

"The villain might have sat waiting to see who won."

She laughed when she should be terrified. "Ye're right,

though I never thought I'd see the day we'd agree on something."

The lord smiled, the sight stealing her breath. His eyes met hers, and her heart thumped with nerves, not frustration. It took every effort to banish the memory of being held tight against his solid body. To forget she'd felt something thick and hard pushing against her bottom.

Mother mercy!

Seeing the spell book today had played havoc with her mind. Was she suffering from delusions? Had she taken to inventing things, concocting erotic fantasies?

Lord Denton must be afflicted by the same fallacy because he stood gawping like a lovesick fool. "Your hair is much like your character, a wild burst of flames amid a bleak darkness. You should wear it in a softer style."

Ailsa clutched her throat, eager for an explanation but too scared to ask. She'd rather tackle the intruder than address his comment.

"My lord, ye will think I'm fit for Bedlam when I tell ye this, but I fear we've both fallen under a spell." Why else would she feel these unwanted stirrings?

She expected Lord Denton to scoff, but a deep furrow appeared between his brows. "A spell? What makes you say that?"

How might she explain without revealing the mystic's prediction?

"Before the auctioneer's assistant read the few lines from the love spell today, we couldnae abide one another."

"That's not entirely true. Yes, we have different opinions, and you enjoy making me angry, but a mutual respect flows between us. We both love books, both have the courage of our convictions."

Good Lord! It was worse than she thought.

He was utterly delirious.

"Ye never compliment me. Now ye cannae seem to stop."

Lord Denton threw his hands up. "What do you want me to do? Berate you for standing there in a thin nightgown? Call you a harlot for letting me gaze upon your silky locks and pert nipples?"

Ailsa almost choked. She cupped her breasts, which only roused a hunger in the man's eyes the likes of which she had never seen.

"Stop this!" *Argue with me. Cut me to shreds with your sharp tongue and razor-edged wit.* "'Tis the spell. That's why ye dragged yer coachman from his bed and made him come here."

"No. I was visiting someone in King Street and made a slight detour." He seemed desperate to prove her wrong, which was a positive move in the right direction.

"Aye, and ye stink of her perfume."

"Rest assured. I'll not *stink* of it again." Sniffing his coat, he shrugged out of the garment and stood there in his shirt-sleeves.

Her traitorous gaze flew to the material plastered to his muscular shoulders and biceps. "Put it back on!" She screwed her eyes tight. "Hurry. I dinnae want the servants thinking we've been intimate."

"Do I strike you as a man who's swayed by a servant's opinion?"

"Nae, ye're a grouch and as stubborn as an ox."

"Damnation! Open your eyes, woman. Anyone would think it's *my* nipples pushing against the fine lawn. A man would need a saint's restraint not to notice."

Her eyes flew open. "A gentleman shouldnae speak like that in the presence of a lady. Does that nae prove the devil is at work?"

"It proves we're so open and honest with each other I can say what the hell I please. Few women have your mettle."

Anger burst forth. "On the graves of my slain kin, ye better button yer mouth before ye say something ye'll regret." Keen to have him focus on any woman but her, she said, "Now, perhaps we should return to the subject of yer mistress."

"I don't have a mistress."

"Then what were ye doing in King Street? And why do ye smell like ye've bathed in a vat of lavender oil?"

"Visiting a friend, though we've decided we're incompatible."

Ailsa was no fool. Besides, this was the perfect subject to banish all thoughts of a love spell. "And while in her bed, ye decided it would be a good idea to come to Pall Mall and spy on me? The woman who riles yer temper? The woman ye chastise for having an opinion?"

"An opinion I happen to admire, despite the fact you're wrong the majority of the time." His gaze swept over her again, and he grinned. "Though it's fair to say you've been keeping some things from me, madam."

She folded her arms across her chest.

Wickedness and arrogance made a worrisome combination.

"What are we going to do about the book? I cannae leave it here? Happen I should take it to the bank in the morning. Make it known it's nae in the house."

"I could take it to Grosvenor Street," he suggested.

Ailsa narrowed her gaze in suspicion. Had he planned this? Had he hired a thug to stage a robbery while he waited outside? And to think she had been foolish enough to believe him.

"Hide not thy poison with such sugar'd words."

Recognising the quote, the lord jerked his head. "You mean to insult me by citing Shakespeare? Question my logic, by all means, but never question my honourable intentions."

"Something is amiss. It's clear ye're nae yerself tonight."

"Why? Because I find your hair attractive? Because I've paid you the odd compliment? Perhaps after spending an hour with a woman who has no interest in my opinion, I'm beginning to see your worth."

Och, the man would try a nun's patience.

"Remember, I'm a wild Scottish lass who browbeats Englishmen into submission." He had said that numerous times. Ailsa stepped forward, jabbing her finger to support her claim. "Ye'll stop this nonsense, else I shall put ye out of this house."

Lord Denton arched an imperious brow. "You might have been bludgeoned in your bed had I not had the foresight to call."

Enough was enough.

"And I thank ye from the bottom of my heart." She strode to the study door, dragged the red ribbon from around her neck and gripped the iron key. "Take the book. I trust ye to keep it safe."

Ailsa unlocked the door and entered the study, aware he followed closely behind, too close. She stopped at the desk and motioned to the wooden casket. "Keep it until I receive word from my father."

Lord Denton threw his coat over the chair and examined the small box. "You've not opened it. Did you not think to check the contents?"

"'Twas late."

"What if there's nothing but straw inside?"

"Why would a man from Chadwick's deliver an empty box?" Granted, there had been something shifty about the fellow. Through subtle means, he'd tried to deter her from checking the merchandise. "The document I signed bore the Chadwick seal."

"If he stole the original, your signature means you cannot hold the auction house to account. Hand me the scissors. They're in my coat pocket. No. Wait. I need something more substantial to prise off the lid."

The lord rounded the desk and opened the top drawer. He removed a silver letter opener and set to work on the box. The wood creaked against the pressure, but he wrenched the lid off easily.

In the gloom, they both peered inside to find a bed of straw.

"The book is buried beneath. I can see the spine." She moved to brush the straw aside and froze. That's when her fingers began trembling, when her heartbeat drummed loudly in her ears, when blind panic tightened her throat.

Much like the night Mr Ashbury followed her from the supper room, attacked her and tore her gown, a coldness chilled the blood in her veins.

She had stared ruin in the face that night.

An ominous energy in the air threatened ruin again.

Lord Denton watched her intently. "What's wrong?"

She managed a shrug. "Will ye uncover the book?"

The night had brought one strange encounter after another. A deep sense of trepidation said to expect a host of disturbing events.

Indeed, when Lord Denton moved the straw, she stumbled and had to grip the desk for support. Hidden in the depths of the box was not Thomas More's vision of a perfect world.

It was Ailsa's worst nightmare.

Chapter Four

Sebastian stared at the red leather grimoire, confusion and shock battling for prominence, though the emotions had as much to do with his body's reaction to the scantily clad Miss MacTavish as they did finding the ancient spell book.

Much like the words bound within the tome's old pages, the lady had her own dark secrets. By day, she posed as a plain spinster. An annoying bluestocking who shied away from convention. By night, she was the epitome of a Scottish temptress. A siren with a flame of red hair and a body made for sin. Curves so soft, Sebastian grew as hard as a butcher's block whenever he touched her.

A vision of pert nipples and round buttocks flashed into his mind.

Why the devil hadn't he noticed before?

But when a man was engaged in verbal warfare, he considered his battle plan, not what lay hidden beneath his enemy's armour. That said, did the Scots not flash their tackle to intimidate their rivals? Had Miss MacTavish thought to unnerve an English gent in much the same manner?

Sebastian mentally shook himself.

His only concern should be how the lady had the blasted grimoire in her possession. And why she'd stumbled back in horror as if the inanimate object might leap out of the casket and seize her soul.

"It cannae be," she gasped, clutching her throat.

"There was obviously a mistake with the delivery," he said, clinging to logic as one might the mast of a sinking ship. "Did you check the details on the docket?"

She blinked rapidly. "I—I cannae remember."

Lord Almighty! What had happened to the shrewd woman he considered his equal in the game of persiflage? This lady could barely catch her breath, let alone form a word.

Keen to get control of his emotions and the situation, Sebastian rounded the desk. He gripped Miss MacTavish by the upper arms and urged her to look at him.

"For a sensible woman, you're acting like a dimwit."

For a sensible man, he was acting like a rakehell. How could he be the voice of reason when his traitorous gaze dipped to the neckline of her nightgown?

Thankfully, she failed to notice. "Ye dinnae understand what this means. This amounts to more than a simple mistake at the auction house."

He understood perfectly well. "At best, it's a mistake we will rectify tomorrow. At worst, it amounts to robbery and deception."

"'Tis worse than that."

"The only thing worse than that is murder."

"Or marriage," she snapped.

"Marriage?" Had she lost all grasp of her senses? Scouring every recess of his mind, Sebastian focused on the

45

only logical conclusion for her odd outburst. "Are you refer-ring to the auctioneer's assistant reading the love spell today?"

"I'm referring to the mystic's prediction at the Bartholomew Fair."

He snorted. "The mystic who told Helen she would marry a man who fell in a cowpat?" It sounded so ludicrous, he had paid little attention to the ladies' excited chatter.

"Aye!"

"It was said in jest. Fortune tellers make their predictions sound exciting. They mean to give value for a crown." And play havoc with an innocent mind. Torture a naive soul.

"All three previous prophecies came true."

Sebastian shrugged. "It's likely a coincidence. Crones persist in being vague. What has it to do with the mistake at the auction house?"

She pursed her lips and seemed reluctant to explain.

"Miss MacTavish, on the scale of embarrassing scenarios, nothing could compare to the awkwardness of this situation. You're standing in nothing but a cotton nightgown. I've seen more of you tonight than some married men see in a life-time." And he was damned angry with himself because he'd like to see more. "Tell me what the mystic said."

The lady might have covered her breasts again but Sebastian still held her upper arms.

When he released her, she hugged herself, preventing him from peering at the thin material.

"She said I would marry a man who put me under an ancient spell. That's why I decided to bid on the grimoire. I thought it better to own it myself than let it loose amongst the fools in the *ton*."

He failed to see the problem. A man couldn't use a love

spell to make a woman marry him. Could he? His thoughts turned to Michael, a sensible fellow who had taken to reading nonsense.

"Is that why you made the wager not to marry?" Did she know her passion for collecting rare books would outweigh anything she might feel for a man? "To protect yourself from falling under a spell?"

By their very nature, incantations were meant to render a person powerless. No wager or attempt to make oneself unappealing could negate that.

"In part," she confessed.

"I see." Was he any different? Had he not overruled her bid because he suspected Michael had died due to his obsession with magic? That he feared she might befall a similar fate?

Damnation! He was rarely so irrational.

Needing to prove the words in the grimoire amounted to nothing but twaddle, he reached for the book and unfastened the tarnished clasps.

"What are ye doing?" Miss MacTavish looked horrified.

"Proving a theory."

"Leave it in the casket."

The book fell open at the love spell, and he managed to recite the first three words before the lady charged forward and slapped her hand over his mouth.

"Dinnae repeat them unless ye want to marry me." Her fingers were soft and warm against his lips. "One shouldnae mock what one doesnae understand. Ye cannae risk breaking yer oath."

Snatching the tome from his grasp, she fastened the clasps with haste, buried the grimoire beneath a bed of straw in the box and slammed the wooden lid on top.

"Now..." Miss MacTavish fought to catch her breath. "Let us stop this nonsense and deal with our pressing problem."

Sebastian cleared his throat and pasted his usual stony-faced expression. "I lost the auction. The problem is yours to solve."

He was rather glad when she raised her chin in defiance. The sooner they returned to normality, the better.

"Then take yer smelly coat and leave. I didnae ask ye to come barging into the house and take control."

A knot of guilt twisted in his gut. "I meant *you* need to take the matter up with Mr Murden. The bill of sale is with you, not me."

"I understand. Ye dinnae want to help a lady in distress."

Sebastian frowned.

Miss MacTavish leaned closer, the nightgown gaping open at the neck, permitting him an eyeful of smooth alabaster skin. "Dinnae stop shouting," she whispered as if spies were recording their every word. "We must keep scolding each other. 'Tis the only way to banish the spell. Heaven forbid we get caught in its clutches."

He might have called her a loon.

He might have called a servant to escort her back to bed because if anyone else heard her ramblings they would consider her deranged.

But the need to feed the beast inside encouraged him to say, "Perhaps you should tell me what you find distasteful about my character."

She nodded, but the flicker of excitement in her eyes died. "In the confusion, I find it hard to think of anything. Och! Do ye see what I mean? Already it has me in its powerful grip."

On the slight chance there might be some truth to her claim, and not wanting Miss MacTavish to fawn over him like the desperate debutantes he encountered daily, he said,

"Then let me help you. Last week, you called me the devil's spawn because I said there's something quite disturbing about a man in a kilt."

"Aye! Ye did." She seemed relieved he remembered. "And I said I'd nae taken ye for a jealous man. That ye've a gripe because yer legs are like spindles."

"Let me correct you on that point. I fence, box and ride frequently. I have a gladiator's thighs, and I'm not being conceited."

Her gaze dared to slide down the length of his trousers. "Muscular thighs doesnae make a man heroic. Empathy and compassion are the qualities ladies admire."

"I suppose you consider racing to a lady's aid part of the strict criteria. How convenient when you have a problem you don't wish to solve yourself."

A mocking snort escaped her. "May I remind ye, I hid in the darkness ready to confront the intruder with nae thoughts of my own safety?"

"Wielding a blunt pair of scissors that could barely cut hair let alone stop a determined thief in his tracks. Admit you lack the brawn necessary to fight with your fists."

Miss MacTavish stepped forward, so close the scent of apples consumed him. "Dinnae underestimate me. Like my forebears, I would fight to the death if need be."

A tension thrummed between them. A charged sexual energy that came from nowhere but left him staring at her bow-shaped lips, left him battling against an inner ache that proved confounding.

"Why are ye looking at me like that?"

"Like what?" Like he was considering doing something as foolish as kissing her? Like he wanted to fist his hands into that mass of red hair and steal the last breath from her lungs?

A blush marred her cheeks. "Like ye're dazed?"

49

Sebastian blinked. "I'm tired."

He never lied, yet he could not tell her the truth.

I think I may have succumbed to the spell.

It would be enough to send her racing back to the Highlands. Enough to make her tear the pages from the grimoire and make a bonfire on the desk. Then she'd make them both dance around the flames as part of a wild Scottish ritual.

Heaven forbid he acted on these unwelcome urges.

A sudden hammering on the front door made them both jump. This woman knew how to turn a sensible peer into a bumbling wreck.

Miss MacTavish looked at him and frowned. "Who on earth can it be at this late hour?"

"As it's not my house, I haven't the faintest notion. But if I'm caught here, we may be forced to marry." And he'd rather sever his tongue than shackle himself to any woman.

"Do ye think the spell works that quickly?"

Drawing on his aristocratic bearing to disguise his own hypocrisy, he said with some aplomb, "Madam, will you cease with these outlandish ideas? I know the Scots believe in folklore and fairies, but this is taking whimsical concepts a stretch too far."

Miss MacTavish pressed a finger to his lips. "Hush now, else ye might offend the Lady of the Lake. Bad luck will befall yer family for a century."

Who in hell's name is the Lady of the Lake? That should have been his query. But three other questions bombarded his mind, each one fighting for supremacy.

If he sucked her finger, would she taste of apples?

Why would a sensible man find this illogical chatter so appealing?

And who in God's name was banging on the front door?

50

"I should see who's knocking," she said, reminding him of their present predicament. "Hide here until the coast is clear."

"You can't go," he whispered. "What about the intruder?"

"I doubt the intruder would want to wake the household."

He gestured to the frumpy nightgown that had such an odd effect on him. "You cannot answer the door in such a state of dishabille. You'll have to wake your footman."

"Miss MacTavish!" came the echoes of a voice Sebastian knew.

"Good God. Is that Lucius Daventry?" Why in blazes would the master of London's most skilled enquiry agents visit the lady's home at midnight? Unless he knew there had been some mishap at the auction house. Though how did a mistake in a warehouse constitute a crime?

"Fail to open the door, and I shall have no choice but to force my way inside." For a man who prided himself on his calm composure, Daventry sounded somewhat anxious.

"Wait here." Sebastian grabbed his coat. "Daventry is not one to judge, and my being here can be easily explained."

Despite her soft gasp when he draped his coat around her shoulders, he drew it firmly across her chest. He'd be damned if he'd let anyone else gaze upon her womanly charms.

Sebastian strode to the door and welcomed the man who thrived on intrigue. "Come inside quickly," he said from behind the door. The street was wide but gossips were resourceful.

"Ah, Denton. I thought that was your coach parked near Schomberg House and wondered if you'd come to read *Utopia*." Daventry did not appear shocked to see Sebastian standing in his shirtsleeves. "Studying old texts must be tiring work."

Sebastian grumbled to himself and broke into a garbled story of how he'd been passing and noticed an intruder. Guilt clung to every word, which was doubtless a result of his lascivious thoughts about his Scottish companion.

"How fortuitous," Daventry said calmly. His gaze drifted to the open study door. "You may come out, Miss MacTavish. I assure you, I'm here on the King's business not to question your morals."

Swamped in Sebastian's coat, the lady slipped out from the shadows. Her cheeks were as red as her hair. Her bare feet poked out from beneath the hem of her nightgown.

His traitorous body reacted instantly.

"Bloody hell," he muttered.

He should have insisted she dress.

"Something wrong, Denton?"

"No. As you're a master at keeping secrets, this should pose no problem." Though it was the closest Sebastian had ever come to being shamed into marrying.

Daventry grinned. "Your nightly habits are your own affair."

The implication they were indulging in a romantic liaison roused Sebastian's temper. "Think what you like about me, but do not presume to tarnish Miss MacTavish's character."

"I merely suggest your passion for old books has led to this unlikely encounter." Daventry did not give the lady time to defend her position. "In truth, I'm thankful you're here. It saves me scouring every club in town."

Miss MacTavish found her voice. "What wicked business keeps ye out at this time of night, sir?"

"Murder, madam. I came to warn you to stay alert."

"Murder?" Miss MacTavish gulped.

"Mr Murden's assistant was found dead at the auction

house earlier this evening. The scene bore the markings of a similar case I investigated many years ago. Such is the unusual nature, I feel it's important to explain what occurred."

"Unusual nature?" The lady glanced at the dark study.

"Might we find somewhere comfortable to sit? This will take time, and you may find some elements disturbing."

Sebastian snorted. "Nothing could shock me more than what has occurred this evening."

How often did one race through foggy streets to apprehend a villain? How often did a man lust for a woman he could barely tolerate? How many times did one find oneself crippled by a spell?

"Trust me. This tale will make every hair stand on end."

Miss MacTavish visibly shivered. "We'll sit in the study. Make yerselves comfortable, and I shall join ye in a few minutes. Ye'll find the brandy decanter in the drawing room."

Daventry inclined his head.

Sebastian fought the urge to watch her mount the stairs, to watch the cotton gown slide over her peachy buttocks. While pouring drinks, he tried not to think about her standing naked in the darkness, her chemise slipping over her porcelain skin.

"This isn't how it looks," he felt compelled to say once they'd lit the lamps and found a seat in the study.

Daventry sipped his brandy. "And how does it look?"

Was the man being facetious? "You know damn well how it looks. Like our passion for old books has led to a passion of a different kind. I assure you. I came to the lady's aid, nothing more."

"What I think is of no consequence."

"Then I trust you will keep your opinion to yourself."

Daventry's curious gaze flicked to the wooden box on the

desk and the strands of straw littering the surface. "Tell me about the intruder, and how you happened to be passing."

Sebastian took the comment as a veiled accusation. "I had my reasons for wanting More's book, but I did not stage a robbery to gain the tome."

"And yet it would be easy to manipulate the lady while she is without her parents' protection."

Sebastian shot to his feet. "I may have a heart of stone, but I would never hurt Miss MacTavish. The implication is reason enough to call you out."

"I'm told you're an excellent marksman." Daventry gave a confident smirk, then knocked back his brandy. "But you're not cold. Your heart growls with the passion of a disgruntled bear that savages anyone in its path. Imagine a life where love replaced hatred."

Sebastian scowled. He did not need a lecture from a man who thrived on punishing wrongdoers. Injustice and fury were sides of the same coin. "You forget I've seen you fight. You've the devil's darkness in you."

Daventry did not deny the claim. "Life is about balance. I'm a different man when I make love to my wife. A different man when I educate my sons on the value of loyalty and forgiveness. But you're right. Woe betide anyone who crosses me."

A tense silence descended.

Sebastian never felt more alive than when fighting in the dank pits at the White Boar or flexing his foil at the School of Arms in Soho. Loving a woman would not bring answers. Hurting men was a means of punishing someone for the mystery surrounding his brother's death.

Daventry gestured to the sinister box. "Were you not curious to study More's *Utopia*? I'm surprised it's not open on the desk."

"Chadwick's delivered the wrong book," Miss MacTavish said from the doorway, the nervous edge to her tone in sharp contrast to her bright demeanour. "'Tis a mistake we must rectify tomorrow."

They stood.

"We were debating the fact it might not be a mistake," Sebastian said. Eager to see what she'd done with her hair, he permitted himself one glance.

The loose braid hung over her shoulder to rest gently against her breast. Errant red wisps escaped to caress her slender throat. She wore no corset beneath the plain green dress, and he was suddenly thinking about rosebud nipples again.

Like a woodland nymph, did she mean to entrap him in her womanly spell or was the damn grimoire conjuring these lewd images?

"Then what's in the box?" Daventry asked.

"The grimoire, sir." Miss MacTavish sat in her father's chair behind the desk, and they resumed their seats. "A spell book from the sixteenth century. The one sold at auction yesterday."

Daventry straightened. "May I see the book?"

"I—I think it's best to leave it buried," she stuttered.

"I'm afraid I must insist, madam. A man was murdered at the auction house, and now you tell me More's book is missing."

"Evidently, the person who won the grimoire now has a copy of *Utopia*," Sebastian countered. Yet a knot in his gut said things were more complicated, not at all what they seemed.

"Tell me what happened tonight," Daventry demanded. "Leave nothing out. It is vital I understand what we're dealing with here."

Sebastian gave a detailed explanation, though did not mention hauling Miss MacTavish against his body in the dark. Said nothing about pressing the hard ridge of his cock against her buttocks.

"Might the intruder have been the shady fellow who wished to purchase the grimoire at auction?" Daventry mused.

"It's possible. He was nimble and fast on his feet."

Daventry nodded before turning his attention to Miss MacTavish. "Is there a reason you keep glancing at the box as if there's a hissing cobra inside?"

She gulped. "I dinnae care if this sounds like the ramblings of a mad woman, but the spell book has a power beyond all rhyme and reason."

"A power?" Recognition dawned, and Daventry said, "Ah! You're referring to the mystic's prediction at the Bartholomew Fair."

"Aye, which is why ye should take the book as part of yer investigation into the assistant's murder. Though ye've still not told us how he died."

The deep furrow marring Daventry's brow conveyed the disturbing nature of the scene. "You might not wish to hear this, madam. The images may return to haunt you at night."

"Like my father, I have a hardy constitution, sir."

Sebastian stole a furtive glance at the woman he'd once considered his nemesis. She had a backbone of steel, but she was soft and feminine in all the right places.

"Very well," Daventry said. The man was easily persuaded and enjoyed discussing the macabre. "Someone stretched Mr Hibbet's body until his bones snapped. His heart is missing. The symbol carved into his forehead looks to be a druid marking."

Miss MacTavish plastered her hand to her mouth.

"Are you suggesting some sort of ritual?" Sebastian scoured his mind. There had been strange images and markings in the spell book found in his brother's quarters aboard *The Perseus*.

"That's what it would seem, though I cannot help but feel the villain staged the scene. A smoke and mirrors effect to hide the true motive."

Sebastian's pulse raced. Was there a retribution spell in the ancient tome? Was fate conspiring to lead him down a path that might shed light on Michael's untimely death?

"Perhaps I might accompany you during your investigation," he said, quickly enough for Daventry to arch a brow. The man was short of agents, and Sebastian needed something to distract his mind.

"Catching criminals is a dangerous business, Denton."

"I'm not afraid to die for a worthy cause." Now Helen had married, he had no one to care for. "I can fight as well as any Whitechapel thug." Like Daventry, inside he harboured Satan's savagery.

Daventry pursed his lips, seeming to consider the prospect. Sebastian wouldn't be the first peer to work for the master of the Order. Not that he would do something so uncouth as to accept payment for his services.

"I'm struggling to understand your motivation, Denton."

"Does it matter?"

"Most definitely."

Damnation! If he wished to learn more about the power of ancient spell books, he would have to reveal his darkest secret.

"My brother died aboard *The Perseus*. Amongst his possessions was an old grimoire. I'm keen to learn what drew a sane man to read such rubbish."

Sebastian could feel the heat of Miss MacTavish's gaze.

Now she knew why he'd tried to stop her bidding on the book.

Daventry fell silent for a time, his gaze moving between Sebastian and the Scottish temptress. "Very well. You can escort Miss MacTavish to Chadwick's tomorrow. Find out what happened to the copy of *Utopia* and how she became the custodian of a magician's textbook."

Every muscle in Sebastian's body tensed. "I'll not have the lady embroiled in this dangerous business." And he had no intention of spending an inordinate amount of time in her company.

Miss MacTavish appeared equally disturbed. "I'm quite capable of visiting the auction house alone, sir. Ye may give his lordship another task. It will save time."

"Denton is the only person who can identify the intruder. You're the only one who can identify the delivery man. You bought the book, but you'll need someone powerful to bring the auctioneer to heel. No. You'll visit Chadwick's together."

That was not the only disagreement of the evening.

Daventry demanded Miss MacTavish spend the night with the St Clairs. Despite explaining that she needed to keep a watchful eye on her sick butler, Daventry agreed to have his own physician attend to the servant within the hour.

"Verra well," she conceded, "but I shall return tomorrow."

Daventry nodded. "Send word to me in Hart Street once you have information on the grimoire." He motioned to the wooden casket on the desk. "Might you hand me the book, Miss MacTavish? I must inspect it before I leave."

Being stubborn, and perhaps because she wished to show Daventry he was right to place his faith in her, she swallowed hard and drew the box slowly towards her.

One would think it *did* contain a deadly snake. With trembling hands, she removed the lid, a visible shiver coursing through her. The second her fingers slipped around the spine, her alarmed gaze shot in Sebastian's direction.

Something passed between them.

An awareness of a newly formed bond.

An understanding that they shared a secret.

A fear their lives may never be the same.

Chapter Five

Home of the St Clairs
Upper Seymour Street

Ailsa had just taken a bite of her toast when Helen appeared at the dining room door, carrying the dreaded casket Mr Daventry had taken home last night.

"Mr Daventry begs your forgiveness but hasn't time to return the book in person. He asks you visit him in Hart Street later today." Helen plonked the ebony casket at the end of the table, and there it sat like a baleful relative. "It's so light one might think the box is empty."

If only it contained nothing but straw. Then Ailsa wouldn't have weird thoughts about Lord Denton. Amorous thoughts of midnight trysts in a dark bedchamber. Lewd thoughts about hard things rubbing against her buttocks at night.

Ailsa swallowed before she choked on breadcrumbs. "On my oath, whatever is in that box will bring nothing but trouble." An ominous energy swirled in the air. One capable of turning a sensible woman's mind to mush. "I feel like I'm already under its spell."

Helen sat when the footman held out her chair. The servant kept an impassive expression, though talk of the supernatural had his hand shaking a little as he poured the tea.

"Yes, I think you've every reason to be worried. The mystic has been right three times so far. Odds are you will marry within a month, two at most."

Ailsa's heart missed a beat.

She couldn't marry.

She couldn't lose her wager with the viscount.

The idea of such an odious man owning her precious books was unthinkable. Mother Mary! How could a simple bid at an auction lead to a night of catastrophe?

"Is that why you're wearing that old thing?" Helen, who possessed the same mischievous blue eyes as her brother, gestured to Ailsa's ugly brown dress. "If you're truly under a spell, dull clothes won't save you. Indeed, there's something different about you today. You exude an air of mystery. Your skin has an almost otherworldly glow."

Ailsa dropped her toast onto the plate. "Has he told ye to torment me? Does he take pleasure in making me look foolish?"

Helen frowned. "Who?"

"Yer brother."

"Sebastian? I haven't spoken to him for two days." Helen snatched a piece of toast from the silver rack. "I know he can be difficult, but you rile his temper more than most. Still, it is not in his nature to be cruel."

No, Lord Denton had been more than helpful last night. With no fear of the consequences, he chased the intruder. He had done his best to persuade Mr Daventry to let them visit

Chadwick's separately. Had muttered an oath every time his gaze ventured to her loose hair.

"This business with the spell book has my nerves in tatters. I pray we resolve the matter today so we can get back to some normality."

Yet a man had been murdered most brutally. And Lord Denton was keen to play an enquiry agent and discover if there was a connection between the grimoire and the disturbing scene.

"I'm sure the owner of the grimoire will be waiting to return your copy of *Utopia*." Helen was so in love with her husband she saw the positive in every situation.

Being under strict orders from Mr Daventry not to mention the murder, Ailsa reached for her teacup and said, "Aye, I'm sure ye're right."

While they broke their fast, Helen felt the need to add insult to injury and recall every detail of their trip to the Bartholomew Fair.

"Without some communication with the Divine, I cannot see how the mystic could have predicted future events. How could she have known Nicholas would fall and land in a cowpat?"

"Did yer brother nae punch him, and that's why he fell?"

"Yes, but how could she have known events would transpire as they did?" Helen sipped her tea. It was a matter of seconds before she turned to the dreaded topic of Ailsa marrying. "Maybe the man who has *Utopia* will be dark-haired and dashing. He will be so grateful for the return of the grimoire he will ask you to ride out tomorrow."

Ailsa inwardly groaned.

Not because Helen was a daydreaming romantic. But because Ailsa envisioned a man with golden hair, erotic hands and a gruff temperament.

Being a realist, she made a confession. "'Tis of nae conse-quence, as I cannae marry. I made a wager with yer brother." She explained the nature of the vow.

Helen almost choked on her tea. "Have you lost your mind? You love those books more than life itself. Why would you risk losing them? Oh, Sebastian must be rubbing his hands together in glee."

Making the wager was foolish. She would never give up her precious collection. "As a gentleman, he wouldnae take my books. He simply wished to unnerve me during the auction." She did not mention the wager was her idea.

"Trust me. Sebastian is quite rigid when it comes to oaths."

Ailsa swallowed hard. Oh, she knew how rigid the viscount could be. The moment was ingrained in her memory. What beggared belief was why a man who despised her had found himself aroused.

Ailsa glanced at the casket—the portent of evil. "Hence why I must get rid of the grimoire and put all thoughts of spells from my mind." The sooner she did so, the better.

Lord Denton arrived moments later, his deep masculine voice echoing through the hall as he conversed with the butler.

Ailsa stifled a gasp when he appeared, his broad shoul-ders filling the doorway, an arrogant grin playing at the corners of his mouth.

The atmosphere grew tense.

Her heartbeat pounded in her ears.

"You're still eating." Annoying cobalt-blue eyes scanned Ailsa's hair. His nose wrinkled with disapproval upon noting the severe knot. "We're expected at Chadwick's within the hour."

"It's very good of you to accompany us," Helen said,

oblivious to the fact her brother had taken work with Mr Daventry. "I know Ailsa is particularly grateful."

Lord Denton's brow rose in disbelief. "I can spare two hours, no more." He stood like he had a sharp stone in his shoe, and the barest movement might cause significant discomfort.

"Then we will ready ourselves at once." Helen dabbed her mouth with her napkin, and the footman helped her out of the chair. "I shan't be a moment. Ailsa will keep you company. She's been ready to leave this past hour."

Lord Denton kissed Helen's forehead as they met in the doorway. "You look a little pale today. I trust you're well."

She patted his muscular arm affectionately. "Yes, quite well."

He nodded and waited for Helen to leave before entering the dining room and dismissing the servant.

Gripping the top rail of the chair, he leaned across the table and whispered, "You've not mentioned what occurred between us last night? You've not told Helen we were alone in the house?"

"We agreed to keep our interactions a secret."

He exhaled a relieved sigh. "Good. If Helen knows I compromised you, she'll think there's some truth to the crone's prediction."

Ailsa shivered at the memory, goose pimples rising to her skin. He had touched her barely clothed body, held her tightly in the darkness. Another woman might use the fact to her advantage.

"Ye had nae choice but to come to my aid. I'll nae see ye punished for that." Being stretched on the rack would be less torturous than a life spent bickering. "Marriage to me would be a fate worse than death."

His gaze roved over her dull dress before he agreed. "I'd

rather gouge out my eyes with a butter knife than make both our lives miserable."

Reassured they were reading from the same page, Ailsa managed a smile. "As we're both quite determined to keep our oath, we should encounter nae problem. Except Helen insisted on acting as our chaperone. I'm nae sure how we'll question Mr Murden while she's present."

Lord Denton considered their dilemma. "Allow me to interrogate Murden first, and then you may speak to him alone."

It seemed like the most sensible solution. With Helen keen for her brother to wed, they should avoid each other's company where possible.

"Verra well." Ailsa stood. "Let us make haste." With some trepidation, she considered the ebony casket. "We should ask Helen to carry the grimoire. She's already deeply in love and is in nae danger of falling under its spell."

"This is ridiculous," he moaned. "I'll not cower before an imaginary force. I'll not be held hostage by a fortune-teller's ramblings." He reached for the casket, tucking the box under his arm as if it were a wayward child. "Come. Let us deal with the matter swiftly."

Though loath to admit it, he was probably right.

Ailsa dressed in her outdoor apparel—a faded blue pelisse and plain bonnet. Not only would she blend into the background, but it was dowdy enough to repel a would-be suitor.

Helen climbed into the carriage first, scooting over to the far side and insisting Ailsa sit beside her.

Lord Denton occupied the seat opposite, his thighs spread wide in a sign of masculine dominance, the bane of their existence perched beside him in the ebony box.

An awkward silence ensued.

Ailsa shuffled her bottom back against the leather squab

to avoid knocking knees with his lordship. Thank heavens they had a short journey across town and not a six-hundred-mile trek to the Highlands. Although the carriage had barely turned into Oxford Street when Helen clutched her stomach and turned a sickly shade of grey.

"I'm sorry, but I need to return home quickly." Helen lowered the window and called for Lord Denton's coachman to stop the vehicle.

"Have you forgotten something?" Concern marred his lordship's tone. "We cannot afford to miss the appointment at Chadwick's."

"I feel so dreadfully dizzy." The carriage came to an abrupt halt and Helen alighted before anyone came to her aid. "Go ahead without me. There's no reason to change your plans. I need to lie down, that's all."

"I'll nae leave ye to walk—"

"I'll escort you home and arrange for a maid to accompany us," Lord Denton interjected, keen to avoid further delays. He vaulted to the pavement, leaving Ailsa alone with the enchanted box. "I shall be but a few minutes, Miss MacTavish."

He sounded haughty, so unlike the man whose rakish gaze roamed over her nightgown last night. At one point, he'd looked like he might lean in for a kiss. Granted, her nerves were frayed, and her imagination had run riot.

Ailsa waited patiently, trying her best not to look at the box.

Why did she get the sense it was silently mocking her?

An agitated Lord Denton returned with Gladys. After exchanging a few words with the maid, the viscount climbed into his conveyance and slammed the door shut.

"Gladys can only ride atop the box," he grumbled. The vehicle rocked on its axis as he dropped into the seat. "But she waited until now to tell me. Perhaps you should return home and let me deal with the matter at Chadwick's."

Wait like a sitting duck while a man dealt with her problems? Trust Lord Denton to act in her stead?

Never.

"'Tis a short journey, my lord." Goodness! She should avoid all contact with him. Only a fool would test the bounds of propriety when in the grip of a love spell.

"Miss MacTavish," he began, his frustration like a trapped bee butting the window. "I mean no offence, but I prefer the termagant to the biddable creature who nods and speaks falsehoods. Say what is on your mind, madam."

Where should she start?

What would she say?

That she wished she'd never visited the auction? She wished he hadn't grabbed her in the darkness, hadn't looked at her as if she were a desirable woman? Hadn't ignited a flicker of something she refused to name?

Merciful Lord!

If only she could chase away every romantic thought, argue and fight with him like they used to. Berate him for the slightest misdemeanour.

"Verra well." She grabbed the lap blanket and threw it over the box, smothering its ominous aura. "Can ye nae see fate is conspiring against us?"

Heavens! She sounded like the loon in Piccadilly who waved his walking stick and warned of the world's end.

"Helen is likely with child," he countered, "and doubtless Gladys has taken a fancy to Jenkins and means to hug his arm as we navigate the bends."

"Has Helen told ye she's with child?"

Excitement warred with inadequacy. All her friends were in love and married and would soon be the proud parents of many children. Ailsa had always been the odd one. The blue-stocking. The spinster. The Scot. The fool.

"No, it's merely an assumption."

"Being an uncle might make ye reconsider yer oath nae to wed," she teased.

"I didn't make an oath not to wed. I made an oath to delay the inevitable. For the next ten years, I shall be a free man."

He made duty sound like a shackle around his neck, one that tightened with each passing year. Did he not want a companion? Did he not yearn for a woman's love?

"Did ye have dreams and aspirations when ye were a wee boy?" The lord possessed a strictness of mind. Had it always been the case?

A compelling twinkle in his eyes hinted at a hidden passion. Like a star in the night sky, had his dreams burned brightly only to fade with the morning sun?

"I would have liked to sail the seas and travel to distant lands. Eat exotic food. Mingle with the locals." The light inside him quickly died. "But the heir to a viscountcy must be sensible, and my brother's demise proved there is nothing romantic about perishing from a tropical fever."

"I cannae imagine how hard that must have been." Ailsa's parents were alive, and she had no siblings. Seeing the destructive nature of grief did not make it easier to compre-hend. "But ye cannae presume yer experiences will be the same."

Five words left his lips.

Five words shrouded in finality.

"It's too late for me."

"'Tis never too late." Perhaps if she could convince him to travel abroad for a time, it would break the spell and save them both a wealth of misery. "There's an old Scottish proverb. Time and tide for nae man bide." Her father used it every time he tried to persuade her to marry. "While ye're more fortunate than most, we're all waiting to meet our maker. When taking yer last breath, ye want to have lived a full life."

An unspoken pain filled his eyes as he scanned her face. She could almost hear his silent plea. The real man crying for someone to unlock his chains, to free him from his prison.

Lord Denton glanced out of the window, realised they were still stationary and rapped on the roof. "We've an appointment and cannot be late. And you seek to distract me at every opportunity, madam."

"Says the man who peeks through the keyhole then grumbles because he sees something vexing."

The carriage lurched, and Ailsa slipped forward on the polished leather seat. The lord came to her rescue, his strong hand gripping her arm, steadying her balance.

Their gazes locked.

Heat infused every fibre of her being.

Confusion marred the lord's brow before he snatched back his hand and resumed a rigid position.

"I didn't peek through the keyhole," he said as they journeyed along Oxford Street. "You left the front door open. And I recall making no complaints about what I found beyond."

No, he had not demanded she make herself presentable and had been most relaxed when standing in his shirtsleeves discussing their dilemma. The man was a monument to contradiction.

She knew the argumentative fellow.

The one who broke his fast with a hearty plate of sarcasm.

"Ye do enjoy taking control of a situation," she said, knowing powerful men liked to grasp the world in their palms.

"Yet you strive to make that impossible." He narrowed his gaze. "Why is that? Do Highland maidens keep their men in manacles?"

Aware his derisive tone was an attempt to lighten the mood, she decided to play along. "Highlanders dinnae belittle women to make themselves seem stronger. To survive in the wild, a man needs a courageous lass who doesnae crumble when the weather turns."

"One who wields scissors to tackle an intruder?" he teased.

"'Twas the first thing I had to hand. I was about to cut my hair when I heard the rattle of a doorknob downstairs." She gestured to where she planned to make the first snip.

His eyes widened in horror. "Cut your hair? Whatever for?"

Anyone would think she'd planned to hack off a healthy limb. "Like the Highland winds, it's wild and has a devil of a temper. It takes Ivy forever to tame it into a tight knot."

His gaze slipped over her with some disapproval. "There is a less drastic alternative. You could wear it in a softer style, as I suggested. Most women seek to enhance their features. You persist in making yourself appear quite plain."

"I'm nae most women."

"No. You're definitely an original, Miss MacTavish."

Was that a compliment? She couldn't tell.

Keen to change the subject, they spent the rest of the journey discussing her issues with More's version of *Utopia*.

"Is that why you persist in making yourself appear unattractive?" he stated, bringing the subject back to her hair. "Because you refuse to objectify yourself? You mean to be no man's trophy? Is that it?"

Ailsa might have mentioned Mr Ashbury assaulting her at

her come-out ball, but the carriage stopped outside Chadwick's, bringing an abrupt end to their conversation.

The viscount alighted, handing the evil box to his groom.

"Allow me." Lord Denton offered his hand.

A fluttering in her stomach held her rigid. Knowing what to expect, she braced herself before her palm slipped over his.

It happened again. Heat and excitement rippled through her body. Her stomach twisted in confounding knots, and she couldn't draw air into her lungs.

Through intense blue eyes, he studied her reaction. "Is something wrong? I heard the hitch in your breath."

Ailsa shook her head and swallowed hard.

She expected him to release her, but he drew her closer. "You never lie to me, so I must question why you're not being honest now." His gaze lingered on her mouth before dropping to their clasped hands. "You feel something, don't you?"

Oh, she felt something.

Something wonderful and frightening in equal measure.

"Aye," she dared confess, preparing to weather the storm.

A low hum rumbled in his throat. "Though loath to admit it, I believe it amounts to quite a profound sexual chemistry, madam."

It couldn't be.

They barely tolerated each other.

"Such things dinnae just occur. We've known each other too long to have a sudden change of heart."

"This has nothing to do with the heart. Our bodies are communicating in an ancient language. It means nothing more than we're compatible bedmates."

She laughed, else she might expire from the sudden panic. "Aye, happen we *have* been possessed by an ancient language —the devil's own witchcraft. Were it nae for the spell book, this would never have happened. Rest assured, I'll nae expect ye to give me a perfect pebble."

The lord glanced at the box in his groom's arms. "I'm beginning to believe you may be right. Lust is a powerful thing. We must fight it with every ounce of strength we possess."

Lust! Now she knew he was possessed by a demon. A man like Lord Denton did not long to bed a plain Scottish lass.

"Aye. 'Tis what I've been saying all along. Ye should avoid touching me. Else we're liable to do something we'll regret. Something that will cause nae end of problems."

Mischief flashed in his eyes. "Something?"

"Ye know what I mean."

"Yes, but I seek clarification. How far do you fear this *something* might go?" The man moistened his lips. "Not all the way, surely?"

"Ye cannae ask an innocent such a question." For a second, she was back in the study, gazing into his hypnotic eyes, her hard nipples aching against her cotton nightgown. The need to kiss him like a plague on her soul.

Ailsa tugged her hand free and marched into Chadwick's Auction House. The sooner this matter was over with the better.

Lord Denton was not far behind, but now he had a firm grip on Satan's casket. Gladys hovered in the background. If a spell could bend a viscount to its will, it would ride roughshod over the maid.

"Wait here while I see if Murden is free." Lord Denton strode into a room off the hall, where a bespectacled clerk sat behind a cluttered desk.

Grateful for a moment to gather her wits, Ailsa made no protest.

Her peace lasted a few seconds before Lord Brockton saw her and smiled. How odd? While she had danced with the dark-haired gentleman once or twice, they were not on familiar terms.

That did not prevent the man from closing the gap between them and offering a graceful bow. "Good morning, Miss MacTavish. I heard you won More's *Utopia* at auction yesterday. May I congratulate you on your fortitude and excellent purchase?"

Suspicion flared.

Gentlemen rarely gave her compliments.

Gentlemen rarely spoke to her in public.

What was this about?

Ailsa offered a polite reply, then added, "I have an important meeting and willnae keep ye, my lord."

"Perhaps you'd like to ride in the park tomorrow. Amongst other things, we can discuss our mutual love of literature."

"Ride together?" she attempted to clarify. Weird didn't begin to define what was happening here.

Lord Brockton laughed. "Of course."

It was then she noticed other men watching them intently. Was there a wager in the book at White's? The first man to seduce a Scot won a thousand pounds and a Derby-winning stallion?

"Sadly, I havenae a free day this week." She would not be used as a pawn in anyone's game.

"Then perhaps you might permit me the first dance at Lady Winfield's ball. I'm told you've accepted her invitation and mean to attend with the St Clairs."

Had this blackguard been snooping into her affairs?

Wickedness was most definitely at play.

Ailsa had mocked Helen's prediction this morning, yet

here was a dark-haired, dashing gentleman keen to pay court. Did that mean the spell worked on all men? Would she be hounded by the male species in the coming days?

On the bright side, that meant she wasn't destined to marry Lord Denton, and these lustful feelings were all in her head. The thought should have left her sagging in relief.

Oddly, it stirred a more disturbing emotion.

One that felt strangely like regret.

Chapter Six

The clerk stood and said something about Mr Murden, but Sebastian was too busy watching the unfolding scene in the hall to respond with any clarity.

"Yes," came Sebastian's curt reply.

What the devil did Lord Brockton want with Miss MacTavish?

The gentleman grinned like the cat who'd found the cream. His eyes would have bulged from their sockets if he'd seen her hair cascading down her back like a fiery mane. He would have broken into a sweat if he'd wrapped his arms around her lithe body and touched every soft curve.

"If you'd care to wait in the hall, my lord, I shall fetch Mr Murden." The clerk lingered in the doorway and lowered his voice, but the damn fellow blocked Sebastian's view. "He's running a little late. Under the circumstances, I'm sure you understand. And if you can refrain from mentioning the murder to anyone at present, we would be—"

"Yes. Yes." Patience was not Sebastian's forte. "My lips are sealed. The mere suggestion of a murder will send your customers fleeing."

Not wanting to prolong the conversation, he ushered the clerk into the hall, pushed past him and headed for Miss MacTavish.

"Brockton," he said, though he was desperate to quiz the devil and demand to know what the bloody hell he wanted. "I didn't realise you knew Miss MacTavish."

Brockton raised a dark brow, a move akin to throwing down the gauntlet. "We've danced together many times over the years," he lied. The lady spent most of her time hiding behind potted ferns and rarely took to the floor.

"We danced together twice some years ago," she corrected. "Lord Brockton asked if I'd ride out with him tomorrow. He's a lover of literature too."

"He is?" Was Brockton keen to get his hands on More's rare volume? Or did he have plans to make merry with an original? "Did you tell him you're engaged for the foreseeable future?"

"The lady agreed to afford me the first dance at Lady Winfield's ball," the smug oaf said, grinning like he'd won a round in the White Boar's fighting pit.

"She meant the third dance. The first two are promised to me." Sebastian never danced, but he'd be damned if he'd let Brockton have the advantage. "Being a dear family friend, I plan to watch her closely the entire evening."

Miss MacTavish looked at him like he'd sprouted a carrot for a nose. Then she offered Brockton a smile to light the heavens. "I shall mark ye down for a waltz, my lord. Understand 'tis a while since I've danced."

A waltz!

Sebastian suppressed a growl. Was she trying to provoke him?

"Have no fear, madam," Brockton said with an arrogant grin. "I happen to be an exceptional lead."

The fop was so self-assured it was sickening.

"Excuse us, Brockton." Sebastian placed his hand on Miss MacTavish's back to guide her away, ignoring the damnable tingling in his palm. "We have an appointment with the auctioneer and haven't time for idle tattle."

Brockton stole a moment to appreciate Miss MacTavish's figure. "We shall continue our conversation at Lady Winfield's ball. Then your surly chaperone will have no choice but to watch from the wings."

Silently seething while forced to listen to her polite reply, Sebastian made his discontent known the second they were alone. "Why do you snap at me but bat your lashes at Brockton?" He drew her closer to the clerk's office while they waited to meet Murden.

The lady ground her teeth together. "Happen because he doesnae act like a doaty bampot. Did ye hear yerself?"

"A doaty bampot? Is that a form of weasel?" It sounded like a bland stew eaten in a remote Highland village, though he suspected it amounted to a mild insult. "Brockton might be amusing, but he's a known cad. You'd do well to rebuff his advances."

"As I'm nae looking for a husband, I dinnae see why it matters. And I agreed to dance, nae tumble in a haystack."

Sebastian smiled to himself. How could a lady be intelligent and so innocent at the same time? "Do mature adults use the word *tumble*, or is it a Scottish thing?"

She stiffened her spine. "What would ye call it?"

He cupped her elbow and drew her close. "That depends."

"On what?"

"On the woman."

Miss MacTavish's gaze dipped to his mouth. "What would ye call it if ye tumbled me?"

An erotic image slipped into his mind. The lady beneath

him in bed, him holding her hands above her head, ramming into her so hard the headboard cracked the plaster. It wasn't making love, and it wasn't fucking. Whatever it was, it left his cock baton stiff. Left his body aching. Left him so damnably intrigued.

"No words could describe what would happen if we found ourselves in bed, madam." Mere days ago, he would have called it a mistake. The thought of bedding an innocent would have been repugnant. "One way or another the earth would shake. There'd be tremors of biblical proportions."

Her eyes widened as if she found the idea enthralling.

Could she imagine sitting astride him, taking him deep?

Would she beg him to pump faster, tug her hair, suck her bud?

"'Tis the book talking." She pointed discreetly to the ebony box wedged under his arm, as if it were an annoying relative one did not wish to offend. "Ye wouldnae say such things otherwise."

No, of the many tense conversations he'd imagined having with Ailsa MacTavish, none related to them fornicating.

"Are you suggesting I'm a puppet and the devil is pulling my strings?" he snapped.

"Something is dreadfully amiss. But I have good news." She lowered her voice so the grimoire couldn't hear her theory. "While we've both fallen foul of the love spell, it doesnae mean we're developing feelings for each other. I suspect we're about to be plagued by a host of compatible mates. Why else would Lord Brockton approach me?"

Sebastian frowned. "Because you're an attractive woman of good fortune." And he was confused why he'd not seen it before.

"My lord, I've gone to great lengths to make myself invisible. I'm the most unapproachable woman in the *ton*, yet half the men waiting in this hall willnae stop looking in my direction. Explain that if ye will."

Sebastian glanced around the vast hall. Brockton wasn't the only man eyeing Miss MacTavish's delightful form. Mr Smythe-Jones gawped with equal fascination, as did Pendleton.

The rats!

"Perhaps they're wondering why we're together."

"Then shall we test yer theory?" She moved to where Gladys stood like one of the grim marble statues. After exchanging a few words with the maid, the lady returned. "Well?"

Did he tell her every eligible man watched her with hawk-like intensity? Did he tell her there was some truth to her claim? She would likely be the object of many a man's desire.

Good God!

Would desperate debutantes hound him?

Would wallflowers cling to him like ivy?

Would scheming mamas trap him into marriage?

His heart raced faster than his brain. "Then I propose we work together to ward off all predators." It was all so irrational, but he'd be damned if he'd take the risk.

"What can we do?"

He thought for a moment. "What if we pretend we've developed an affection for each other? I'll take you riding in the park. We'll visit a museum or two. Dull places for courting couples. We'll let others think I'm considering proposing."

Lost in thought, she pursed her lips. "Once we've broken the spell, we could say we realised we're nae suited."

"Yes, I'll say you were too opinionated."

She jerked her head. "I'll say ye're as gruff as a bear."

"I don't suffer fools. That doesn't mean I'm hot-tempered."

"My lord, Hostile should be yer middle name."

"I'm not so belligerent with you."

An incredulous snort escaped her. "Admit ye love riling my temper. Ye challenge my opinion at every turn."

Sebastian shrugged. "Very well. I shall endeavour to be more accommodating. That way, people are more likely to believe I've developed some affection for you."

She looked like she doubted his ability to appear convincing. "Aye, but when we're alone, ye should be yer usual domineering self."

"Agreed."

The auctioneer arrived, scurrying along the hall at such speed he was liable to trip over his feet. "My lord, forgive the delay. We expected to remain closed this morning. It's been a terrible strain on all those involved." He peered at the customers crammed into the hall, all waiting to be summoned to the auction room. "Let us continue this conversation in my office, away from prying eyes."

They followed the gentleman to a room at the end of the corridor and instructed Gladys to wait outside the door. The mound of papers on the desk suggested a heavy workload. The green bottle must have contained liquor because the auctioneer snatched it away and hid it in a cluttered cupboard.

"Please, sit down." Mr Murden motioned to the chairs flanking his desk before staring at Miss MacTavish through dirty spectacles. "Madam, perhaps you would rather remain outside. I fear your delicate sensibilities would crumble beneath the weight of this dreadful burden."

Clearly, the man had never met an assertive Highland lass.

Miss MacTavish smiled. "When one lives amid the wilds

of Scotland, one cannae afford to be delicate. Be assured, sir, I'll nae swoon at the first mention of blood."

Murden seemed too agitated to debate the subject. "Mr Daventry said I must afford you every courtesy. I'm told you're assisting the Metropolitan Police Force but have a pressing issue of your own."

Sebastian placed the ebony casket on top of the papers. "This does not contain Thomas More's *Utopia*. Miss MacTavish took delivery late last night. The devil roused her from her bed."

"It was most inconvenient." Being sharp-witted, she added, "I didnae have time to inspect the box before the fellow jumped into a hackney and charged off into the night."

Murden straightened his spectacles. "If you did not take receipt of *Utopia*, what's in the box?"

"The grimoire," Miss MacTavish stated. "The anonymous bidder must have my copy of Thomas More's book. We seek to make an exchange."

A sudden apprehension coiled in Sebastian's gut. What if the intruder had come for the grimoire? What if he'd killed the assistant to gain information? Either way, was the lady's life in danger?

"We want answers," he demanded, knowing Miss MacTavish would object to his next proposal. "We need to know how the mistake occurred and be sure it had nothing to do with your assistant's murder. Only then can we part with the grimoire."

Miss MacTavish's head shot in his direction. "What? We want rid of the spell book today. I'll nae take it home."

"I'll take it home." He'd love nothing more than to pummel the blackguard who'd terrified the lady. And it meant he could examine the pages at length.

"I think ye're missing the point," she said, wagging her brows.

"Murden, we need to question your delivery man," he said. Now was not the time to argue about spells. "We need the name of the fellow who won the grimoire. I advise you to send someone to his property to ascertain if he has More's book."

Murden flapped his hands. Could the man not sit down? "Yes, yes. I should see to that right away. This business has taken its toll. Do you know how long I've worked with Mr Hibbet? Nigh on fifteen years."

"I pray you weren't first on the scene." Such a gruesome discovery would plague one's mind for years. "I'll have questions about alibis later, but for now—"

"Alibis!" Murden clutched his chest. "Surely you don't think a colleague had anything to do with the murder. Why would anyone want to hurt such a gentle soul?"

"That is what we mean to establish. In the meantime, we need you to fetch the delivery man, and we need the name of the person who bought the grimoire."

The auctioneer nodded vigorously. "Yes, yes, I shall find Woodbury. He'll be able to sort out the mistake with the tomes. I shall be back shortly."

As soon as Murden left the office and closed the door, Miss MacTavish was on her feet. "What were ye thinking?"

Sebastian stood. "Be specific, and I'll tell you."

"We must get rid of that thing." She jabbed her finger at the box.

"Though I loathe sounding like a parrot, we cannot hand over a book that may have been the motive for a murder." And he needed to compare it with Michael's book. He could only do that if he took it home.

"We cannae keep it."

"We need to keep it until we determine what happened. The intruder will try to steal it again. We'll lay a trap and catch him in the act. The matter will be resolved in a few days."

It was simple enough for an intelligent woman to understand.

"In a few days!" She threw her hands in the air and began pacing. "We almost kissed last night. What do ye think will happen if this drags on for days?"

Would they have kissed?

He recalled being swamped by erotic thoughts but had no clue she might have been equally bewitched.

"We're strong-minded people," he professed, though his resolve was being tested to the limit. "I'm sure we'll be able to resist the temptation. Besides, there's every chance it will be a disaster."

More like an utter catastrophe.

She blinked like she'd had a sudden epiphany. "Of course. Why did I nae think of it before? 'Tis a sure way to break the enchantment. Kissing ye would be like kissing a brother."

He was about to agree, but a seed of doubt took root.

The volatile nature of their relationship might make her the perfect bed partner. Passionate. Demanding. Dominant.

Then again, the taste of her lips might turn his stomach.

How was he to know without sampling the forbidden fruit?

"What are you suggesting, madam?"

"Is it nae obvious?"

He did not want to be presumptuous. "Not to me."

She squirmed on the spot, her gaze darting between him and the closed door. "Maybe just a quick peck would suffice."

"You're asking me to kiss you?" He pretended to sound horrified.

"I'm asking ye to break the spell." She grumbled under her breath, then berated herself for losing her mind and considering such a foolish notion. "Forget I said anything. We'll muddle along, safe in the knowledge it would have—"

He was on her in a heartbeat.

Their mouths met, clashing together with a force that defied logic. There was no awkward fumbling. No trying to find the right angle to avoid the brim of her bonnet. No hesitance. No tentative strokes. Just a desperate need to feed the craving. A rampant mating of mouths that hardened his cock.

Merciful Mary!

Miss MacTavish gripped his coat lapels, anchoring him to her as he pushed her back against the desk. Paper fell to the floor. The ink pot rattled on the metal stand. They were kissing open-mouthed. Panting. Frantic. Hungering for more. His blood coursed hot and wild in his veins. He needed to grip her buttocks and squeeze hard. Rub his erection against her stomach to ease the damnable ache.

Unable to control the primal urge to thrust, he breached the seam of her soft lips with his tongue.

A sweet moan rumbled in her throat.

But the Highland lass did not surrender. She fought him, the seductive dance of her tongue driving him to the brink of insanity. Never had he wanted a woman more. Never had he considered bending a woman over a desk in another man's office and pounding deep.

Miss MacTavish pulled away on a ragged gasp, desire burning like wildfire in her eyes. "Good Lord!"

"Quite," he managed while trying to gather his wits. Damn, he shook like a virgin schoolboy reaching his first climax.

"What possessed ye to do that?" She batted her skirts, evidently annoyed that their brief clinch hadn't been an utter disaster. "I said a quick peck, nae a thorough ravishment."

"Madam, you put your tongue in my mouth. What was I supposed to do? Ignore the delightful intrusion?" And if he'd meant to ravish her, she'd be spread on the desk, his face buried between her thighs. Indeed, the fact they'd stopped so abruptly left him as randy as a feral dog.

She pressed the backs of her fingers to her flaming cheeks. "On my oath, ye breached my lips first."

"Perhaps it was a simultaneous devouring." He might have taken the lead. Who knew? They'd been so rampant he'd lost use of his faculties. "Regardless, it cannot happen again."

The damn grimoire meant to manipulate events until he breached her maidenhead. Then he'd be hurtling down a slippery slope to marriage.

"I'm nae sure how it happened at all."

"We were attempting to break the spell. It was your idea."

Her eyes widened. "Perhaps it worked. We've nae argued like this for days." With a quick glance at the box, she whispered, "Tell me it was a terrible kiss."

Sebastian swallowed past the truth. It had been the most memorable kiss of his life. "It was so dreadful, I couldn't bear the thought of doing it again."

"Aye," she said, lifting her chin as if about to take to the stage to recite a rousing monologue. "Yer coldness chilled me to the bone."

Her acting skills were poor at best.

The woman had moaned in his mouth on three occasions.

Murden returned, though he said nothing about the paper strewn over the floor. "Forgive the delay. Woodbury has just come back from a delivery." The auctioneer ushered the tubby fellow into his office. "You're at liberty to question him for as long as you need."

Woodbury dragged his cap off his head and held it between his meaty paws. "How can I help you, milord?"

"You can begin by—"

"Mr Murden, how many men work here delivering goods?" Miss MacTavish interjected, a nervous hitch in her voice. "Do ye have other employees? Men other than Mr Woodbury?"

Sebastian turned to her. "Why do you ask?"

The lady swallowed deeply, a shadow of alarm passing over her features. "Because that's nae the man who delivered the casket."

Chapter Seven

Ailsa stared at Lord Denton, making every effort not to look at his mouth and imagine it moving expertly over hers. Kissing him had been a mistake. Her motive for doing so seemed ridiculous now. An otherworldly force had planted the seed in her mind, daring her to indulge in a wicked fantasy that might break the spell.

"Are you certain Woodbury didn't bring the casket?" the lord said, gently cupping her elbow as if compelled to finish what they'd started. "It was dark, and a fog had settled. It may have been difficult to identify him."

She shivered against his touch and fought to concentrate on the simple question. "Aye. The person who gave me the casket had whiskers and lank brown hair. The scar on his knuckles said he'd recently cut his left hand."

Had he cut it while subduing the assistant, while scoring a druid symbol into his forehead?

Mr Murden frowned. "Woodbury was the only one working yesterday. And the document says he delivered your parcel at three in the afternoon. You signed it, madam."

The auctioneer produced the docket.

Lord Denton snatched the paper and scanned it through narrowed eyes before showing her that Mr Murden spoke the truth.

"It states you received the package at three." Lord Denton's gaze met hers, his blue eyes softening when he would usually mock her for the error.

She studied the evidence. "Dinnae try to shift the blame, sir. The servants will testify that the package arrived at ten o'clock. If ye look closely, the time is written in a lighter ink."

Lord Denton's lips curled into a satisfied smile, and he gave her a sly wink of approval. "It seems you have something to confess, Woodbury." Arrogance infused his tone as he approached the fellow. "And please, do not dare call Miss MacTavish a liar, else I might be forced to make you eat your words."

Mr Woodbury's nervous gaze dipped to his feet. He wrung his cap between shaky hands. "I'm not sure what you mean, milord."

"Then let me speak plainly." Lord Denton paused for dramatic effect. "Tell the damn truth, else I'll have you arrested for conspiracy to pervert the course of justice. Who delivered the casket to Miss MacTavish?"

His angry outburst brought some relief. This was the man Ailsa knew, not the one who fired her blood with his wandering hands and rampant kisses.

"Ye had better have an alibi," she added. "Else we might think ye paid someone to run an errand so ye had time to commit murder."

"I swear, miss, I had nothing to do with what happened to poor Mr Hibbet." The man struggled to hold her gaze. "I've been a fool, that's all. Tricked into handing over the box."

"Tricked?" A sudden anger lit Mr Murden's tired eyes.

"Tricked by whom? From the smell of ale on your breath, am I to assume it's someone at the Old Crown tavern?"

Mr Woodbury winced. "Sir, the devil knew what he was doing. He plied me with drink and arranged for me to spend the afternoon with the buxom serving wench. Said he'd take care of my deliveries."

"You gave a stranger our clients' possessions?" Mr Murden rubbed his forehead to ease the mounting tension. "As if I haven't enough to deal with at present. Now I shall have to contact all those who won auctions yesterday and ensure they received the right books."

While Mr Murden continued haranguing his employee, Ailsa tried to determine if either man might have killed Mr Hibbet.

Was Mr Woodbury a naive fool, or was he part of a sinister plot? Did Mr Murden have a reason to murder a man he'd known for fifteen years? Thankfully, it was up to Mr Daventry to decide.

"Has nae one contacted ye about a possible error?"

"Not at present."

"We'll need the name of the person who won the grimoire," Lord Denton said with an aristocrat's arrogance. "Else I shall charge into the auction room and enlighten your patrons. Tell them Woodbury gave Miss MacTavish's book to a thief so he could bed a tavern wench at the Old Crown."

Mr Murden paled. "Do what you must, but I cannot divulge confidential information." He turned and jabbed his finger at his employee. "Wait for me in the packing room. I intend to get to the bottom of this mess. You'd better pray all the books are accounted for, else you'll face a private prosecution."

"Wait," Ailsa said, anticipating the questions Mr

Daventry might ask them later this afternoon. "We need a description of the person at the Old Crown."

Mr Woodbury described the delivery man to a tee, which meant Mr Daventry would have to visit the Old Crown to corroborate the story. "The scar looked to be a few days old."

So, not one inflicted during a struggle with Mr Hibbet.

Mr Woodbury left, and the auctioneer waited a few seconds before whispering, "I shall give you the name. I'm not sure who to trust anymore, and I did not want to reveal his identity to Woodbury."

"But Woodbury had the delivery address," his lordship said, confused.

"He was to deliver it to the milliners on Newport Street. Once I give you the name, you'll understand the need for secrecy. The professor is often subjected to a torrent of abuse."

"The professor?"

"I'm not sure he's an actual professor," Mr Murden admitted. "That's to say, I'm not sure one can obtain a certificate when training in the dark arts. Professor Mangold runs the Guild of Unexplained Phenomena. They meet weekly at a secret location near Leicester Square. I know this because he often purchases curiosities."

That explained why someone would pay handsomely for an old grimoire. The sinister man seated in the front row that day must be a competitor or a minister keen to burn the devil's work.

"We'll need the name of the man who bid against me," she said, a chill creeping over her shoulders as she recalled his evil stare. "As everyone had to register before bidding, that shouldnae be a problem."

Mr Murden moved to the desk and rifled through the jumbled papers. "Here it is. Oh! His name is Smith. There's an address in Tavistock Street, Covent Garden." He found a quill pen, wrote the details on a scrap of paper and handed it to Lord Denton.

"Should Professor Mangold complain about his missing grimoire, say you'll look into the matter." His lordship scanned the note. "It will give me time to investigate the guild."

Investigate the guild?

He had agreed to assist Mr Daventry, not take matters into his own hands. But what did one expect from a man who took command of every situation? No wonder he refused to relinquish the ebony box. Doubtless he suspected the professor had a motive for murder.

"Before we leave, can ye tell us anything about Mr Hibbet?" Hopefully, he would not relay every gruesome detail.

"There's not much to tell. He was unmarried and lived on the upper floor." Mr Murden sniffed and gave a mournful sigh. "He was not just an assistant but custodian of Chadwick's. Old Mr Chadwick gave him the apartment just before he took ill."

"Mr Chadwick is still alive?" she said.

"Yes, though he's bedridden and leaves the running of the auction house to me these days." Lowering his voice, Mr Murden added, "His daughter prefers it that way. The ailing fellow is not always of sound mind."

Preparing to depart, Lord Denton snatched the box off the desk. "We'll need to search the apartment before we leave."

"I'm afraid that's impossible. It's considered a crime scene until the Great Marlborough Street men have finished their investigation." He pulled his handkerchief from his pocket and mopped the sweat from his brow. "It will take a week to clean the bloodstains. In all my days, I've never seen anything so sickening."

A heavy silence ensued.

"We shall leave ye to deal with Mr Woodbury." She looked at Lord Denton, who nodded in agreement. "Mr Daventry will keep ye informed of our progress and arrange for the grimoire's return."

They made for the door, but struck by an intense curiosity, Ailsa turned. "I almost forgot. I need the name of the person who paid for my copy of *Utopia*. Ensuring I won may have been part of a plot to swap the books."

Mr Murden shifted uncomfortably. "I can confirm it was a generous gesture by someone who wanted you to own the rare volume."

"As much as we'd like to trust your word," Lord Denton snapped, "under the circumstances, you can see why that's impossible. You'll give us the name."

Mr Murden tutted while having a brief tussle with his conscience. "I suppose you'll find out eventually, but in the meantime, I must ask you to keep the information to yourself." He did not need to scour his records. The name slipped off his tongue with ease. "Mrs Sybil Daventry wanted you to have the book, madam."

Hart Street, Covent Garden
Office of the Order

"If you care to wait in the drawing room, I'll have Mr Daventry attend you as soon as he returns." The friendly housekeeper pointed to a room off the hall. "He's at Great Marlborough Street and won't be long." She offered a beaming smile, then took Gladys to the kitchen to help with the tea tray.

Ailsa wondered if this was a conspiracy.

At every given opportunity, she found herself alone with Viscount Denton. Even strangers sought to nurture this unlikely relationship. Perhaps they were receiving other-worldly cues from the wings.

Lord Denton gestured for her to lead the way.

The second they were alone, the atmosphere changed along with his demeanour. His stern gaze softened, his mouth curling with satisfaction rather than remaining in a rigid line. Intimacy swirled between them, warm like a gentle summer breeze.

She did not need to look at him to know his gaze wandered over her figure. She sensed his mounting interest, his need to study her as if she were a complicated addition to his library. Something he was determined to decipher, keen to understand.

In a bid to settle her pulse, she scanned the room.

Mr Daventry's business premises was more like an aristocrat's mansion house than a place of work. The plush decor and expensive furniture confirmed it was on par with the wealthiest homes in Mayfair.

Ailsa was deciding where to sit when Lord Denton touched her lightly on the arm. "I've never known you be so quiet." Concern marred the lord's tone, along with this confounding familiarity. "Are your lips pursed because you fear I might slip my tongue into your mouth again?"

The devil!

Did he have to remind her of their amorous interlude?

"So, ye admit ye're to blame for it being more than a peck?"

Amusement danced in his eyes. "I'm happy to accept responsibility if it eases your embarrassment."

"I'm nae embarrassed." She was shocked. Shocked, she had been so free with her affections. Shocked that kissing him had felt as natural as breathing air. Lord Denton was the last man she thought would fan the flames of desire. "I find it hard to understand how matters progressed so quickly."

Her confession was met with an impressed grin. "You mean how the mere brush of our lips ended in a rampant tongue tangling? Why we were minutes away from stripping off our clothes and indulging in every wild pleasure?"

Och, this man loved making her squirm. "At nae time did I think about removing my garments."

"No," he drawled. "It's clear we weren't thinking at all. But if my mouth sends you into such a frenzy, one wonders what would happen if my hands found their way up your skirts."

Mother Mary!

"Thankfully, we're in nae danger of finding out." She dared to glance at the box he'd placed on the chair. "Mr Daventry will take the grimoire for safekeeping, and our problems will be solved."

"He seemed keen for us to keep it."

"'Tis evidence in a murder investigation." A thought entered her head, and she glanced at the door before whispering, "What if Mrs Daventry arranged for me to have the wrong book? What if she believes in spells and premonitions and wants me to fall in love? What if the intruder came to steal More's *Utopia*?"

The viscount frowned. "Mrs Daventry is a staunch

believer in women's reform. I suspect she didn't want you to lose the book just because you're a woman with limited funds."

"Aye, ye may be right." Yet she couldn't shake these suspicions. Perhaps because she was unused to Lord Denton being the voice of reason.

He arched a brow. "You agree? This is becoming a habit."

"Enjoy it while it lasts. When this is over, I shall go back to calling ye a doaty bampot."

His smile reached his beguiling eyes. "When this is over, I doubt we'll snipe at each other like we used to."

No, she feared their relationship had changed. She would always wonder what might have happened had she allowed him to put his hands up her skirts. Whenever he opened his mouth, she would remember that passionate kiss.

"Then we should begin now, before it's too late. Teasing ye is the highlight of the London Season." Struggling to find anything unpleasant about him at present, she returned to their old jibes about his excessive use of cologne. "Though after suffering yer sickly scent for days, I long to fill my lungs with Scottish air."

He hit her with a maddening smirk. "Cologne is my weapon of choice. This is new from Truefitt & Hill and is said to repel stubborn Scots."

"It didnae work and smells like old leather carriage seats."

"It does? Can you not pick out the notes of musk and vanilla?" Strong fingers captured her wrist, tugging her closer. He turned his head, offering his sculpted jaw and a chance to inhale the fragrance.

Ailsa craned her neck and sniffed, ready to wrinkle her nose and feign a sudden coughing fit. A week ago, she would have mocked him, sought a means to knock him off his pedestal. Not anymore.

Mingled with cologne was the earthy essence of the man. A bewitching scent that assaulted her senses, left her so dizzy she placed her hand on his chest.

The hard planes flexed beneath her fingers. "It can be rather overpowering," he said. "A cologne should reflect something of the man who wears it. Do you not agree?"

"Aye," she breathed.

He turned his head. Their mouths were but inches apart. The close proximity proved more dazing than the masculine fragrance. His hot breath on her lips sent a bolt of heat to her core.

"Perhaps I'm not as dominant as I profess," he said.

"What makes ye say that?"

He looked at her mouth, a moan rumbling in his throat. "Because despite everything I've said to the contrary, I'm like a fly trapped in your womanly web."

Ailsa swallowed. This man knew how to make her feel desirable. "'Tis only lust, my lord." And a mindless curiosity. An insatiable hunger. "Surely ye've battled against it many times in the past."

"Never like this."

Having grown tired of blaming the grimoire, she sought another explanation. "This often happens when two unattached people spend time alone together. 'Tis why we need a chaperone."

"What if I don't want a chaperone? Neither of us wants to marry. What if we give in to our whims and begin a romantic affair? It's obvious we're compatible."

She blinked as her body and mind went to war. "Ye're suggesting we become lovers?" It was outrageous—as tempting as it was terrifying.

Lord Denton shook his head as if to jolt his logical brain from slumber. "Forgive me. Doubtless, it's the greatest insult of your life."

And yet she wasn't offended.

"I have the utmost respect for you, madam," he said, though he did not straighten or pull away. "Too much respect to take liberties when I cannot offer marriage. Again, forgive me for speaking out of turn."

"We're not acting like ourselves. And the strange events these last two days have left us questioning many things."

They fell silent, though their gazes remained locked.

"A case of road dust in the eye, Miss MacTavish?" Mr Daventry's amused voice dragged them from the spell.

Lord Denton released her abruptly. "Quite."

Ailsa coughed to hide her embarrassment. "After the poisonings at the perfumery last month, Lord Denton wished me to smell Truefitt's new cologne."

"I'm surprised you couldn't smell it from the doorway." Mr Daventry motioned to the sofas and waited for them to sit before dropping into a chair and updating them on the case. "I've just returned from a meeting with the coroner. He believes the murderer had some knowledge of anatomy. That, or he has committed other ritualistic killings in the past."

He removed a piece of paper from his brown leather portfolio and gave it to Lord Denton. The lord studied it carefully before handing it to her.

It was a pencil sketch of the murder scene. The villain had tied Mr Hibbet's wrists to the legs of his desk, bound his ankles in fetters.

"What can you tell me from looking at the scene?"

Lord Denton shuffled closer to her, his arm touching hers as they both examined the frightful image. She tried to concentrate but was distracted by the sound of his breathing, by the deep rise and fall of his chest.

"There are no defensive wounds," the lord said, pointing to the annotated drawing. "Mr Hibbet knew his killer."

"Or was plied with drink and subdued," she added.

Mr Daventry nodded. "Excellent. They lock the doors to the auction house at seven. Mr Hibbet must have let his killer in. They found a bottle of expensive Armagnac on the desk but only one glass."

It seemed odd that a mere assistant could afford to waste money on liquor. "Maybe the killer had a key and brought the Armagnac with him." Something else struck her as strange. "Ye came to warn me just before midnight. How was the body found so quickly if the auction house was locked?"

Mr Daventry grinned. "At nine o'clock, a woman approached the watchman and said she heard screams coming from the auction house. The door was open. I happened to be dining with the magistrate when a constable informed him of the murder."

Lord Denton gave a short hum. "Did you find Mr Hibbet's waistcoat and cravat near the body?"

"No, his clothes were folded neatly in the armoire. Why?"

"Based on his relaxed dress and there being one glass, we might assume he was entertaining a woman, a lover. I trust the watchman gave you a description of the informant."

"A vague one at best." Mr Daventry flicked to a page in his notebook. "Thirty. Dark hair, though it may have been a wig. Pretty face. Nothing to help identify her amongst a crowd."

"A woman didnae do this." Ailsa doubted one person could have managed it on their own. "She had an accomplice. She couldnae have held a pistol to Mr Hibbet's head and made him shackle himself to the desk. And she couldnae do it herself while holding a weapon."

"Agreed," Mr Daventry said.

"The woman's claim seems dubious." Lord Denton's long, elegant finger came to rest on the sketch of Mr Hibbet's chest. "Had she heard Hibbet scream, the watchman would have caught the murderer in the act. In all likelihood, the man was killed quickly. A stab to the heart before the killer mutilated the body. One suspects the ritual aspect is a means of disguising the real motive."

Mr Daventry's gaze shifted between them. "You really do make quite a remarkable couple. Equally insightful. Tell me what you discovered today."

Ailsa felt a blush rise to her cheeks. Amongst other things, they'd discovered this confounding attraction could not be tempered. That when they kissed, the world blurred into the background. That they lost their heads whenever they were alone together. That she suddenly found the lord's gruff manner appealing.

While she recalled Lord Denton's indecent proposal, he revealed what they'd learned from the auctioneer. He spoke about the plot to fool the delivery man and named Professor Mangold as the person who won the grimoire.

"I know of the guild," Mr Daventry said. "On the surface, Mangold seems harmless. Just another man disgruntled with his maker and seeking answers elsewhere. We'll need to probe deeper."

"We were told he's unpopular with the masses, hence why he did not attend the auction." A thread of excitement in Lord Denton's voice said he welcomed the prospect of interviewing the professor.

Did it have something to do with the book found in his

brother's quarters aboard *The Perseus*? Was the lord seeking spiritual answers to cope with his grief?

"I shall contact him to arrange a meeting." Mr Daventry took his pencil and scribbled a reminder in his notebook. "You'll say you're investigating the power of incantations but will not mention having his grimoire."

Ailsa swallowed past a lump in her throat. "Sir, Lord Denton agreed to act as yer agent but 'tis best if ye send someone else to assist him." It was the only way to ensure she didn't fall under his spell.

"There's no one else, madam. And your insight will be invaluable to the case. Denton will keep you safe if that's your concern."

Safe!

He'd behaved just as recklessly.

Despite being a strong Highland lass, she was in danger of succumbing to temptation. That said, did the professor know of an antidote, a way to break the enchantment? As a disbeliever, Lord Denton wouldn't think to ask.

"I suppose I could go with his lordship to meet the professor." Heavens, Mr Daventry must think she had the discipline of a young pup. "It will add credibility to the story."

Lord Denton didn't tut or grumble as he'd been wont to do that day at the auction. The lord's mischievous grin spoke of a desire for her company.

"And I'll need you to visit the Old Crown with him," Mr Daventry said. Anyone would think he got paid for every hour they spent together. "It would be wise to have a woman's perspective when taking the wench's statement."

The gentleman removed a letter from his portfolio and gave it to Lord Denton. "Should you encounter any resistance during your investigation, this will help to secure the suspects' co-operation."

The viscount read the letter before leaning closer. "It's from Viscount Melbourne." He did not presume her ignorant of the fact the peer served as Home Secretary. "He grants us the same rights as the magistrate."

Some men would not welcome a woman or a Scot interfering in English business. But Lord Denton conveyed such a powerful masculinity, she doubted many would argue.

Mr Daventry closed his portfolio. "Miss MacTavish, I suggest you remain with the St Clairs. Your butler is bedridden but recovering well, and we still don't know the intruder's identity. I shall send word there when I've arranged for you to interview the professor."

Lord Denton sat forward. "We could visit the Old Crown tavern later tomorrow. See if we can find the fiend who delivered the wrong book."

"Yes, see if the wench knows his name." Mr Daventry stood and fixed the viscount with his penetrating gaze. "I trust you will also reside with your sister until the matter is concluded. As you uncover evidence, the killer will seek to secure your silence."

"I'm quite capable of protecting myself, though I'll not endanger my sister. I shall take the grimoire to my house in Grosvenor Street."

The master of the Order frowned as he shook his head. "The gruesome nature of the crime lends me to err on the side of caution. As you say, we may be dealing with two villains." He looked between them while deciding what should be done. "Having lost a man once, I refuse to take a chance with your lives."

"What are you suggesting?" Lord Denton said impatiently.

"You'll both reside at a location of my choosing."

Ailsa jumped to her feet in protest. "But we cannae live

together. I'll nae put his lordship in a situation where he is forced to propose." And if the kiss was any benchmark, they'd be writhing in bed before the week's end.

Mr Daventry raised a reassuring hand. "We'll take tea while I think on the matter. Then I'll tell you what I have planned."

"What you have planned?" the viscount scoffed. "I'm not a boy of ten. I answer to no man."

He had a valid point.

Was Mr Daventry conspiring with fate?

Mr Daventry's eyes darkened. "You made a gentleman's agreement to act as my agent. Your word is your bond. And I promised Lord MacTavish I would take care of his daughter. If you want to solve this mystery, you'll both do exactly as I say."

Chapter Eight

Fortune's Den
Aldgate Street

"They'll use my unmarked carriage. Mr Gibbs will act as their driver and brawling companion should they encounter any difficulties." Daventry relaxed back in the gilt chair, the scales of justice engraved on his signet ring visible as he gripped his brandy glass. "Agree to let them stay here, and I shall be in your debt."

Aaron Chance, known as the King of Clubs to the men who frequented his gaming hell, stared at Daventry. "You know my views on ladies living under this roof. I guarantee my brothers will find it equally insufferable."

Sebastian silently cursed. All four Chance brothers lived on the premises. He had to wonder if the strain of working long hours had affected Daventry's logic.

It was Miss MacTavish who offered a retort. "Desperate times call for desperate measures. In truth, I'd rather nae suffer the fools who gamble their fortunes here, sir. For the life of me, I cannae understand the attraction."

Aaron Chance's brow quirked. "All men have their vices, madam. Have you never felt your blood course wildly in your veins? There's nothing quite like the risk of ruin to make one feel alive."

A blush touched the lady's cheeks.

One that doubtless had nothing to do with the dissolute lords of the *ton*, and everything to do with an erotic kiss in the auctioneer's office. Realising women felt lust as keenly as men, she'd stolen more than the odd glance at Sebastian's lips.

"I'm not a petty man," Daventry said, an air of warning in his tone, "but you wouldn't have known about the plot to kidnap your sister had I not brought it to your attention."

Aaron gritted his teeth. "You gave your word you would never mention the *incident*. I had you marked as a loyal man. Now Denton and Miss MacTavish are party to my personal affairs."

"My agents have signed a non-disclosure agreement."

Daventry had given Sebastian little choice in the matter. To learn more about Michael's grimoire, he had to play by the man's rules. And a pang deep in his gut said his brother hadn't died from a tropical fever.

Aaron tossed back his brandy and slammed the glass on the side table. "So, you have me by the ballocks." He glanced at Miss MacTavish. "If you're going to spend a few nights here, madam, you'll discover gamblers have the mouths of sewer rats. Perhaps you should find somewhere else to rest your pretty head if you find that offensive."

Sebastian's chest tightened. Aaron never complimented a woman. He was cold, as hard as new dice. Was he captivated by the Scottish temptress or enchanted by the damn spell?

Sebastian hoped neither was true. Else he would challenge the King of Clubs to a round in the basement's fighting pit.

Miss MacTavish gave a mocking snort. "Clearly, ye've never had dealings with my father, sir, else ye'd know I dinnae find coarse language offensive."

"Excellent. Let's hope you're accustomed to hearing creaking beds and pleasurable moans in the dead of night. Gentlemen sometimes rent the rooms on the first floor to enjoy not-so-quiet moments with their mistresses."

The lady showed no outward sign she found such matters distasteful. "If ye'd ever held a clan meeting in yer home, Mr Chance, ye would know pleasurable moans bring light relief. I trust none of yer patrons ever hack the dining table with a claymore."

A sudden flash of amusement in the man's eye roused Sebastian's ire. "So, you're more an original than a bluestocking, Miss MacTavish."

"I'm a Scot, sir. Where I'm from, there's nothing original about hardiness. Though I thank ye, for I recognise 'tis an English compliment."

"I hoped Miss MacTavish might have a bed in your sister's room," Daventry said. "I trust Delphine is home at present. I know she likes to escape the metropolis whenever possible."

Aaron narrowed his gaze, evidently wondering if Daventry knew something he didn't. "I'm sure she will be delighted to have female company. It will break the monotony." Aaron turned to Sebastian. "You're quiet, Denton. Surely you think this whole idea is absurd. As a man who's saving marriage for his dotage, staying under the same roof as an innocent is akin to putting your neck in a noose."

Sebastian slid his fingers under his collar. Dallying with

Miss MacTavish was the closest he'd ever come to experiencing rope burn.

"The lady's life is in danger."

They had both stayed with Helen last night and had barely slept a wink. Every noise had them leaping out of bed. Miss MacTavish had peered around the door jamb to find him lingering on the landing, wearing nothing but a burgundy silk robe.

"As a gentleman, her welfare is my primary concern," Sebastian continued. "We're both strong enough to weather the storm."

Mischief danced in Aaron's eyes. "Tell that to MacTavish. I never gamble, but I'm inclined to make a wager on the outcome."

He might have challenged the devil, but Miss MacTavish gave an insightful reply.

"Ye should never gamble with fate, Mr Chance. The odds are poor at best. The outcome is often unpredictable. Have ye never found yerself in a situation nae one could have predicted?"

A darkness passed over Aaron's features, and the atmosphere thrummed with tension. "Almost every day of my life, madam."

Daventry cleared his throat. "Well? Can they stay for a few days?"

Aaron dragged his hand through his black hair and swore beneath his breath. "If they follow the rules. Miss MacTavish cannot leave her room during opening hours. She must remain on the third floor and keep her door locked." He shot Sebastian a wary glance. "Denton is not allowed in her chamber. If they must discuss the case, they will do so in the dining room. Is that clear?"

Miss MacTavish nodded. "What if we need to go out at

night? Can I gain access to the upstairs rooms without entering the club?"

"Denton will knock on the viewing hatch while you remain hidden. Sigmund will sneak you inside, madam." Aaron Chance faced Daventry, a determination in his gaze. "Three days. No more."

"A week," Daventry countered. "And I shall give you information about a certain lord's interest in Delphine."

Aaron shot out of the chair. "You'll give me his name now. Is it Pendergast?"

"No." Daventry reached into his portfolio, withdrew a folded note and handed it to Aaron. He kept a firm grip on the paper until Aaron agreed to let them stay for a week.

Protecting one's sister was difficult enough. Protecting one's sister when half the men in the *ton* wished you dead must be nigh on impossible.

Aaron tore back the folds and glared at whatever was written inside. Regardless of what people said about the King of Clubs, he would protect his kin with his life.

The man's reaction reminded Sebastian of his own short-comings. He should have put a pistol to Captain Wainwright's head and demanded answers. He should have interrogated the crew and learned what had really happened to Michael.

But by the time *The Perseus* had returned to England's shores, his father had died, and Sebastian's responsibilities became a significant burden.

Still, anger lived inside him like a bloodthirsty wolf.

And by God, he needed his pound of flesh.

"I despise being in anyone's debt, Chance," Sebastian said, keen to prove he had power in his own right and was not at Daventry's beck and call, "and I always pay my dues. Should you need assistance in any matter forthwith, you only need ask."

Aaron screwed the paper in his fist, throwing it into the fire before saying, "I shall hold you to that, Denton."

Then Miss MacTavish did something surprising and jumped to Sebastian's defence. "Lord Denton is quite rigid when it comes to keeping oaths. You can trust his word. And kindness begets kindness. If ye would like me to talk to Miss Chance on any matter, know I shall oblige."

Aaron considered the lady, his gaze lingering on her person for far too long. He professed to have no time for women, but Miss MacTavish's forthright manner doubtless had great appeal.

While Sebastian's blood simmered, Aaron gave a curt nod. "Wait here. Help yourselves to refreshment. I shall speak to Delphine and see what rooms we have available."

As soon as Aaron left the plush office, Sebastian crossed the room and pulled the stopper from the brandy decanter, keen to soothe his mounting ire.

Daventry appeared at his shoulder to offer one of his banal truisms. "Love is never without jealousy."

What the devil?

Was Sebastian's slight possessiveness so obvious?

Had the serpent writhing in his chest started hissing?

"I wouldn't know. I'm not jealous, and I'm not in love." Yes, he was eager to protect a woman he considered a friend. When it came to the spell, was it not right to show concern over a man's sudden interest? "We may be friends, but do not presume to know what I'm feeling."

"I was referring to Aaron Chance," Daventry said, amused.

Damn. Sebastian rarely jumped to conclusions. "I see."

"When a man has fought his way up from the streets, he seeks to keep his family close and is fearful of change."

Daventry gestured for Sebastian to pour brandy into his glass. "Aaron won't cope when one of his brothers leaves the nest."

What would Aaron do if his brother died under mysterious circumstances? "They share a lucrative business. I doubt they plan to sail the high seas, cross oceans and live a thousand miles apart."

"No." Daventry glanced at Miss MacTavish, who had taken a book from the side table and was busy scanning the pages. "That reminds me, Mr Kirkwood is a regular patron here. I'm told he served with your brother Michael aboard *The Perseus*. Perhaps you might play a game of hazard together."

Suspicion flared.

Daventry knew something.

"For what purpose?"

Daventry shrugged. "To reminisce. To discover what life was like aboard the vessel." *To delve into your brother's private affairs*, he might have added.

"Is this where you tell me that nothing is coincidental? That one must make the most of every opportunity?" Was Daventry manipulating events from the orchestra pit? A maestro directing him and Miss MacTavish, forcing them to dance to his tune.

"Am I that predictable?" he teased.

"Yes, and I'm well aware of your motivations here."

"What are his motivations?" Miss MacTavish said, joining the conversation. "Do ye speak of the grimoire?"

Daventry replied, revealing the connection to Mr Kirkwood before Sebastian had time to draw breath. "A death abroad must rouse many questions. I merely thought Denton might use the opportunity to address concerns over his brother's sudden demise."

"Concerns?" Miss MacTavish's brow furrowed. "I thought he died of a tropical fever."

Every muscle in Sebastian's body stiffened. The memories did not live in his mind. To speak of them would mean dragging a net deep into the belly of the beast and hauling the debris to the surface.

"He did," Daventry said, keen to dredge up the past. "But Denton clearly has unresolved issues. He fights the hardest man in the White Boar's fighting pits every anniversary. He has to punish someone for what happened to his brother. That's where he gained the scar on his jaw. My agent, Mr D'Angelo, always attends the event."

Sebastian met Miss MacTavish's wide-eyed gaze. He expected her nose to wrinkle, to see the sour pout of disapproval, but she looked at him as if he were a Highland warrior come to rid the village of a scourge.

He could imagine the mechanisms in her mind smoking from overwork. Later would come questions he would refuse to answer, and they'd be back to bickering.

The lady's gaze softened. "Men have a way of dealing with pain that women rarely understand. But from what I've seen of my father, I know inaction breeds self-contempt."

Sebastian stared at her. Somehow, she had managed to see into his soul and identify the crux of his problem. He wasn't angry with the world. He was angry with himself.

"Here, let me give you this before Aaron Chance returns." Daventry reached into his waistcoat pocket and handed Sebastian two keys on a brass ring. "They're for Chadwick's Auction House. One is for the front door, the other for Hibbet's apartment. Delay your visit to the Old Crown until tomorrow. This matter is a priority."

Glad of the distraction, Sebastian dropped the keys into

his coat pocket. "I thought we were forbidden from entering the apartment."

"You are. I need the keys back tonight. Bring them to the Hart Street office before midnight. I'm dining with the magistrate Sir Oswald and need to slip them into his coat before he leaves."

"What are we looking for?" Miss MacTavish said.

"If I knew that, madam, I wouldn't need to give you the key. Use your intuition. But you cannot remove evidence from the scene." Mr Daventry hardened his gaze. "And whatever happens, do not get caught on the premises."

Leaving Fortune's Den under cover of darkness should have been a simple affair. But with a host of rowdy gentlemen queuing to gain admission, it was a feat of military precision.

"What kept you?" Lord Denton said from the dark confines of Mr Daventry's unmarked carriage. "It's almost nine, which doesn't leave much time to search Hibbet's apartment."

Ailsa considered him sitting amid the gloom, all broad shoulders and solid thighs. "Delphine insisted I wear her clothes, and I had to wait until gameplay began before Sigmund could usher me safely outside."

Delphine, who dressed in the height of fashion and adored blue, had literally emptied her armoire to find something suitable.

Lord Denton gave a hum of approval as his gaze slipped over the midnight-blue dress and matching cloak. "The dress fits you like a glove. And it's good to see you in something other than that brown monstrosity."

"Ye mean the dress ye said resembled a sack?"

"The dress you use to disguise your womanly attributes."

Panic fluttered in her throat. She knew the next question before it left his lips but pretended she hadn't heard him ask why. "Must we keep the blinds closed? 'Tis so dark in here it feels like Satan's boudoir."

Something about the lack of light lent itself to the illicit. Being alone with Lord Denton made this feel like a clandestine affair.

"We must do everything possible to prevent being seen. And you're avoiding my question."

Her tongue grew thick, her throat tightening.

Dare she admit to being a naive fool?

"Why do you persist in drawing attention away from yourself?" He spoke so bluntly she knew he would not rest until he had an answer.

"For the same reasons ye avoid dancing with debutantes. So, I cannae be drawn into a compromising situation." The memory of Mr Ashbury's assault flashed into her mind. A fiend grabbing her in the blackness. "So a reprobate cannae use me for his own gain."

He must have heard the thread of anger in her voice. "You've encountered such a fellow before?"

"Aye, at my come-out ball." She kept her tone even, determined to disguise the cracks in her voice. She breathed through the painful stab to her heart. "Thankfully, he didnae take my virtue." He'd stolen a young woman's hopes and dreams instead. Shown her the world was a wicked place where romantic fantasies were for fools. "He tore silk from my gown and kept it to bribe my father, though the matter was resolved quickly."

The lord's breathing deepened like that of a beast hunting prey. "You will give me his name, madam."

"His name? Why?"

"So I might ensure he never lays a damn finger on you again."

"'Tis nae yer concern."

"I am making it my concern." He spoke like a champion of justice. "Tell me his name, else I shall hound your friends and family until I discover the truth."

Despite the hardness of his voice, the frostiness clinging to every word, heat warmed Ailsa's chest. Perhaps one needed Scottish blood to find a warrior's ruthlessness attractive.

"The man is dead."

Lord Denton huffed as if robbed of the need to seek vengeance.

"I appreciate yer brotherly concern, my lord, but—"

"My interest in you is by no means brotherly. If that frightens you, be assured this possessiveness will pass."

Ailsa couldn't stop the smile forming or the chuckle escaping her lips. The man tried to rationalise and control every human emotion. "Doubtless ycr need to play protector stems from us working together on the case."

The viscount rubbed his muscular thigh like it pained him. "No, it stems from my sudden desire to bed you. A raw primal need that defies logic. One made worse by our close proximity."

"Oh!" Ailsa glanced at the empty seat next to him. Such talk was to be expected when in the grimoire's company. But they had locked the item away in Mr Chance's steel vault. Still, she decided to tease him. "Of course, it wouldnae be logical to *want* to bed me. Hence why ye need to find some other explanation."

He sat forward, his masculine presence filling the small space. "I meant the compelling nature of these lustful feelings can rob a man of his will. I imagine you're a woman most men would like to bed, but the very thought leaves me seething. That damn grimoire has a lot to answer for, madam."

"So, ye admit we're under its spell?"

"I admit I'm not myself at present."

They fell silent, both gazing at the blinds, at the black leather upholstery, at anything except at each other.

Amid the stillness, an alarming thought struck her. Truth be told, she rather enjoyed Lord Denton's attentions. Despite his shocking declarations, she felt safe in his company. And that kiss! Well, she was almost desperate to feel the heat of his lips and the rampant plunges of his tongue.

Hmm. How many times would she need to kiss him before it grew tiresome? Men rarely kept the same mistress for more than a few months. Was that not proof sexual attraction fizzled to nothing? Yes, maybe the more they locked lips, the more their passion would wane.

The coachman, Mr Gibbs, brought the carriage to a sudden halt. A quick peek beneath the blinds confirmed they were in Broad Street, a short walk from Chadwick's Auction House.

Mr Gibbs had made it clear he served as a guard, not a peer's lackey, and so Lord Denton sat forward and reached for the door handle. "If you would prefer to remain here, I'm happy to search the premises alone."

The painful constriction in her chest said she needed to protect him, too. "Mr Daventry suggests two minds are better than one, and it would kill me to sit here imagining all manner of horrors." With their knees so close they touched, she tapped him playfully on the thigh. "And with spindles for legs, ye may need my support."

He captured her hand and let her feel the power in the

firm muscle. "I've the legs of an Olympian, madam." He smoothed her hand back and forth. "Feel the proof beneath your fingers, then you need never doubt my word again."

Magic swirled in the air between them.

So intense it left them both breathless.

Ailsa swallowed past the lump in her throat, resisting the urge to flex her fingers and explore every hard contour. "My lord, ye should raise the barricade and ready yer defences. I fear there's every chance we will kiss again tonight."

He ran his tongue over his bottom lip. "Yes, I have every reason to think you might be right. Perhaps now is as good a time as any. Then we might concentrate on the case."

Her galloping pulse sent heat coursing through her body. "Do ye nae want to fight the urge? Resist the temptation?"

"Not in the slightest," he drawled, his thumb stroking the back of her hand. "Though loath to admit it, I lack the strength needed to resist, and we're quite alone."

They moved closer.

Pulled together by an otherworldly force.

A coiling need wound tighter in her belly.

But then Mr Gibbs thumped the carriage roof and yelled in a broad East London accent, "Have you fallen asleep in there?"

Lord Denton firmed his jaw and muttered a curse. "That man has the manners of a gutter rat. When it comes to it, he'd better be handy with his fists, else there'll be hell to pay."

Trying not to acknowledge her disappointment, Ailsa focused on their current task. "Mr Gibbs said it's his job to keep us healthy, not happy."

"If I don't kiss you again soon, I'll likely expire from desperation."

Ailsa laughed. This profound desire was absurd. "Two

weeks ago, ye couldnae bear my company for more than a few minutes."

"That's not true. Our spats have been my only source of amusement for some time. Arguing with you was the highlight of my week."

Her breath caught in her throat. While his passionate kisses stole her sanity, confessing his feelings posed a greater danger. Having inherited her mother's gentle heart, the need to soothe Lord Denton's woes would leave her vulnerable, too exposed.

"Time's a ticking!" came Mr Gibbs' warning.

Lord Denton shoved open the carriage door and vaulted to the pavement. "I'm well aware of my duties this evening," he snapped.

"Then happen you should get a move on. We need to be in Covent Garden before the stroke of midnight. You've an hour at most to see to your business."

The lord handed Ailsa down. "Park at the end of the street, Mr Gibbs. That way, ye'll be able to ring yer bell to warn us if ye see anyone enter the auction house."

Mr Gibbs doffed his weather-beaten hat. "Beggin' your pardon, ma'am, but I'm equipped with a handbell, not the might of St Paul's."

"I'm from the Highlands, Mr Gibbs. I'm trained to hear the ring of the supper bell from a mile away."

The man gave a hapless shrug. "Have it your way, but if you're caught with your fingers in the pie, don't expect me to clean up the mess."

Chapter Nine

They slipped into the auction house. The air grew thick with nervous energy when Lord Denton locked the heavy oak door behind them. Alisa squinted amid the never-ending blackness, though the white marble floor gave a modicum of light.

They paused in the hall and listened.

Quietness crept through the place like an invisible spectre, raising the hairs on Ailsa's nape, twisting the knot in her stomach.

A murderer had stalked these walkways, his intention clear as he mounted the stone staircase. Had Mr Hibbet pleaded with his attacker, or had the first plunge of the knife caught him unawares?

"We have little time to waste." Ailsa would not breathe easily until they were in the carriage, charging through the fog-filled streets back to Aldgate.

Being strangely attuned to her thoughts and fears, Lord Denton placed a comforting hand on the small of her back as they climbed the stairs to the upper floor. Taking tentative steps, they stopped outside a door at the end of the stark landing.

Lord Denton faced her. "Are you sure about this?"

Sure about what? Witnessing the blood splatters or the promise of sharing a passionate kiss? "Aye. Let us get the matter over with and return the keys posthaste."

Lord Denton unlocked the door and prised it slowly from the jamb. He guided her into the unlit hall, though their eyes were already accustomed to the gloom.

He locked the door behind them and slipped the keys into his coat pocket. For long, drawn-out seconds, they paused in the narrow space before he said, "We'll stay together. Work methodically. Search one room at a time."

"What are we looking for?"

He sighed. "I don't have a clue."

For the first time since entering, Ailsa dared to inhale deeply. She didn't wretch, for her nostrils failed to detect the pungent smell of death. There was no whiff of noxious gases, no metallic tinge of blood. Just a trace of lye soap.

"Mr Daventry said nae one has touched the scene since the coroner removed the body. Unless my nose fails me, someone has scrubbed this hallway clean."

He drew in a breath. "I can't smell anything."

"Because ye're choking on Tiffin cologne."

"It's Truefitt, and you made no complaints in the auction-eer's office while ravishing me senseless."

A delightful shiver raced through her at the memory. "Because I was intoxicated by the fumes."

"Oh, you were intoxicated, but it had nothing to do with the notes of musk and vanilla." His voice dropped to a husky drawl. "Admit, you couldn't get enough of me. And before you offer another explanation, we both know a spell cannot make a woman moan into a man's mouth."

Had she moaned? It must have been when she lost her wits.

"Liar. I didnae make a sound."

His lips curled in amusement. "You were panting, love, begging for more with each ragged breath." He surprised her by clasping her hand. "Come. We shall continue this discussion on the journey home. When I intend to provide proof of my claim."

Nerves mingled with excitement. Ailsa gripped his hand tightly, refusing to admit nothing in her life had ever felt so right.

"So, let's assume the murderer or his accomplice cleaned the hall to remove evidence. To hide two sets of footprints." One person could not have subdued Mr Hibbet and tied him to the table.

"It's possible." Lord Denton tugged her hand gently and drew her into the vast drawing room that served as a living space, study and dining room. The curtains were open, a sliver of moonlight giving faint illumination. "Mr Hibbet was well read," he said with admiration.

Ailsa's heart warmed upon seeing the rows of leather-bound volumes in the bookcase. "I doubt a man on Mr Hibbet's pay could afford to purchase such an extensive library."

"They could be heirlooms, though I'd wager the antique furnishings in this apartment do not belong to an auction house assistant."

"They must belong to old Mr Chadwick."

"Indeed. Else a next of kin would have come to claim their inheritance." He gestured to the imposing walnut desk. "We should search the drawers."

Practically hugging his arm, she moved with him until they caught sight of the ruined Persian rug, the burgundy bloodstain stopping them dead in their tracks.

Mr Hibbet had bled profusely.

"Does a man nae lose less blood when stabbed in the heart?"

"Yes, death is quick."

"Then how do ye account for this?"

He shrugged. "There were no other wounds on the body."

"The murderer would have made a sizeable cut to remove the organ and would have had to break the sternum." Feeling the heat of Lord Denton's gaze, she glanced up. "I own a copy of Vesalius' *Anatomy Humani Corporis*. My father knows Mr Jordan from the School of Anatomy in Manchester. He gave me a brief education on the text."

He grinned. "Of course."

"Do ye find something amusing?"

"No, it's just that few people impress me, madam." He turned his attention to the vast red stain. "This may not be Hibbet's blood. To stage the perfect scene, the villain may have used pig's blood."

Ailsa considered the remnants of rope still fastened to the desk and recalled something her friend Lillian had said. "I've something to ask, though such a question should nae grace a lady's lips."

Keeping a firm grip on her hand, Lord Denton faced her. "As our relationship has already breached the bounds of propriety, you can ask me anything."

She pushed aside her embarrassment. "Might the lady have lured Mr Hibbet into playing a game? He may have asked her to restrain him. She could have taken her pleasure while sitting astride his helpless body. Would that nae place her in the perfect position to thrust a knife into his chest?"

"What an interesting notion." Mischief danced in his eyes. "Now I'm wondering what other books you have in your library, Miss MacTavish, and who else has offered tuition. Your knowledge of relations is more extensive than I expected."

Heat flooded her cheeks. "One only need study the history of the Romans to learn of the many ways people perform congress."

"I'm sure it will make for an interesting conversation at a later date. I'm beginning to understand what you meant when you said talking makes kissing better."

She'd said talking was as important as kissing when it came to attraction but was in no mind to argue now. "Let us search the desk."

They spent a few minutes rifling through the drawers, finding nothing but loose coins, a comb and a pile of unpaid bills. Despite studying the spines of many volumes lining the bookcase, nothing captured their attention.

"There arc nae creases in the bedsheets, so we know the couple were nae frolicking," she said when they moved to Mr Hibbet's chamber.

Lord Denton strode around the room, looking in the armoire and chest, dropping to his hands and knees to check under the bed. "If you had a letter from a secret lover, where would you hide it?"

A secret lover? Her mind conjured an image of a shirtless Lord Denton. Did he have the capacity to write flowery love poems? No doubt such words were foreign to his vocabulary.

Ailsa assessed the room. "Under a loose board. Or on top of the armoire, too far for someone to reach without standing on a chair."

The viscount snatched a chair from the corner of the room, stood on the seat and searched the armoire. Finding nothing, he brushed dust from his hands and coat before using his strength to move the heavy furniture.

Something hit the floor with a thud.

"I suspect we've found Hibbet's secret papers," he said, grinning.

Ailsa crouched and reached behind the armoire, stretching to grasp the spine of a small book. It wasn't dusty, and a quick flick through the pages showed numerous annotations. "'Tis a book of magical sigils."

She handed the book to Lord Denton, watched a frown appear between his brows as he examined the ancient symbols.

"These are identical to the ones found in Michael's grimoire." The pain of losing a beloved brother darkened his features, gathering in his blue eyes like a violent storm.

How long had he silently sought answers?

How many times had she mistaken grief for arrogance?

She touched him gently on the arm. "Perhaps ye might let me look at Michael's book." A problem shared was a problem halved. "Together, we might attempt to understand his frame of mind before he died."

He looked at her hand before slowly meeting her gaze. "You have enough to contend with at present. And I've never spoken to anyone about Michael. I wouldn't want to burden you."

"'Tis nae trouble. Friends should help each other."

"Is that all we are? Friends?"

His intense stare brought a change to the atmosphere. A wind of enchantment breezed over her, stirring the carnal hunger she fought to keep at bay. An invisible power compelled her to brush the rakish lock of hair from his brow and caress his cheek.

He closed his eyes briefly, a soft hum leaving his lips.

The sound held her captive until the distant ring of a bell in the street ruined the intimate moment. "Is that Mr Gibbs, do ye think?"

Like a hawk, his ears pricked.

Then they both heard the clip of footsteps on the landing.

"Quickly." Lord Denton slipped the book into his pocket, grabbed her hand and drew her behind the closed curtain in the bedchamber. Thankfully, it overlooked the alleyway and not Broad Street. His finger came to rest on her lips. "Don't make a sound."

The space was so small they were squashed together—her breasts crushed against his solid chest.

"Who do ye think it is?" she whispered, trying to think about their predicament, not the sudden rush of heat pooling in her loins.

"We're about to find out," he said as the lock clicked and the front door creaked open. He snaked his arm around her waist, holding her tight to his body.

Ailsa's heart hammered so hard she had to concentrate on calming her breathing. What if the murderer had been waiting to return? What if he needed to search the apartment and found them hiding behind the curtain? What if nothing ever felt as good as being held in Lord Denton's embrace?

"If we're found, I'll attack him while you run," he whispered against her temple. "Run and don't stop until you reach Mr Gibbs. Do you understand?"

Now was not the time to argue, so she gave a curt nod.

Sensing her anxiety, the viscount pressed a kiss to her forehead, a reassuring brush of the lips to remind her she was not alone. Needing to reinforce the point, his mouth came to rest on her cheek, moving slowly back and forth in a caress that did nothing to settle her rising pulse.

Madness was in the air tonight.

Why else would she turn her head and kiss him?

Amid the quietness, they stood still, their mouths touching, their breath mingling, mating. He coaxed her lips apart with soft teasing strokes, tightening the coil of lust in her belly.

The need to ravish him, to grab his lapels and thrust her tongue deep into his mouth, left her dizzy. They could not make a sound. No pants. No moans. Just the gentle glide of lips, their restraint painful yet beautifully seductive.

While the intruder opened the desk drawers and rifled inside, she dared to let her tongue slide over Lord Denton's.

Heavens! She could hardly breathe.

He tasted divine.

Of earthy male and forbidden pleasures.

He pushed his erection against her abdomen, letting her know how much he loved tasting her, too, even if he couldn't say so aloud.

"Where the devil are they?" came an angry cry from the next room. "They must be here somewhere."

They froze, their mouths still joined, as the clip of footsteps came closer. The intruder had entered the bedchamber. Any second, he might whip back the curtain and find them in a clinch.

The villain opened the armoire and spent minutes muttering to himself, calling Mr Hibbet a traitor, the worst kind of Judas. He moved to the drawers on the nightstand. Then the creak of the bed preceded the rustling of the sheets.

Was he looking for the book of sigils?

No, he was looking for more than one item.

Ailsa said a silent prayer of thanks when the devil marched back into the drawing room, but events took another shocking turn. One that had nothing to do with her desire to devour Lord Denton's mouth.

Someone else entered the apartment.

Was it the accomplice?

"You're working late, Mr Murden," came a woman's

sultry voice. "Though I'm assured your duties do not entail rummaging through your employee's belongings."

Mr Murden!

Lord Denton's eyes widened at the revelation.

"M-Miss Chadwick." Mr Murden started stuttering before offering an excuse for his presence. "The m-magistrate said I might remove any paperwork relating to the running of the auction house. Mr Hibbet often left the delivery dockets in his desk drawer."

The lady's light titter rang with mockery. "Come now. I think we both know what you're really looking for. Else why would you scurry around like a rat in the darkness?"

"I'm looking for the delivery dockets," Mr Murden affirmed.

"No, you're looking for evidence Mr Hibbet enjoyed relations with your wife." Amusement coated her tone. "It pays to keep abreast of auction room gossip, sir, though the husband is often the last to know he's a cuckold."

Mr Murden cursed. "One might ask what you're doing here. Returning to the scene of your crime? Admit you had more reason than most to drive a blade through Hibbet's heart."

"You think I'm responsible for his murder? Don't be ridiculous. I haven't the stomach or strength to commit such a heinous act." The lady must have moved closer to the desk. "Good Lord! It's hard to believe a man could lose so much blood. Poor Mr Hibbet."

"Don't act like you give a damn."

"Mr Hibbet was the devil incarnate," Miss Chadwick snapped. "He tricked an old man into letting him have this apartment. He persuaded a confused man he was kin."

Mr Murden gasped. "Kin?"

"Did you not question why a mere assistant was suddenly

given the role of custodian and allowed to live in such luxury?"

"Hibbet said it was a temporary arrangement. After the robbery last year, Chadwick wanted someone to guard the premises."

Miss Chadwick's disdainful snigger echoed through the room. One could imagine a pretty face twisted with bitterness. "Was there a robbery? We only had Mr Hibbet's word. What exactly was stolen? An old spell book that barely raised fifty pounds."

Ailsa suppressed a gasp.

A grimoire had gone missing?

It couldn't be a coincidence.

"My guess is he stole it himself," Miss Chadwick continued. "So he might gain more leverage with my father. Mr Hibbet spent hours at his bedside, whispering, filling his head with nonsense."

The sudden slam of the drawer preceded Mr Murden saying, "Stay back. Don't come any closer. I didn't kill Hibbet. But as we're the only two people with a motive for murder, I must presume you're guilty."

Miss Chadwick laughed. "And what are you going to do? Stab me with that letter opener. I'm inclined to believe that's the murder weapon, the item the constable overlooked."

A brief silence ensued.

Pins and needles prickled Ailsa's toes. She tried to move, but Lord Denton held her tight to his body. To ease the crippling sensation, she screwed her toes in her boots, rested her head against Lord Denton's chest and focused on the wild thump of his heartbeat.

"If you didn't kill Hibbet, why come to the apartment under cover of darkness?" Mr Murden asked. "You must agree it looks suspicious."

"There has to be something here to prove Mr Hibbet lied to my father. Why would a man who trusts no one, a man who's secretive about his personal affairs, suddenly confess all to the auction house clerk?" The lady's temper got the better of her, and she thumped her fist on the desk. "Joshua Hibbet was not my half-brother. I don't care what he claimed. We look nothing alike."

Mr Murden sighed. "And I can't imagine Marjorie betraying her marriage vows. But she received a letter from Hibbet written in silly code. She swears it was a mistake. A missive meant for someone else."

The pair continued grumbling about their misfortune.

"Perhaps we might be useful to each other," Mr Murden said, sounding desperate rather than optimistic. "I know Hibbet's mother lives on the corner of Wentworth Street and Petticoat Lane. She may shed some light on her son's claim."

Ailsa made a mental note of the address.

Mr Daventry would want to send an agent to question the woman.

"And it's pointless searching these rooms," Mr Murden added. "There are no personal effects here. It's almost as if Hibbet used it as a place to rest his head. His mother might know of other lodgings."

Miss Chadwick gave a curious hum. "I could speak to Mrs Murden. Say Hibbet mentioned an affair and judge her reaction."

The couple conspired together, made plans, traded favours. Determined to search the desk drawers, Miss Chadwick removed every item for inspection while Mr Murden flicked through the books, hoping a letter proving his wife's guilt might slip out.

Long minutes passed before the pair agreed to meet in the apartment in a few days and exchange information.

Even when the suspects left—both had a motive for murder and were the only suspects at present—Ailsa remained locked in Lord Denton's embrace.

"We should wait for ten minutes before moving." His breath drifted over her lips like a warm breeze. "In case Miss Chadwick returns without Murden."

Only ten minutes?

She could remain like this for a lifetime.

Ailsa raised her eyes to find him watching her. "There's something to be said for kissing when ye're trying nae to make a sound."

His masculine essence had teased her senses.

The tightening in her core had left her with a confounding ache.

"There's something to be said for kissing when you're grabbing my clothes and moaning against my mouth. I like both but perhaps we should try something new."

She swallowed. "Something new?"

How many ways could one kiss a man?

She was more than eager to find out.

"Let me touch you." He stroked her cheek with the backs of his fingers, her skin tingling from the faintest touch.

"Ye're holding me, touching me now."

"I mean intimately. I want you to come while you're kissing me."

She had never heard anything so scandalous, yet every fibre of her being wished to indulge in these wicked pleasures. "What here?"

"We've ten minutes to spare, and Aaron Chance won't let me within ten feet of your bedchamber." He glanced at the alley below. The passageway was obscured by a spectre-like fog, shifting with every gust of wind. "I've never felt such a clawing hunger. And I've felt nothing but anger for such a long time."

They were on dangerous ground.

She was a slave to his charms.

The more time they spent together, the harder it was to resist. Soon, kissing would not be enough. Touching intimately would not settle the beast. They would gift each other the use of their bodies, but where would that leave them?

What would happen when they revoked the spell?

Lord Denton took the long silence as her answer. "I understand. You do not feel the same. I'm pressing you too hard."

He moved to open the curtain, but she caught his arm to stall him. "It's nae that. I need yer touch like I need air to breathe. But what happens when this is all over?"

He captured her chin between his elegant fingers. "Who can say? Maybe we won't break the spell. Maybe we will, but these perfect memories will mean something. Maybe you'll forget me."

The last comment struck a nerve.

What if she forgot how it was to feel worshipped?

"I want ye to touch me," she said, panic rising. She wanted to remember every precious second spent in his arms. The feelings of adoration would sustain her for a lifetime.

"You're certain?"

"Aye."

He wasted no time. His mouth closed over hers, moving in the slow, drugging way that tightened the muscles in her abdomen. His lips were soft, intoxicating, the first stroke of his tongue hardening her nipples.

She moaned into his mouth, felt him smile against her lips.

"You're so responsive to my touch," he murmured

between kisses, his voice dark and deep. "It's like our bodies are in tune. No two people have ever been so compatible."

"Magic holds a power we cannae comprehend." Her breath caught in her throat as his hand slid up her skirts. Blood raced through her body, pooling hot and heavy between her thighs.

Oh, Lord!

"This isn't magic." The first glide of his fingers over her sex sent a shiver to her toes. "It's the touch of a man who finds you irresistible."

Did he find her irresistible?

No man had ever taken such liberties.

Still, she could not get enough of him.

"'Tis magic," she whispered as he moved his fingers back and forth in an erotic rhythm. "Ye hold me spellbound with every wicked stroke."

"You're not the only one held captive by the things we do to each other. I'm a slave to your wants and desires. I'm obsessed with the prospect of pleasuring you."

"I like how ye touch me," she panted. The intense tingling in her sex made her moan aloud. "Oh! Oh! Did ye know it would feel so good?" The heat building in her lower abdomen spread like wildfire.

"Your reaction to me is what makes this exceptional." His hot mouth settled on her neck, sucking softly as he brought her closer to a dazzling climax.

She clung to him, a gasp escaping as he probed her entrance and pushed a longer finger slowly into her, stretching her, claiming her.

"You're so wet," he moaned against her ear as a second finger joined the first to open her wider. "The next time I make you come, I mean to own you. I want you hugging my cock, taking me deep."

His crude words did not shock or offend. They were like a potent aphrodisiac, stimulating every nerve.

He kissed her, his tongue plunging into the moist depths of her mouth, mimicking the gentle pumping of his fingers.

She was close to losing her mind.

Every muscle tensed.

An intense pressure built inside.

He stopped kissing her, but his lips lingered on hers as he waited for her to come apart on the last delicious stroke. Then her world exploded, all tension disappearing.

They stared at each other as she bore down on his fingers and rode every wild convulsion. He swallowed every pant, drank in her moans. Held her tight to his body, absorbing every shudder.

Chapter Ten

Sebastian sat at Aaron Chance's dining table, flicking through the book of sigils while sipping coffee. Pretending to examine the symbols when he could think of nothing but Miss MacTavish shuddering beneath his touch. The woman stirred something carnal in him. A beast he couldn't contain.

Things were progressing just as he feared. Kissing wasn't enough to ease the craving. Touching barely fed his addiction. He'd spent half the night trying to tame his cockstand, the other half dreaming about her sleeping naked beside him in bed.

But it went deeper than that.

He didn't want to go back to bickering. He wanted to indulge every wicked fantasy—make love to her, to no one but her.

What the hell did it all mean?

One thing was certain. He was being manipulated by a force he didn't understand. Had Michael suffered a similar fate? Had he met a temptress ashore? Was he held captive by her charms? Had he died of heartbreak, not a tropical fever?

Christian Chance strode into the dining room, his arrival

providing a much-needed distraction. "I didn't take you for an early riser, Denton."

"I couldn't sleep." Not while yearning to hold Miss MacTavish in his arms. "I decided to use the time to study the evidence we found last night." Christian doubtless thought all peers were dissolute devils who slept until noon.

The man sat opposite, though there were eight other chairs around the table. Known as the King of Diamonds because of his golden hair and sparkling blue eyes, Christian was a scholar. One who studied facts and figures. A sturdy fellow with brains and brawn.

It came as no surprise when he said, "Show me the book you found."

"By all means." Sebastian handed Christian the small book, then took a sip of coffee. "We found similar symbols in the grimoire locked in your vault."

He did not mention Michael's book or his eerie suspicions.

Christian drew his spectacles from his coat pocket and wiped them on a napkin before sliding them onto his nose. He flicked through the pages, his eyes shining as bright as the diamond stick pin adorning his cravat.

"Sigils are symbols that are said to have magical powers." Christian pointed to a specific image in the book. "This one for lust is a combination of different ink strokes. Whereas the annotations in the book are of a runic alphabet."

"An alphabet?"

Christian nodded. "Each rune represents a letter. Each sigil represents an idea or a symbol of a supernatural spirit or deity. People assume they're one and the same. But the alphabet is about human language. The symbol is a means of otherworldly communication. Now you just need to under-stand the connection."

To say the man's knowledge impressed Sebastian was an understatement. "I need time to study the grimoire, but the investigation keeps us busy night and day."

"I can examine the spell book once I've finished the monthly accounts. There seems to be a pattern to the markings in the margins."

Sebastian wished he'd noticed, but since touching Ailsa, logical thought had abandoned him. "I'm not sure you should study the grimoire. Not unless you want to be bound by a magical spell."

Not that Sebastian was complaining.

He liked his current obsession.

Christian laughed. "Spells are just a figment of the imagination. Only one's mindset has the power to alter one's destiny. Ask Aaron." He looked up as his eldest brother marched into the dining room. "While he can kill a man with a single punch, it's his mental agility, his determination in the face of adversity, that makes him a force to be reckoned with."

All the brothers had a powerful, masculine presence. Aristocratic blood flowed in their veins, yet years of surviving in the rookeries had made them an indomitable force.

"It doesn't matter how hard a man punches," Aaron said, taking his seat at the head of the table. "He'll lose everything if his mind isn't in the game." Curiosity clouded his black eyes. "Delphine said Miss MacTavish struggled to sleep last night."

"Perhaps it's the unfamiliar surroundings," Sebastian said.

Or did she remember every delightful tremor?

Was she desperate to experience them again?

"You were out quite late." Aaron spoke like a domineering father.

"Daventry instructed us to visit him at midnight." Not that he had to explain his actions to anyone, least of all the notorious owner of a gaming hell.

"I'm surprised someone of your ilk would sully his hands by working for a duke's bastard. But then Daventry knows how to grab a man by the ballocks and cut off his blood supply."

Daventry certainly had the power of persuasion.

"Sometimes men of *our* ilk are forced to take matters into their own hands. Like you, I'd fight to the death to protect those I care about."

Aaron grinned. "You care about Miss MacTavish?"

"I wouldn't tolerate your endless jibes if her safety were not my priority."

A discreet cough behind him brought the object of his desire.

He turned, his heart lurching.

The dark shadows beneath Ailsa's eyes confirmed she'd struggled to sleep. Her jade green irises had lost the magical sparkle that held him mesmerised last night.

"Good morning, gentlemen." A guilty blush touched her cheeks.

They all stood.

Sebastian drew out the chair beside his. *They don't know what we've done*, he wanted to say, but Aaron seemed to find something amusing.

"Had I known lack of sleep was a Scot's weakness, I'd have hired a violinist to play soothing music at the tables." Aaron resumed his seat. "You don't seem at all yourself, Miss MacTavish."

The lady gathered her wits and smiled. "We came close to being caught at the murder scene by a potential killer, Mr Chance. Would that nae unsettle any lady's nerves?"

135

"You led me to believe you cope well under stress."

"Ye led me to believe ye're a hard, nae-nonsense man, yet ye persist in making mindless comments."

Aaron snorted. "Did Delphine encourage you to provoke me?"

"If ye find honesty provoking, it explains why ye surround yerself with deceitful men. Desperate gamblers often lie and cheat."

Sebastian poured the lady tea while enjoying the friendly banter.

"I've met more than my share of deceitful men, Miss MacTavish. Most wear expensive coats, ride in elegant carriages and have seats in the House of Lords."

"Then it's clear we move in different circles, sir." She glanced at Sebastian, her smile broadening. "The men in my life are nothing but honourable."

Sebastian inwardly grimaced. His behaviour last night was that of a randy reprobate. He should whip himself with a birch, yet he was neither ashamed nor sorry. He'd touch her again in a heartbeat.

The other Chance brothers arrived, and the conversation turned to the raucous events of the previous night. While they ate ham and eggs, Christian revealed the wins and losses that resulted in Sigmund turfing two lords out onto the street.

"I shall visit both men today and remind them of their obligations," Aaron said in a sabre-sharp tone. "They need to know I'll not tolerate disrespect."

Aaron Chance was a man of action. He made sure men toed the line. He did not let his responsibilities prevent him from seeking justice.

Sebastian would do well to follow the man's lead. When it came to Michael's shipmates aboard *The Perseus*, he would no longer condone their silence. He would find the men and gut them like fish until they spilled their secrets.

Sidney Alley
Off Leicester Square

"Are ye sure this is the address Mr Daventry gave ye?" Miss MacTavish glanced at the trays of sweet treats in the bow window and licked her lips.

Sebastian tore his gaze away to compare the writing on the hanging sign to the words *George Beard Confectioners* scrawled on the note in his hand. "This is the right place, though I wasn't aware you had a sweet tooth."

"Only for cherry liqueurs covered in praline."

They were not his preferred choice, still he imagined buying every last one just to please her. "They're too hard to eat without spilling cherry liquid down one's chin. And I hate to sully a newly starched cravat."

She batted him playfully on the arm, her vigour much restored. "Catching the dribbles is part of the fun."

"Do I strike you as a man who does anything for fun?" he teased, though there was a wealth of truth to his assertion. He had forgotten how to laugh, how to enjoy frivolous pursuits. He had forgotten one could find joy in simple pleasures.

Miss MacTavish looked at him beneath lowered lids. "Did ye nae have fun last night when we kissed behind the curtain?"

The memory of her panting against his open mouth fired his blood. "I doubt I have ever enjoyed anything more. Perhaps there's much you can teach me, madam."

She grinned, barely able to contain her excitement. "Then wait here. We've a few minutes before we meet Professor Mangold."

Tugging her reticule off her wrist, she hurried into the shop and returned with a small paper bag. She removed her kid glove and retrieved one cherry liqueur, gripping it between two slender fingers.

"We take it in turns. Ye must take a bite while I hold it." Her eyes glistened like dewdrops beneath a moonbeam. "Whoever dribbles the least wins."

Had someone asked him to play a week ago, they'd have felt the sharp whip of his tongue, yet the desire to indulge this woman left him a slave to her whims.

He bit into the treat, the sweet liquid filling his mouth with an infusion of cherries. Catching one drip with his tongue, he licked his lips clean.

Her shoulders sagged. "Must ye be good at everything?"

"Last night, you were rather glad of my skill."

"Dallying with a novice must prove tiring. Ye did an awful lot of panting." She pushed the rest of the liqueur into his mouth. A drop rolled down his chin, and she giggled as she wiped it with her finger.

Captivated, Sebastian watched her suck her finger clean. "I believe it's my turn." He reached into the paper bag. "And like you, I pant when I'm aroused."

Miss MacTavish laughed. "Never in my wildest dreams did I think *we'd* discuss intimate matters. In truth, I thought ye were incapable of feeling anything but disdain."

"You said you need a passionate man, not one who gives

you cold shivers." He held the confectionary between his fingers. "Open your mouth."

She locked gazes with him, slowly opened her mouth and bit down. The praline cracked, the cherry liquid bursting out and coating her lips. Amusement danced in her eyes. A sight so bewitching he couldn't tear his gaze away.

He hoped the juice trickled down her chin, down the slender column of her throat, but the minx was an expert in this game.

"I believe ye owe me a boon, Lord Denton," she teased after finishing the treat without making a mess. "I shall call it in at a later date."

"Why do I feel like I've been duped by a master?"

She batted her lashes. "Should a lady nae have the upper hand in some things? Else how might she make a good impression?"

"As I despise falsehoods, I'd rather she call me a doaty bampot."

Miss MacTavish touched his upper arm. "There'll be plenty of time for that later. But for now, we should focus our efforts on fooling Professor Mangold."

Lying to the professor shouldn't be difficult.

Their imagined story did not stray far from the truth.

They would claim to be under the grip of a spell and plead for help to break the curse. In reality, these romantic interludes felt more like a blessing.

Entering the confectioner's shop together, Sebastian approached the assistant and presented his calling card. "We have a midday appointment with Professor Mangold, and he gave this address."

The tubby fellow eyed them suspiciously. "What's it concerning?"

Sebastian kept his temper. "A private matter. Let's just say we find ourselves enchanted and require advice on the matter."

The man tucked the card into his apron pocket. "Cross the road to Coventry Court. When ye come to the end of the alley, look for the evil eye. Ye'll find Mangold below ground."

The cryptic clues proved more amusing than alarming. Was Mangold so consumed by his own self-importance he shrouded himself in an air of mystery?

Sebastian escorted Miss MacTavish through the narrow alleyway. The houses stood so close together the occupants could shake hands out of the upper windows.

"We cannae be looking for a real eye," the lady said once they reached the branch in the L-shaped lane. "It must be a puzzle."

"Not so great a puzzle." Sebastian gestured to the large eye painted on the brickwork of the end house. "My groom could have invented something more taxing."

"There's a flight of steps behind those iron railings."

"Yes." He sighed, disappointed the challenge had proven rather lame.

They descended to a small courtyard. The solid wooden door leading to the basement dwelling was paint-chipped and had no number.

Sebastian knocked.

Failing to hear the hurried clip of footsteps, he raised his fist to thump harder, but after a series of odd clicking noises, the door creaked open.

No one stood in the dim, candlelit corridor.

No one stood behind the door.

Miss MacTavish clutched his arm. "I feel like a ghost has trampled over my grave. It's like we've stepped into Lucifer's lair."

"There's nothing sinister here." He noticed the pulley system and a series of cogs running flush with the ceiling. "Just a simple piece of engineering."

Still, she gripped him tightly. "The man means to intimidate us."

"This is the Guild of Unexplained Phenomena. He means to show us that sorcery is nothing more than a trick of the mind."

"Perhaps."

They proceeded down the long corridor. Paintings of sigils, forked-tailed imps and witch hunts lined the black walls. The sconces looked like twisted devil horns, the candle flames flickering as they passed.

Upon arriving at a large basement cellar with stone walls and a low beamed ceiling, they saw a cloaked gentleman sitting behind a stone desk.

"It looks like an altar," Miss MacTavish muttered.

"Or a sacrificial slab," Sebastian agreed.

Head bowed, Mangold peered through a magnifying glass, examining text in an old tome. Despite being aware of their arrival, he did not tear his gaze away from the page to greet them.

"Professor Mangold?" Annoyed, Sebastian stepped closer.

The fellow glanced at them through his magnifying glass, his overly large eye less intimidating than the one painted on the brickwork outside.

"Lord Denton, I presume." Mangold stood briefly to bow and remove his tasselled black cap. "I trust you found me without too much trouble. Forgive the secrecy, but there are those amongst us who think the unexplained should remain a mystery."

The only mystery was why this man spent hours in a

dingy basement. "Allow me to present Miss MacTavish. We've both been affected by a strange phenomenon and pray you're equipped to offer expert guidance."

That said, there was nothing strange about lusting after a beautiful woman. What proved confounding was Miss MacTavish's interest in him.

The man's beady gaze shifted to the lady in question. "You come on Lady Perthshore's recommendation. She said you spoke to her about this unusual problem."

Miss MacTavish managed a smile that conveyed naivety. "I didnae know who else to confide in, sir. Lady Perthshore said ye came to her home to give a talk on the supernatural. She was kind enough to write to ye for help on my behalf."

As luck had it, Daventry was firm friends with the matron.

"Lady Perthshore makes regular donations to our efforts. As such, we consider her a valued friend." He rubbed his boney hands together as if his palms itched for coin. "Investigating the unexplained can be a costly business."

Daventry had advised they make a donation, and so Sebastian removed the signed bank note from his pocket and handed it to the professor. "Allow me to offer a small token, recompense for your time."

The professor mumbled and stuttered, acted flabbergasted by the generous gift. "Well, this is a welcome surprise. And will pay towards the study and purchase of ancient texts." He motioned to the chairs flanking his desk. "Please sit. I'm afraid I cannot offer refreshment at present."

He did not say why.

Perhaps his cauldron was away for repair.

"We merely seek any advice ye can give us regarding love spells." Miss MacTavish settled into the seat. As soon as Sebastian sat, she looked at him with a mix of soul-deep yearning and lusty desire. "Ever since that devil recited the love poem, we cannae control our feelings."

She spoke the truth.

Though the problem ran deeper than the need for physical gratification. When a man wanted to share his darkest secrets with a woman, that was cause for concern.

Professor Mangold removed a clean piece of paper from the drawer and dipped the nib of his quill in the ink pot. "Where did this occur?"

"At Chadwick's Auction House." Sebastian saw the nervous flicker in the professor's eyes. "We sat together. We both wished to purchase the rare copy of More's *Utopia*."

The professor froze. Ink dripped from his nib and stained the page. He muttered to himself before grabbing another sheet. "Someone recited the spell without thoughts of the consequences?"

Miss MacTavish mentioned the assistant. "He read from an old grimoire, sir. Ever since, we cannae bear to part company. I fear we're under the spell. That we've nae choice but to fall in love."

Sebastian listened to her heartfelt account. Whatever existed between them had always been there, lingering beneath the surface. They thrived on every argument and heated exchange. All the grimoire had done was turn rivalry into lust.

One kiss had led to many.

One touch would lead to something far more intimate.

He felt the inevitability of it deep in his bones.

"But there must have been other men in the room," came the professor's logical reply. "What makes you think you're in love with Lord Denton?"

A rosy blush stained her cheeks. "Sir, the need to be with

him is like a hunger I cannae sate. He fills my waking thoughts, plagues my dreams, too."

Days ago, Sebastian might have praised her acting ability.

Now he knew there was truth to that claim.

"I see. It sounds like a classic case of infatuation." The professor scribbled a few notes. "Can you remember anything about the spell?"

"I believe I can recite the first few lines."

Quill at the ready, the professor nodded for Sebastian to continue.

"*Attract to me my deepest desire. From this minute, this hour, let my heart speak only thy name. With our bodies entwined, set our souls aflame.*"

Miss MacTavish swallowed deeply. "Does the spell sound familiar, sir?"

"I have heard it before and believe it's early medieval in origin."

"Then ye know of a way to break it?" she said with much enthusiasm.

The professor pushed out of the chair and hobbled to a mahogany cupboard containing many books. He perused the volumes before taking one and returning to the desk.

"You must perform a releasing ritual to stop the manifestations. Write down your intention to break the spell and list each other's names. Beneath the moonlight, you must burn the paper and recite…" He paused while he found the relevant page in his necromancer's journal.

Sebastian locked gazes with Miss MacTavish.

Did he want to break the spell?

Did he want to spend his days occupying an empty shell?

If he didn't believe in sorcery, would it matter if he performed the ritual? And yet there was a hesitance within him he couldn't explain.

"Ah, here it is." Mangold pointed to the relevant page. *"This spell no longer serves me. With the last wisp of smoke, set my soul free."*

The lady blinked. "That's all we need to say?"

"Yes, as long as you repeat the words with heartfelt intention, the power that binds you should be broken. Best you do it at night beneath the waning crescent. Sometime in the next five days should suffice."

"The sooner, the better," she said, though Sebastian wasn't sure if her eagerness was part of the act.

An awkward silence descended.

Mangold wanted rid of them because he closed his books, pulled his watch from his waistcoat pocket and checked the time.

It was then Sebastian noticed an inking on the inside of the professor's wrist. For a second, his heart stopped beating. Perhaps Michael had sent a sign, a prompt to begin a conversation.

"One often sees such inkings amongst sailors." He pointed to the strange symbol on the professor's wrist. "They rub gunpowder or ink into the wound for artistic effect."

The professor jerked in response, his gaze darting to the door as if willing them to leave. "When dealing with the supernatural, one must shield oneself from harm."

"It's a protection symbol, then?"

"Y-yes. A colleague marked me some years ago."

"I only ask because I found similar markings amongst my brother's belongings." An unexplained force urged him to confess. "He served aboard *The Perseus* and died of a tropical fever. There was an old grimoire amongst his possessions."

"A grimoire?" The man's chin quivered.

Should he not be used to conversations about sorcery and magic?

Was Mangold a fraud?

A trickster who used the paranormal to take money from clients?

"Amongst the printed symbols were pencil drawings of runes, done by hand after publication. They were littered throughout the book."

While Miss MacTavish's eyes were awash with pity, Mangold paled.

"Seafaring men have an innate fear of omens." The professor spoke as if sailors were as evil as Satan's minions. "The cramped conditions play havoc with the mind."

Sebastian had presumed the same.

Now, he wasn't so sure.

"I'd need to see this grimoire if you still have it," Mangold added. "I could study the drawings and attempt to decipher their meaning."

Every instinct said not to trust this charlatan.

"That's rather generous of you." Sebastian kept the sarcasm from his tone. "I shall bring the grimoire here so you may cast your expert eye over the text," he lied. He refused to let anyone put their grubby hands on Michael's book.

The professor's watery smile failed to hide an inner agitation. "I shall do my utmost to make sense of the markings in the hope it will give you some clarity."

He omitted to mention a donation and made no bid for extra funds. That's when Sebastian knew Mangold had a secret. Was it a secret relating to witchcraft? Was it something more sinister?

Did he know what the drawings meant?

Did he know what happened aboard *The Perseus*?

Chapter Eleven

One expected to see a familiar reflection when peering into a looking glass. Yes, the faint mole on Ailsa's cheek was visible. One eyebrow was not quite as arched as the other, and the fiery red curls tickling her earlobe were still the bane of her existence.

Yet she looked nothing like herself.

Delphine's maid has styled her hair in a soft, sweeping coiffure. She had added a little powder to even her complexion, a dab of rouge to redden her cheeks and lips. Such things enhanced one's features, they didn't alter them drastically. Still, Ailsa felt different. Beautiful. Feminine. Exposed.

"The blue silk will look divine on you." Delphine clapped her hands in glee. "You will be the belle of Lady Winfield's ball. There'll be stories about you in tomorrow's *Scandal Sheet*. Wagers on which gentleman has caught your eye."

Ailsa suppressed a groan. Gossip was often halfway around the *ton* before the truth had its boots on. She met the dark-haired beauty's gaze through the glass. "If there's ever a way I can repay yer kindness, ye must tell me."

Mischief danced in Delphine's wide brown eyes. "I suspect there might be. When I am ready, I shall need your support. I only pray you're living in London and not rusticating in the Highlands."

Any curiosity surrounding Delphine's cryptic comment died. The thought of leaving London filled Ailsa with dread. It wasn't the busy metropolis she would miss. It wasn't trips to the theatre or visits to the quaint bookshop tucked away in a narrow snicket. It was him.

"I promised my father I'd return to Scotland after the auction. He'll be expecting me home within a few weeks. But I shall be back in September."

September seemed like a lifetime away.

Scotland a million miles.

"I would visit you in the Highlands if I could persuade Aaron to let me travel that far. Still, I shall look forward to your return." Delphine came closer and placed her hands on Ailsa's shoulders. "Every eligible bachelor in the *ton* will want to dance with you tonight."

She didn't want to dance with every man.

Only one.

In the next few days, they planned to break the spell. Then she would be living for her books and hoping her married friends would spare an hour of their time. There would be no teasing banter with the viscount. No lustful kisses. No promises of something illicit.

The chime of the mantel clock drew Ailsa from her reverie. "Heavens. I should hurry. Helen will be here in half an hour, and Mr Chance said I must leave before the first customers arrive."

Since meeting with Professor Mangold yesterday, Lord Denton had been acting strangely. During the journey to the

Old Crown, he had hardly spoken a word and seemed glad the place was closed because of a fire in the taproom.

He'd spent hours at the gaming tables last night, waiting for Michael's shipmate, Mr Kirkwood. Delphine said he'd cursed the man to the devil when he failed to show, and resorted to guzzling brandy with Mr Chance.

He had missed breakfast this morning, rising late before leaving Fortune's Den at noon on the pretence of preparing for Lady Winfield's ball. Perhaps there was somewhere else he'd rather be. It certainly felt like he was avoiding her.

Had he already performed the ritual and broken the spell?

It would account for his distance, for the lapse in his attentions.

Ailsa was still thinking about the viscount when Delphine helped her into the vibrant blue gown. The material hugged every curve and was sure to capture Lord Denton's eye.

A muscle in Ailsa's jaw twitched.

Attracting a man had never been a priority.

She disliked the game of flirtation. Despised these mistrustful feelings. Hated the suspicious train of her thoughts.

Perhaps she should suggest breaking the spell tonight. Take comfort in the knowledge things would return to normality. Persuade herself she didn't long for his passionate kisses. Didn't crave every forbidden touch.

When the St Clairs' carriage arrived to ferry her to Lady Winfield's ball, it was Nicholas St Clair who stepped down to the pavement to greet her. He must have sensed her disappointment. Where was the man who stole her breath? The man who'd made indecent proposals?

Nicholas smiled and offered his hand. "How are you finding life at Fortune's Den? With Aaron at the helm, it must be like living in Hades."

Ailsa pushed her troubles aside and managed a chuckle. "Mr Chance is quite rigid in his opinions. He rules with an iron fist." It was obvious the King of Clubs loved his family. However, she feared his need to protect his kin was a terrible weakness.

Nicholas handed her into the carriage. "I've never known a man work so hard. How he survives on four hours sleep is anyone's guess."

Ailsa sat next to Helen, who still looked peaky. Lord Denton was noticeably absent, though Helen made excuses on her brother's behalf.

"Sebastian agreed to meet us there. He went out earlier and was somewhat delayed. Doubtless he's taken it upon himself to find your missing *Utopia*."

Or he was burning notes and reciting the releasing spell.

"I've not spoken to him since last night." Not since they'd returned to Fortune's Den after visiting Professor Mangold. Now Helen knew about the intruder and Mr Hibbet's murder, Ailsa added, "He was supposed to be my protector yet seems consumed by his own problems of late."

Helen patted Ailsa's hand. "You know how he is. Stubborn to a fault. Today, he asked if I still had Michael's letters. If he'd mentioned his friends aboard *The Perseus*. I fear he's letting grief consume him again."

The marked change coincided with his conversation with the professor and the discussion about Michael's grimoire. Perhaps he'd had a sudden epiphany. Either way, she would confront him tonight and seek an explanation.

"I'm sure the ball will revive his spirits," Helen added.

Ailsa used the thirty-minute journey across town to ask about Lord Denton's vow to remain unmarried until he was fifty. "Was he upset when ye broke yer vow?" she asked Nicholas.

The man shifted in his seat. "Upset is an understatement."

"Did ye nae think to tell him ye were in love?"

"It was difficult," Helen said, blinking back tears. "The day we lost Michael, the old Sebastian died too. He put everything into his relationship with Nicholas and presumed they would be companions into their dotage. In his grief, he was looking for a distraction, a replacement. I didn't want to be the one who took that away from him."

Lord Denton appeared confident and self-assured, a man in complete control of his destiny. To some extent, he was. But now she knew loneliness clung to him like a malevolent spirit. A demon he couldn't shake.

"He seems happy you're married." The viscount spoke fondly of the couple, and Ailsa had witnessed how caring and attentive he was to his sister.

"He is." Helen glanced at Nicholas. Silent words passed between them. "Though we don't see him as often as we'd like."

"Have ye told him ye're with child?"

Helen's eyes widened, and her hand fluttered to her throat. "Good heavens! Is it obvious? I told him I'd eaten something disagreeable."

"We decided to wait before confirming the news," Nicholas added, though his tone said he didn't necessarily agree. "Even so, Denton is astute enough to guess."

Only a week ago, Ailsa would have made a joke at the viscount's expense, called him gruff and incapable of sharing in anyone's good fortune. Now, the need to defend him and fight his battles flowed in her blood.

"May I be so bold as to ask why?"

Nicholas' weary sigh said he had struggled with the decision. "Deep down, Sebastian has a fear of losing those he

151

loves. Loss has been an ever-present theme in his life, hence his desire to delay forming meaningful attachments."

Yes, Lord Denton preferred to observe life from behind a barricade, to command those around him from a high tower. When one stripped away the impenetrable armour, what lay beneath?

She had glimpsed the carefree man in Mr Hibbet's apartment, and the sight had stolen her breath. She had tasted surrender on his lips. Seen the vibrant glimmer of freedom in his compelling blue eyes.

"He would be hurt if he thought ye'd kept the news from him." Ailsa's lungs constricted as if anticipating the viscount's pain. Despite beginning the journey annoyed at the lord's sudden disinterest, a desire to comfort him took hold. "Perhaps he needs something positive to cling to, a reason to look forward to the future."

Nicholas tilted his head and arched a brow. "When did you decide to champion Denton's cause? I thought you could barely tolerate him."

Words from an old book had changed everything.

"When working together on a case, one gains a different perspective." Her disdain had grown into an obsession. An obsession that began in the auction room when he offered his seat and explained why he wanted the rare copy of *Utopia*. "Lord Denton has gone to great lengths to help me. I shall be forever grateful."

They arrived promptly in Mortimer Street, and talk turned to their hostess' lavish birthday celebration.

"Only Lady Winfield would invite every member of the *ton* and instruct them all to arrive at eight." Nicholas yanked down the window and peered out. "Unless we want to sit here shivering for the next two hours, I suggest we walk the last fifty yards."

They agreed and alighted.

Carriages blocked the street in a scene of pure carnage. Coachmen yelled amid their horses' agitated snickers as a hundred or more guests descended like an army of ants on Lady Winfield's London abode.

"It's sure to be a crush tonight," Helen said, as if she would rather be at home nestled in her husband's embrace.

Ailsa scanned the horde of people jostling to beat the crowds and be the first to reach the matron's front door. Some were loud and far too boisterous. Perhaps that's why the hairs on her nape stood to attention. Why every muscle tensed as if intuitively sensing danger.

Instinct drew her gaze to the entrance of the mews.

That's when she saw him—the ominous figure dressed in black lurking in the shadows. He raised his head and peered at Lady Winfield's townhouse from beneath the rim of his overlarge hat.

A gasp caught in Ailsa's throat.

It was the man from the auction house. The sinister fellow who wished to purchase the grimoire. The potential murderer.

Why would the fellow come to Lady Winfield's ball?

Was he following her or Lord Denton?

She dared to look again but the devil had disappeared. Was her mind playing tricks and conjuring frightening visions?

Consumed with thoughts of the baleful rogue, Ailsa was still picturing his pale, skeletal face when she curtsied to Lady Winfield, was still trembling when the attendant coughed and offered to take her cloak.

"Good heavens! Ailsa! You look beautiful in blue." Helen grasped Ailsa's hands and gave them an affectionate squeeze. "It's unlike you to visit a London modiste. And your hair looks divine in a softer style."

Ailsa spoke of Delphine's desire to play fairy godmother. "Miss Chance gets a thrill from turning a spinster into a temptress."

"Well, her efforts have been noted by the masses. Men are gawping." Amid a flurry of curious whispers, Helen led the way into the mirrored ballroom. "Prepare to be hounded by every man under forty."

With her pulse pounding in her throat, Ailsa dared to raise her gaze. Fifty pairs of eyes stared back, stripping her bare, scanning her as if she were the fatted calf and they'd not eaten for a week.

Mother Mary!

Surely they weren't compelled by the love spell.

And if they were, why was she not drooling and lovesick at the sight of them? Why was she frantically searching the sea of heads for one man in particular?

"Has your father increased your dowry?" Helen asked, sounding equally baffled by their sudden fixation.

"If he has, he's nae said a word to me."

Had he hired a matchmaker?

Employed an agency to find unmarriageable ladies husbands?

"Good Lord! They're all heading this way." Helen looked for her husband, relieved to see him approaching. "We're about to be ambushed by every eligible male in London."

The urge to raise her skirts and race to the retiring room had Ailsa's heart pounding against her ribcage. The handsome Lord Brockton bounded past his competitors and was first to the gate.

"Miss MacTavish." The lord captured her hand and bowed. "Please say you've marked my name on your dance card." He stepped closer, the smell of sickly cologne invading her nostrils. "You look remarkable tonight," he whispered for her ears only. "The belle of the ball."

The compliment turned her stomach.

Holding this man's hand made her want to wretch.

Mr Frampton grew tired of waiting and pushed forward, snatching her hand from Lord Brockton to press his moist mouth to her glove. "Will you accompany me to the supper room, Miss MacTavish? Shall I secure us refreshment?"

Nicholas St Clair stepped into the fray and muttered a curse. He looked ready to beat back her eager admirers, round them up and shut them in their pens.

But then warm fingers gripped her wrist and her head shot in the newcomer's direction.

She met Lord Denton's gaze, though his eyes flamed with the devil's fury. "Loath me to break up the party, but get your hands off my betrothed before I break your damn necks."

It wasn't the threat of violence that had everyone gasping.

"Your betrothed?" Lord Brockton mocked. "I don't recall reading the announcement in the broadsheets."

"You'll read it soon enough."

Lord Brockton sneered. "You said you have no intention of marrying until you reach your dotage."

The viscount puffed his chest and straightened to an intimidating height. "Are you calling me a liar? Will you insult Miss MacTavish's moral character? The lady agreed to be my wife, and that's the end of the matter."

Ailsa stole a glance at Helen, who stood staring like a virgin in a brothel.

Nicholas came to his friend's aid, saying, "Let me assure you, those closest to Denton are aware of the couple's plans."

Still, that did not appease her suitors. It was Mr Frampton who said, "But only five minutes ago, we saw you in a clinch with Miss De Luca. Men are listing bets in the book at

White's, laying odds she's the only woman who can persuade you from bachelorhood."

In a clinch with Miss De Luca?

The sudden pain in Ailsa's throat made it hard to swallow. Tears gathered behind her eyes.

"One might think you invent gossip for the *Scandal Sheet*, Frampton." Lord Denton's tone was as biting as an arctic wind. He reached for Ailsa's hand and clasped it tightly. "That damn rag is full of inaccuracies, but allow me to give you the facts. Miss De Luca accosted me by the potted fern, where I made it clear my attentions were engaged elsewhere. You may have seen her grabbing my coat, though I did not lay a hand on her person."

Amusement passed over Mr Frampton's dark features.

"Seeing you maul my betrothed has put me in the mood for a fight." Lord Denton hit the man with his piercing stare. "One more word and I'll make sure you cannot eat solid food for a month. Now bugger off."

Lord Brockton raised his hands and stepped away. The other men followed suit, scattering into the crowd like spooked vermin.

A tense silence ensued until Helen said, "Well? Do you mean to tell me what on earth is going on?"

"Not now, Helen." The lord spoke in his usual dogmatic way. "Be patient. All will become apparent in due course."

"And that's it?" she snapped.

"Not quite. I mean to dance with Miss MacTavish, discuss our shared interests and escort her safely home."

Safely home? Whatever happened when they were alone together in his carriage would be deemed scandalous.

"Home? Or to that iniquitous den in Aldgate?" Helen whispered.

"Forgive my lack of clarity. Yes, to the gaming hell where

you stayed when you left me in Haslemere and chased after Nicholas."

Nicholas pursed his lips. He seemed to find the situation amusing. "You're sure you can handle the lady's fanatical suitors?"

Lord Denton arched a brow. "I can deal with the likes of Frampton and his cronies." He bowed his head and met Ailsa's gaze. "I hear the strains of a waltz. Will you dance with me?"

Ailsa swallowed. A stubborn Scot would refuse and berate him for being absent today. "It's been some time since I've taken to the floor."

"Yet I have every reason to think you will be exceptional."

With a firm grip on her hand, he drew her away.

She followed, gliding across the polished parquet, entranced.

Her sex clenched the moment he slid his arm around her waist. Her breathing quickened, her mouth falling open on a pant. "People are staring."

"It's the spell." His gaze lingered on her hair as they moved in time to the music. "You look so beautiful tonight I can barely breathe."

Desire unfurled in her belly. "Delphine agreed a softer style suits me. Apparently, blue provides the perfect contrast when one's hair is a halo of fire."

"Yet it's the suggestive glint in your eyes that robs me of decent thoughts." A low growl rumbled in his throat. "I've missed you."

"We saw each other yesterday." And she hadn't stopped thinking about him for a second. "Though ye've made yerself scarce ever since."

He winced, the torment in his eyes softening her resolve.

"Don't mistake my absence for indifference. I spent the time searching for Michael's last known associates." Then he made a shocking confession. "I need to solve this case on my own. I cannot protect you when my mind is consumed with thoughts of my brother."

Like a bud in spring he was slowly opening up to her, revealing thoughts he usually kept hidden. But the viscount took command of every situation and she had to make him see she would not surrender her position so easily.

"This is my case," she stated. Despite his earlier declaration, he was not her husband. As partners, he could not make decisions on her behalf. "The grimoire was delivered to Pall Mall. The intruder entered my home."

"And you wanted done with the matter days ago. Daventry had to force you to attend the meeting with Mangold."

He was not wrong. "Regardless, ye should have spoken to me about yer plans, nae spent the evening getting drunk with Mr Chance."

He bent his head to whisper, "Getting drunk with Aaron was the only way to stop myself from entering your bedchamber. The need to pleasure you flows like opium in my veins. I want you. And my resolve hangs by a flimsy thread."

I want you!

Had they been alone, she would have claimed his mouth in fierce possession. "Why did ye nae tell me that?"

"Because you would have looked at me like you are now, doe-eyed and dying for my touch. Because I can barely form a word without imagining driving deep into your body. Because I can't help but think Mangold is dangerous. He knows something about Michael's death, and I cannot cope with the thought of losing you, too."

Ailsa blinked rapidly against this sudden wealth of information. She wasn't sure which to address first, but she couldn't think about him wanting her, needing her, not right now. "I was at the meeting with Mangold. He said nothing to give you cause for concern."

"It's based on a feeling, a hunch." He looked almost embarrassed to admit it. "That, and Mangold's eagerness to study Michael's grimoire without the need of payment."

"He studies unexplained phenomena."

"Yet something about him screams charlatan. Christian Chance knows more about rune symbols than the professor."

They fell silent as they twirled around the dance floor. Doubtless his mind whirled as fast as hers. If they meant to catch a murderer, there was much to do. Still, thoughts of kissing him and lying naked in his arms took precedence.

Oh, Lord!

Guests gathered around the dance floor like they would the ring of the travelling circus. Ladies gawped at her and exchanged wicked whispers, perhaps debating if Lord Denton had lost his wits. Why else would a confirmed bachelor propose marriage? And to a Scotswoman, no less.

Lord Denton noticed a dozen men watching her and muttered his disdain. "I shall find myself at a dawn appointment if we don't break that damn spell. I cannot bear to watch you dance with Brockton tonight. If he puts his hands on you, I'm liable to snap his fingers."

Suspicion flared.

Was the spell responsible for drawing men like moths to a flame?

If so, why did she feel nothing but annoyance? Why did her heart beat fast for one man? The wrong man. The only man determined not to marry.

"Then we should break the spell tonight." Sickness

swirled in her stomach at the thought. She liked feeling giddy. Liked feeling a little bit in love. "We need to accept the truth."

"The truth?"

"Unless we temper these feelings, we've nae hope of catching the killer."

Chapter Twelve

What the devil was wrong with him?

Should he not drag Miss MacTavish from the dance floor, send word to his coachman and make haste? Should he not race to Lady Winfield's study and write the notes they needed to burn? Breaking the spell had always been the priority, the impetus for meeting Mangold.

Yet the thought left Sebastian sick to the pit of his stomach.

If they broke the enchantment, Miss MacTavish wouldn't want him. There would be no more passionate kisses. No tearing at each other's clothes. No forbidden touches. No frantic need to make love.

Hellfire!

The loss was like a cavernous hole in his chest. He enjoyed being held captive by her charms. He wanted her with a desperation that defied logic.

"Break it tonight?" he said, despite the frog in his throat.

"Is it nae for the best?" Her gaze flitted briefly to the group of women watching them dance. Miss De Luca stood amongst them, staring as if she might singe their souls with her irate glare. "Ye must have feelings for Miss De Luca, else there wouldnae be bets in the book at White's. She's the most beautiful woman in the room."

"No, she's not," he snapped, unable to tear his gaze away from his Scottish temptress. It wouldn't matter if Cleopatra appeared wearing a golden kalasiris. No other woman could turn his head. "You're the most beautiful woman here." Plump lips and the soft swell of her breasts roused a hunger he'd never known.

A blush touched her cheeks. "'Tis the spell talking."

"It's not the damn spell." Why could she not accept a compliment? He took a calming breath. "Forgive me. Tensions run high tonight. But just so we're clear. I feel nothing for Miss De Luca."

She raised a brow. "That's easy to say when ye're bewitched. Tomorrow, ye may think differently."

Tomorrow, he might be grieving.

Longing to feel this all-consuming lust.

Finding nothing but the dreaded emptiness.

"Have it your way," he said, suppressing his reluctance to sever the ties. "We'll break the bond tonight. You'll return with me to Grosvenor Street. We'll light a fire in the garden and dance beneath a waning moon."

The music stopped.

Coldness invaded the space the moment he released her.

"Then let us leave now, my lord. But we must do so discreetly." Eager to cast him aside, she drew him from the dance floor. "I'm convinced I saw the devil from the auction house lurking in the street when I arrived."

"You saw Murden?" He brought them to an abrupt halt.

"Nae Murden. The man who stormed out after losing the grimoire."

"The fellow in black? Why didn't you say so before?"

"Because we've been busy avoiding our admirers."

To prove the point, Miss De Luca approached them. The lady forced a smile, but like a wolf on the hunt, her eyes were savage.

"Miss MacTavish. May I be the first to congratulate you on your good fortune?" Her assessing gaze moved to Ailsa's vibrant red hair, her nose wrinkling in a sly sneer. "It takes a certain woman to drag a man like Lord Denton to the altar. Who knew he had a fondness for Celts?"

Miss MacTavish stiffened at the veiled slur. "I knew." She lowered her voice as if to impart a secret. "He can barely keep his hands to himself, and so we mean to marry quickly."

The lady firmed her jaw and practically growled. "The Scots are known for their wild ways. A man might find that appealing in the short term. But such feelings soon wane."

"'Tis unlikely. Scotswomen have a fire in their blood, a fire a man cannae resist. The same fire makes us fine warriors, equips us to slay our enemies." Miss MacTavish offered a serene smile. "In short, dinnae insult a Scot unless ye want to get burned."

The lady's lips quivered. "I—I'm just surprised."

"Surprised a confirmed bachelor would marry?"

"Surprised at his choice."

Compelled to defend his decision, Sebastian said, "Kindness, modesty and a passionate spirit are important to a man." He slipped his arm around Ailsa's waist. At no point had he encouraged Miss De Luca. But he knew she had set her sights high and craved a title. "Miss MacTavish has those qualities in abundance."

He drew Ailsa away, but like a naughty imp, she turned to Miss De Luca and whispered, "And when we kiss, the whole world tilts on its axis. A love like that is sure to last a lifetime."

Yes, the kiss had left his head spinning.

Rocked him to his core.

"Did you enjoy rubbing salt into the wound?" he said, escorting Ailsa into the hall to retrieve her cloak.

"The lady struck the first blow. But she needed to know her weapon is nae match for a claymore." Her amusement died. "Though it will be embarrassing when I explain I cannae marry ye because ye're as gruff as a bear."

Standing in the queue for the cloakroom, he drew his fingers over her hip in a teasing circle. "And yet I've not been so gruff lately."

She inhaled sharply. "Aye, 'tis almost a shame to break the spell."

The churning in his gut returned. His chest grew tight. The need to cling on to something—that in all likelihood was a grievous deception—sent his pulse soaring.

Don't leave me.

Don't leave me to face the world alone.

The confounding words burst into his mind to threaten a bachelor's resolve. This was precisely why he avoided these entanglements, why he kept his emotions locked in an impenetrable fortress deep in a fathomless sea.

But this was different.

Ailsa MacTavish treated him like a strong, virile man, not a pompous viscount or failing brother. In her company, he did not feel bound by traditions, rules and laws. He felt free.

"I should fetch Helen and have her play escort." He was in danger of ruining the only woman he wanted to protect. What if she felt nothing for him tomorrow and was forced to spend a lifetime in his bed? It would be a living hell. "We shouldn't be seen together outside, not without a chaperone."

Being desperate for an excuse to leave the ball early, and

keen to ask the question burning on everyone's lips, Nicholas and Helen jumped at the chance to ferry them home.

On the pretence of informing the ever-opinionated Gibbs to return to Grosvenor Street, Sebastian covered the length of Mortimer Street on foot, scouring every dark recess for the blackguard from the auction.

What business would he have spying on Lady Winfield's abode?

Unless the devil wished to follow Ailsa in the hope she might lead him to the grimoire. But only those who worked at the auction house knew of the delivery man's mistake.

He explained his position to Gibbs and briefly described the rogue in question. "Keep your eyes peeled. There's every chance he's following us. Trying to determine what we've done with the book."

"Happen it's better if *I* take you home, milord. You can identify this villain, whereas I might accost the wrong man."

Good grief! Must Gibbs disagree with every order? "I must protect Miss MacTavish, and we cannot be seen climbing into this carriage together."

"Perhaps the lady can ride home with your sister, milord. And we can scour the streets and see if we can find this fellow."

Damn. It was the most logical suggestion. "Gibbs, sometimes a man must follow his gut. Park outside Grosvenor Street and watch the house until we're ready to leave for Fortune's Den."

And with that, Sebastian turned on his heel, keen to march away before Daventry's insolent lackey protested. That's when fate handed him a boon and sent him crashing into Mr Kirkwood.

"Kirkwood?" Sebastian gripped the man's arm to keep them both upright. "Forgive me. I didn't see you there."

Kirkwood straightened his coat. "Pay it no mind, my lord."

Suspicion stirred the hairs on Sebastian's nape. What was Kirkwood doing in Mayfair? Aaron Chance said he lived near Temple Gardens. The man wore black but was considerably younger than the rogue from the auction.

"Did you attend Lady Winfield's ball? I don't recall seeing you there." Sebastian kept all traces of accusation from his tone. As the nephew of a baron, Kirkwood may have been extended an invitation.

"No, I have a friend in Langham Place." Kirkwood pointed into the darkness. "I thought I'd walk and try to hail a hackney."

"My coachman can take you home." Sebastian nodded to Gibbs.

Kirkwood jolted in surprise. "Thank you, but I'll not put him to any trouble, and I'll likely end up drinking in a tavern." Keen to be on his way, the man stepped to the side.

Sebastian blocked his escape. "Can I ask you something? Something about Michael?" Something he should have asked years ago.

Kirkwood nodded, though Sebastian sensed his hesitance. "It's been a long time since I served aboard *The Perseus*."

"It may sound odd, but I wondered if you'd seen Michael with a spell book. There was an old grimoire amongst his personal effects. Perhaps you might know if he bought it ashore. I know you spent time in Simon's Town on the Western Cape."

Kirkwood stared blankly. "A grimoire? Michael read Shakespeare and had a fondness for Byron. He said it was a form of escapism while at sea. He wasn't the sort to read nonsense."

"That's why I found it odd." So why the hell did he have

the grimoire in his possession? Had Sebastian invented a connection merely to stop feeling so damn useless?

"If you still have it, maybe I can offer some insight," Kirkwood said with a hint of compassion. "Confirm if Michael did buy it in Simon's Town."

Every muscle in Sebastian's body tensed. Instinct said he would be a fool to trust anyone who'd served aboard that ship.

"I keep it amongst my books at home. I'm out tomorrow, but you could call at Grosvenor Street on Sunday evening. It's the servants' half day, but I plan to return from my club at nine."

Kirkwood smiled. "If you think it might help answer any unresolved questions, I shall see you on Sunday evening."

They parted ways. Kirkwood would prove himself false, or he would offer insight into Michael's life aboard ship. If Sebastian had to bet on the outcome, the odds were even.

Sebastian wasn't the only one seeking insight. Within seconds of him settling next to Ailsa in Nicholas' carriage, Helen blurted, "Well? Are you and Ailsa betrothed? She wouldn't answer without you being present. Oh, please say you are."

Sebastian silently groaned. Helen would give anything to see him wed. "We're examining the possibility we might be more than friends." It wasn't a lie.

Helen clapped her hands, happiness brightening her tired eyes. "But this is marvellous news. I thought you despised one another."

"Passion can take many forms."

Nicholas did not share in his wife's excitement. "I imagine it has something to do with the case, my love." He captured Helen's hand as if preparing her for a blow. "Or it's a pact made to ward off their many admirers."

Helen shook her head. "No. There's something noticeably different about the way they react to one another. And they never dance. Never."

"Doubtless they needed to discuss the case."

Like Ailsa, Sebastian wasn't sure what to say. The truth was always best, but anger had surfaced when he saw men fawning over her. And therein lay the problem. He couldn't shake the overwhelming desire to possess this woman.

"It's complicated," Sebastian said truthfully.

Tomorrow, things might be less confusing.

Ailsa cleared her throat. "All I can say is I admire Lord Denton a great deal."

"See!" Helen pointed at them. "Did you ever expect to hear such praise from Ailsa's lips?"

"No, my love." Nicholas shot Sebastian an irate glare. "I just hope you're not disappointed if they discover they do not suit."

"Of course they don't suit. That's what makes it so marvellous."

They arrived in Grosvenor Street promptly.

Sebastian drew their attention to Gibbs, who had parked Daventry's unmarked coach fifty yards from the house. "I've papers to collect from the study. Then we shall return to Fortune's Den until the murderer is caught."

"Is there a way I might help with your enquiries?" While Nicholas' voice was as calm as a windless sea, a storm gathered in his eyes. "Helen would feel better if this matter were dealt with quickly. If the truth were brought to light."

Understanding Nicholas' need to protect his wife and feel useful, Sebastian thought of the least dangerous thing his friend could do. "You could visit Hibbet's mother. I'll have a footman deliver a note to you in the morning with her address and a list of questions."

Nicholas nodded. "I'll come to Fortune's Den and let you know what I discover."

They said farewell and alighted.

Yanking down the window as the carriage pulled away, Helen shouted, "Take care of each other!"

Miss MacTavish sighed as she watched the vehicle disappear into the night. "I hate lying to her. Helen wants to see ye happy."

Guilt ate away at him, too. "I'll explain everything to Nicholas tomorrow evening." He glanced along the dimly lit street, his attention caught by the wavering shadows. "We shouldn't linger out here. I fear the murderer may come looking for the spell book."

Her breath caught in her throat. "Ye think the murderer thought Mr Hibbet had the grimoire? Ye think that's the motive?"

"I don't know what to think, but every instinct says this entire case revolves around that dratted book." Taking advantage of any excuse to touch her, he cupped her elbow. "Come. Keep your hood raised until we're safely inside."

They entered the house and gave the bemused butler their outdoor apparel. Sebastian had never brought a woman home and acted like it wasn't a shocking occurrence.

"You may retire, Cumpson. I shall lock the door on my way out."

Having mastered a butler's bland expression, it was somewhat surprising when Cumpson smiled. "Will you require refreshment, my lord?"

"We'll help ourselves." Noting the pink flush on Miss MacTavish's cheeks, he added, "We've casework to study and may venture outdoors to burn a few documents. If you smell smoke, know there's no cause for concern."

Cumpson's bushy grey brows twitched as if the words

carried a salacious undertone. "Yes, my lord. I shan't trouble you unless you ring for assistance."

"Before you go, I need you to deliver a note to the coachman waiting in the unmarked vehicle across the street."

Sebastian meant to warn Gibbs they might be detained for an hour. How long did it take to repeat an incantation beneath a crescent moon?

For some reason, he hoped it took a lifetime.

He quickly scribed a message for Gibbs, then escorted Miss MacTavish to the library to retrieve Michael's book. While lighting the lamps, he mentioned his brief conversation with Kirkwood.

"Kirkwood agreed to visit tomorrow and examine the tome." Sebastian closed the door. Intimacy swirled between them the instant they were alone. "Are you cold? Shall I light the fire?" He pictured himself smoothing his hands over her naked body, warming every numb extremity.

"Ye do such menial tasks yerself?" she teased.

"A man should know the basic skills of survival."

Her gaze dipped to his mouth. "It seems pointless lighting the fire when we're to venture outdoors." She ignored the expensive books lining the dark oak cases, studying only him. "Perhaps a dram of brandy will heat our blood."

His blood was already simmering.

Lust's insistent call thrummed in every cell, an inner tug urging him to reach for her, hold her, kiss her, fuck and make love.

Despite standing in his impressive library, he had no desire to boast of his rare collection or impress her with his copy of Shakespeare's *Venus and Adonis*. She held his complete attention. Nothing he owned compared to the prospect of owning her.

Mother of all saints!

It had to be witchcraft.

"Brandy it is." As he pulled the stopper from the decanter, his hand shook like a callow youth's. They were minutes away from banishing the spell. The hunger would fade. The pleasurable waves sweeping through him would dissipate with the charred paper in the wind.

He crossed the room and handed her the glass. Their fingers brushed in a deliberate caress that confirmed she feared the haunting emptiness, too.

"Do you have your note, Ailsa?" Saying her given name did strange things to his insides. He meant to wring every drop of pleasure from these final moments. "When we left Mangold, we agreed to keep them on our person, to cast them into the flames at the first opportunity."

She swallowed a sip of brandy, inhaling to cool the burn. "I know what we agreed but I havenae had a moment to myself all day."

Relief raced through him.

"I've not written my retraction either."

Her brow quirked in silent challenge. "Ye could have written it last night while drinking with Mr Chance."

"You could have written yours while Delphine rummaged through her armoire. It's only two lines."

"And pray where would I have kept it?"

He used the opportunity to stare at her breasts. "Have you never tucked a secret love note into your bodice?"

"As a spinster, I've never had cause to entertain the notion. Only a cad would draw attention to my failings."

He found himself smiling. "Would you like to?"

"Like to what?"

"Slip a secret love note into your bodice."

"And who would write it?" she mocked.

"Your betrothed."

She looked heavenward and tutted. "What do ye know of love?"

He knew losing someone close hurt like the devil.

He knew a wounded heart took forever to heal.

He knew real love could not be conjured by a spell, but he'd still mourn the loss of this fantasy long after it ended.

"Perhaps I'd write something crude to make you pant." He tossed back his brandy. "Something to turn your blood molten."

He might distract her for a few days so they missed the waning moon. That would give them another month to indulge their whims.

"Verra well. Ye can write me a note while we're scribbling our recantations." She scanned the room. "Do ye have paper and ink?"

"In the side table drawer."

They both looked at the drawer, though neither moved.

"Make use of it while I visit my study." He left the room, entered the study and snatched paper from the desk, slicing the leaf in half with a letter opener.

A grin formed as he imagined putting his lewd thoughts to paper.

I want to be inside you when you come.

It summed up his present mood perfectly, but it wouldn't do.

I want you to ride me so hard I forget my failings.

It sounded pitiful and self-absorbed.

She would want something personal. A meaningful message she would read endlessly even when the paper developed brown spots and tatty corners. An honest explanation of what this relationship meant to him.

The time spent with you has been the happiest of my life.

The truth of the statement resonated deep in his bones. He

could not recall ever feeling so content. But many men had spouted the mawkish words, many times before.

Keen to do better, he searched his mind.

A broad smile formed with the sudden epiphany.

He dipped his pen into the ink pot.

I could scour the shores for a lifetime and never find a pebble perfect enough to honour you.

He blotted the ink and folded the note. Upon his return to the library, he discovered Ailsa had written her recantation and had taken to examining his books.

"Is this Michael's grimoire?" She trailed her finger over the gold lettering on the red leather spine. Being smaller in size, it was at odds with the rest of his collection. "'Tis the only one I could see."

Sebastian swallowed hard. Hidden within the pages had to be a clue to understanding Michael's death. "Yes. We need to take it with us when we leave. Don't let me forget."

"I cannae promise. I doubt I'll remember a thing once we've broken the spell." She held out her hand. "Do ye have my love note?"

He prowled towards her. "Yes, and I mean to deliver it personally." Coming to a halt mere inches away, he trailed his fingers along the delicate slope of her collarbone. "I don't want you to lose it and miss reading my inspiring prose."

Despite a visible shiver, the minx held his gaze. "Conveying any sentiment must have proved taxing."

"On the contrary. It's easy to relay the words constantly filling one's head." He slid his fingers into the low neckline of her gown, pushing the note between her warm breasts. "Allow me to paraphrase. I've never wanted a woman the way I want you. Now, you need never forget the power of magic."

Her breath quickened.

The air crackled with suppressed need.

He stared at her parted lips. One kiss might ease the ache. But he pulled another note from his coat pocket. "I wrote my retraction while in the study. Shall we venture outside while the moon is still visible? Shall we put an end to this exquisite madness?"

Biting down on her lip, she looked at the words on the paper as if they were written in blood. "We need to do something to stop the influx of admirers. Breaking our bond will help us focus on the case."

Disappointment sat like a heavy weight in his chest.

"You're right." It killed him to admit the truth. The quicker they got this matter over with, the sooner he could gather his wits. "Come. Let us take our notes and go out into the garden."

No longer able to gaze into her eyes without experiencing a pang of regret, he snatched the candle lamp from the side table.

With slow, hesitant steps, Ailsa followed him out through the terrace doors and down the stone steps into the verdant shadows.

The waning crescent was like a golden smile lighting the night sky. It was said to represent a period of reflection and inner peace, yet Sebastian had every cause to be miserable and irate.

Ailsa remained silent as she followed him along the narrow path. Every breath sounded like a sigh. Every footstep seemed heavy with the weight of this burden.

He came to a halt outside the orangery at the end of the garden. Once his mother's beloved space, he never had cause to enter the hothouse. Simms, the gardener, still grew an abundance of fruits and flowers there, his fondness for life never fading.

With a glance heavenward at the threatening clouds drifting closer, Sebastian bit back a curse. "We should begin before the storm breaks." He held the candle lamp aloft and gripped the paper, ready to recite the magical words. "This spell no longer—"

"Wait!" Ailsa darted forward, pressing her cold fingers to his lips. "Dinnae say it yet." Struggling to contain a restless energy, she tried to explain the reason for the interruption. "Ye still owe me a boon."

Confusion and relief made a heady combination. "You wish to claim it now?" he said against her fingers.

"Aye." She didn't snatch her hand away but moved to cup his cheek. "It cannae wait. I'd rather bargain with the passionate man than the one who gives me cold shivers."

He couldn't be cold towards her if he tried. This undeniable attraction was a palpable thing, a hot pulsing energy. "What do you want from me, Ailsa?"

She gulped, hesitated, the anticipation almost unbearable. "What if I never feel like this again? What if I've no hope of experiencing it with any other man?"

His heart thumped an erratic beat. "It?"

She stared at his mouth, her lips parting before they touched his briefly. "This all-consuming need to have you. Make love to me, Sebastian. Make love to me before we break the spell."

Chapter Thirteen

Had Sebastian known the price of losing the game was a night of debauchery, he'd have dribbled cherry liqueur down his chin, slathered it over his face and declared himself a failure.

"Do you know what you're asking?" While his body ached to release the mounting tension, a gentleman should err on the side of caution.

"Aye." Ailsa's nervous smile touched a place deep in his chest. "I'm asking ye to grant me a boon and forget our troubles for an hour or two."

An hour or two? One plunge into her wetness, and he would blow as quick as a young buck taking his first strokes.

"I'm asking ye to pretend we're lovers."

He didn't need to pretend. They had been building up to this moment for days, maybe years. They thrived on every intense encounter. The fire between them blazed as hot as hell's flames.

"You're asking me to ruin you." To push deep into her exquisite body, to ride her hard until they were sweat-soaked and sated.

"I'm asking ye to make me feel like a woman. To show me the true depth of desire." She averted her gaze, hiding behind a veil of timidity. "If the prospect is unappealing, then—"

"Unappealing!" Sebastian laughed. He spent as much time trying to tame his erection as he did hauling air into his lungs. "Do you know how hard it's been to keep my hands off you?" How many times he'd palmed his cock while uttering her name?

Her eyes met his, the sensual smile behind her gaze unmistakable. "But I thought ye were desperate to end this witchery."

I'm desperate to lose myself in your naked body, love.

The tightening in his abdomen confirmed he could rise to the challenge in seconds. "To hell with dancing beneath the crescent moon. It can wait."

Her sultry stare caressed him. "How do we begin?"

"How do you want to begin?"

"Dinnac ask me. I'm the novice."

"You don't kiss like a novice." The woman had near blown his mind with her teasing tongue. "You don't moan like a novice. And I doubt you'll make love like one."

"That has nothing to do with skill and everything to do with—"

"Don't mention the five-letter word that rhymes with hell." He placed the lamp on the ground, took both their notes and slipped them into his coat pocket. "Where do you want me?"

She blinked as if English were a foreign language.

"It's your boon," he reminded her playfully. "As I am at your beck and call, madam, I will do whatever you command." Keen to give her minimal guidance, he added, "Follow your instincts. Take your pleasure."

Her confident smile proved promising. She peered through the gloom at the glow of candlelight spilling from the house. He'd wager she would choose his bedchamber. Somewhere comfortable where they could frolic undisturbed. Or maybe the library, the sight of rare books heightening her desire.

As he waited, his body throbbing with anticipation, the first spots of rain fell.

Plump drops landed on her cheeks and lashes, but she did not squeal or gather her skirts and seek shelter. The minx glanced at the mass of dark clouds swallowing the crescent moon and laughed.

"Fate has given us its blessing." Looking like a woodland nymph in his secluded garden, she reached into her hair and began pulling the pins, discarding them on the ground and shaking out her fiery locks.

Mother of all saints!

Blood pooled low in his loins. "Come. We should seek cover before you catch a chill." He was desperate to sink his hands into her hair, anchor her lips to his and ravage her with maddening kisses.

"Catch a chill?" she mocked, opening her arms wide and surrendering to the heavens. "Have ye never entertained a Scotswoman? We're made to withstand the harsh weather."

The rain lashed down, bouncing off the hothouse roof. Droplets trickled down the slender column of her throat, the rivulets creating an enticing path to the valley between her breasts. He needed her out of that damn dress. To feast on her flesh. To rid himself of this blasted ache.

Like a fool, he had laid down the gauntlet and could do nothing but watch in awe as she turned her back and said, "Quickly. Help me out of Delphine's gown. I mean to take my pleasure here."

"Here?" He almost choked in shock. The garden was cold and damp. Nothing good would come from joining bodies while battling the elements.

Still, he fiddled with the tiny gilt buttons, slid the silk off her shoulders and helped her out of the sumptuous gown.

A lump tightened his throat.

Her hourglass silhouette left his mouth dry.

Upon her command, he loosened the laces of her corset, the power of each tug pulsing deep in his ballocks. "Don't forget about your love letter," he muttered, kissing her bare shoulder.

She shivered at his touch. "How could I? 'Tis the first gift ye've given me. It may be the last."

While he battled with the sudden heaviness in his chest, she retrieved the love letter, gathered her garments and deposited them carefully in the orangery.

She returned moments later, dressed in nothing but her chemise, shoes and stockings. He might have suggested they move the deflowering to the hothouse, but raindrops glistened like diamonds on her porcelain skin. The sodden garment clung to her lush breasts, breasts he longed to fondle and caress.

His cock thickened in his trousers.

"We need to get ye out of these clothes." Like a consummate seducer, she pushed his black evening coat off his shoulders and ran her hands over the hard muscles. "Let the rain wash away yer Tiffin cologne."

No woman had ever undressed him.

No woman had ever stripped him naked in the rain.

Her delicate hands made light work of his waistcoat, her delightful pants coming quicker when the garment joined his coat on the wet grass.

"Allow me." He removed the sapphire pin from his

cravat and yanked the fashionable knot. With mounting impatience, he dragged his shirt over his head and threw it to the ground.

The lady inhaled sharply, her gaze focusing on the rain-water running over the muscles in his chest. "In case I forget to tell ye once we've broken the spell, yer body does strange things to me."

"Strange things?" he said, smiling.

"Aye, a fluttering deep in my belly."

"The sight of erect nipples pushing against wet cotton causes me equal discomfort." He captured her hand, smoothing it down the solid ridge in his trousers. "This is what you do to me, Ailsa. This is how much I want you."

Hell! The merest touch made him weep.

Her eyes widened. "Just promise ye'll nae get me with child."

It should have been an easy promise to make, yet he faltered. Unlike others of his acquaintance, he never broke a vow. "I assure you, there will be no child from our love-making *tonight*." The distinction seemed important.

"But ye plan on removing yer trousers?"

Sebastian glanced towards the house. Although they were hidden in the dark depths of the garden, about to answer lust's persistent call, he couldn't quite find the impetus needed to surrender.

When conditioned to be a pillar of society, one did not chase their dreams. One did not indulge their desires. One remained firm. Steadfast.

You'll be a viscount, not a damn wastrel.

Your brother hasn't a sensible bone in his body.

You must be strong for both of you.

Weakness isn't an option. Do you hear me, boy?

Sebastian fought against the memory of his father's

outrage. "If we do this, there is no going back. Perhaps it's wrong to—"

"Nothing about this feels wrong." Ailsa stroked his solid shaft, her innocent touch sending his need spiralling. "Our bodies are in perfect tune. We deserve to be selfish for once, to know what it is to be free."

Wet tendrils of hair clung to her cheeks. Rain dripped from her lashes. Despite shivering against the cold, she smiled like she found nature liberating. The sight fed a lost desire for adventure. A hidden need to break free from convention and take risks. The thrill of dicing with danger.

Respect for one's birthright had been rammed down his throat from infancy. He knew how to be an arrogant aristocrat. Knew how to follow rigid rules, embrace loneliness, marry for wealth, not love. In the process, he had forgotten how to be a man.

Ailsa sighed. "I should have suggested somewhere indoors."

"No!" He reached for her, snaking his arm around her waist, fisting the drenched cotton and pulling the garment tight. "I need you now. I want to make love to you in the rain." The urge was primal. More powerful than lust and longing. "I shall take pleasure in warming every cold extremity."

Her mouth found his in an almost violent assault. Rainwater coated her sensuous lips, lips that coaxed his apart with ease, plump pillow-like lips that dragged him deeper into a dreamlike state.

Her tongue sought his, not to dance but to wrestle and wrangle. To feast, to fuck his mouth with a passion she couldn't contain.

The hunger writhing in his veins was just as ferocious. A guttural growl rumbled in his throat. Their teeth clashed.

With frantic hands, he gathered her chemise to her waist, grabbed her bare bottom and ground his erection against her abdomen.

"Holy Mother of God!" he uttered against her mouth. "We should slow down. Else this will be over before it's begun."

"I want to savour every second," she confessed, raining kisses over his jaw, digging her fingers into his muscled back. "But I cannae control the impulse to hurry. 'Tis like I'm possessed."

He understood perfectly.

He'd be in Bedlam if he didn't consummate this union soon.

"Then we shall do both." He drew her towards the cherry tree, a billowy canopy of pink and white blooms, unbuttoned his trousers and freed his engorged cock. "We'll sate our lust now. Focus on your pleasure when in the comfort of my bedchamber."

Her wide-eyed gaze fell to his jutting length. "I'm nae sure this will work. Perhaps we should just concentrate on kissing."

"We were made to fit together, love."

In more ways than one.

Somehow, he had always known it.

An idea burst into his mind. He scanned the garden to ensure no one could see them, then dropped to a sitting position, his bare back resting against the tree trunk.

"Stand over me and grip the trunk with both hands. Grip it hard." Committed to enjoying this wild adventure, he'd make sure they climbed to the highest peak.

"What do ye mean to do?"

"You'll see. Take off your chemise." Noticing her gaze flitting about like a trapped bird in a cage, he added, "Trust me. No one can see you. No one but me. Your betrothed."

A coy smile curled the corners of her mouth. "Nae man has ever seen me naked." She gathered the hem of her sodden garment and, with some hesitance, drew it over her head.

"No one but me."

"Aye." She held the chemise tight to her body.

"Let me see you, love. Don't be afraid."

With a sigh of surrender, she let the garment fall.

Sebastian wondered if he'd died and gone to heaven. His cock jerked at the sight of raindrops racing over her porcelain skin. Sucking those rosebud nipples topped his list of priorities. Imagining those stocking-clad thighs gripping his hips almost made him spurt over his trousers.

"I pray I never forget this night," he drawled. "I pray this moment is ingrained in my memory until I take my last breath. Grab the tree, Ailsa, and put one foot on my shoulder."

"A foot on yer shoulder?"

"Trust me, love."

Taking tentative steps, she came closer, close enough for him to smooth his tingling hands over her thighs and palm her soft buttocks.

He encouraged her to follow his command.

Then he set his mouth to her sex, holding her firmly in place while he inhaled her sweet scent, drawing her essence deep into his body.

"Sebastian!" Panic marred her tone.

"You were right," he groaned before sliding his tongue over her swollen bud. "To one's mate, one's natural aroma is addictive. Soon the rain will wash away all traces of my cologne, and you may find my scent equally appealing."

He gripped her wet buttocks, securing his mouth to her sex as he tongued her silky folds. Her legs shook when he licked the centre of her desire and lapped the evidence of her arousal.

"I—I've a confession," she panted. "Oh, Lord! I knew ye had a mischievous mouth but never knew it was this wicked."

"That's your confession?" The way she arched her back and rocked against his lips said she was close to finding her release. "Hold the trunk tightly."

She shook her head as she clung to the tree, causing drops of water to land on his bare shoulders. "I love yer scent. I always have. I dinnae care about yer cologne."

He rewarded her honesty with a few fast flicks of his tongue.

Her keen cry burst from her, escaping into the damp night air as her body convulsed and trembled.

Sebastian drew her down to straddle his thighs.

Raindrops dripped from her rosy nipples. The fevered look in her eyes hardened his cock, standing bold and rigid between them. The angry veins bulged with the need for pleasure.

"We don't have to continue," he said, keeping the strain of disappointment from his voice. "You may want to remain intact."

Ailsa threw herself forward, wrapping her arms around his neck, kissing him, slipping her tongue over his in a slow, hypnotic rhythm.

She stilled, her mouth moving featherlike over his, her heated gaze fixing him to the tree trunk. "Tell me what to do. Show me." Rising up on her knees, she edged forward until the swollen head of his manhood was but an inch from her entrance.

"I cannot promise it won't hurt. But I'm told it passes quickly." He gripped his shaft, couldn't resist stroking it back and forth over her clitoris.

184

"Do it. Do it now, Sebastian. Before the crescent moon appears." The minx gripped his shoulders, lowering herself down.

He firmed his jaw as he pushed inside her an inch, no more. Hell, it took every ounce of willpower he possessed not to thrust home.

She didn't fight the intrusion but welcomed it, her body stretching to take more of him. The feel of her hugging his cock was beyond divine. But the powerful sensations rioting through him amounted to more than sating a carnal need.

No wonder she wanted to make love while still bound by this enchantment. A potent energy flowed between them, an intense electricity that heightened the senses and made every small thrust seem magical.

"I need to push deeper." He wrapped his arms around her waist, sucked raindrops from her rosebud nipples, suckled the peaks.

"Oh!" She gripped his hair and tugged hard, riding the waves of pleasure. "Take me. Dinnae wait." She dragged his mouth to hers, the urgency to mate evident in the punishing strokes of her tongue.

Forgive me, he uttered silently as he crushed her to his soaked body, filling her in one long thrust.

Blessed saints!

While the action tore a guttural groan from him, she froze.

Guilt ripped through him. He stilled to allow her time to breathe. "You need to move. You need to ride me, love. I swear the pain will subside if you keep to a gentle rhythm."

"'Tis nae pain I'm feeling."

"What then?"

"It doesnae matter."

Did she feel this strange form of possessiveness, too? Did

she want to own him, lock him in her bedchamber and throw away the key? Did she fear one night of passion would not ease the crippling ache? Was an otherworldly force in control of their actions?

He might have analysed every question, but Ailsa began moving, rising up on her knees and sinking slowly back down.

The sight of her held him enthralled.

The rain fell, drenching their skin. A sudden gust of wind shook the boughs of the cherry tree, showering them in pretty white and pink petals. Never had he experienced such a wicked ravishment.

As she became accustomed to the feel of his cock pumping hot and deep into her soft flesh, desperation surfaced.

They kissed until they couldn't breathe.

He devoured her breasts, stroked her throbbing bud, pounded into her fast and hard, impaling her with unbridled savagery.

In a tangle of wet limbs, she milked his manhood, finding her release again with a cry of sweet agony.

God, he couldn't get enough of this woman.

Somehow, she had found a way under his skin.

He withdrew with barely a second to spare, spilling his seed over her stockings when he wanted to empty himself deep inside her. Brand her. Mark her as his. Stake his claim.

Chapter Fourteen

Barefooted and dressed in a clean shirt and trousers, Sebastian returned to the hothouse carrying linen towels and a wool blanket.

Ailsa watched him approach, the heat in her chest rising to her cheeks. He had been gone for a few minutes, yet she'd missed him. She'd missed his smile, missed the glint of passion in his perfect blue eyes.

Despite their rampant lovemaking, lust still coiled low in her belly. The need to feel full with him, to remain forever entwined, brought tears to her eyes and a ripple of fear to her throat.

She had made a foolish mistake.

She had given all of herself, opened her heart, and could not take it back. Thoughts of him filled her head. Nothing mattered but the next touch, the next kiss. She wanted to devour him, consume him.

"Wouldn't you rather dress before a warm fire?" Along with a hairbrush, he placed the towels on the rickety wooden chair, then draped the blanket around her shoulders and rubbed her arms vigorously. "We can return to the library without anyone noticing."

"What if Cumpson appears?" Ailsa fought to stop the tears falling. She had never experienced grief, but she would feel the loss of this man keenly.

"He won't." He stared at her cold lips, at the tangle of wet copper curls, at the petticoat covering her modesty, and grinned. "You look like a nymph, a siren sent to lure a man from the doldrums with her passionate promises."

"Forgive me," she uttered despite her chattering teeth.

She'd thought having him would sate the hunger, but it writhed deep in a place a sworn spinster had no need to navigate.

His smile faded. "For what?"

"For making the coming days harder. For making it impossible to continue our friendship now we've been intimate."

His stoic expression added to the tension. "We're both adults, Ailsa. Nothing need change. The only difficult thing will be concentrating on the case."

What did that mean?

Was he plagued by lustful thoughts, too?

Undoubtedly.

They were at the mercy of medieval magic.

"Then we must break the spell tonight, as originally planned." The rain had stopped. Nature had worked *its* magic, turning the barren into something beautiful, restoring their withered hearts. But the storm clouds had parted to reveal the crescent moon and soon their fate would be in their own hands. "I pray it helps us to see this relationship for what it is."

"And what is that?"

Sheer madness! An act of lunacy!

"Merely two lonely people seeking comfort."

"Who said I'm lonely?" He plucked a blossom petal from her hair, studied it and rolled it between his fingers.

"Who said I'm lonely?" she countered.

He laughed. "You did."

"Aye, because my mind is nae my own." Part of her was still sitting astride him beneath the cherry tree, hugging him tightly, panting with pleasure. "Let us bring an end to the confusion."

He snatched a towel and began patting her hair dry. "I'm not confused. I want you. You want me. Thirty minutes of frantic lovemaking proved that."

"What are ye saying? That we begin an affair?"

"Why not?" The devil continued his caring ministrations, gently pulling the hairbrush through her damp tendrils so as not to hurt her. "We're free to do as we please."

Why not?

Because she was already more than obsessed with kissing him. Because she would likely fall deeper under his spell.

"Because, in case ye've forgotten, an intruder broke into my home. An intruder who is still at large. A man who probably murdered Mr Hibbet in the most dreadful fashion. We must focus on finding him."

He sighed like solving the case was a dreaded inconvenience.

"And what about yer brother?" she added, seeking ways to strengthen her argument. "Should we nae read his grimoire and try to understand what happened aboard *The Perseus*?"

Sebastian stopped brushing her hair, the serenity in his eyes fading. "We'll repeat the recantation tonight, but I suspect it won't make a blind bit of difference."

"A difference to understanding yer brother's plight?"

"A difference to understanding ours."

She feared he was right. She would have to live with this yearning for a lifetime. "Still, we must try to solve the mystery. We owe it to those who've lost their lives."

"Then let me help you dress. Gibbs is probably so tired of waiting to ferry us back to Fortune's Den that he's taken an axe to the front door."

Her soiled stockings and chemise were fit for the bonfire. Though Sebastian folded the garments neatly and placed them with his own sodden clothes.

He played the role of maid, tightening her corset and buttoning her into Delphine's dress. Finding a reel of string, he cut a length with the gardener's knife and suggested she use it to tie back her hair.

His blue eyes blazed hot as he watched her fasten her locks into a braid and secure it with string.

"Here's the note renouncing the spell." His hand shook a little as he removed the folded paper from his coat pocket and placed it into her palm.

The instant they touched, the air sparked to life.

He did not stop looking at her, drinking her in like a man parched.

Ailsa tucked the note into her bodice, next to the message he had written earlier to remind her of the power of lust. Words that would fade with time, just like their passion.

He led her outside.

The crisp air breezed over her, raising goose pimples on her skin. Amid the smell of damp earth and sweet blossom, she detected the faintest trace of his cologne.

She hid a smile while watching him strike the sulphur-tipped spill and light the lamp. Tomorrow, she would visit

Truefitt & Hall, scour the shop for cologne with notes of vanilla and musk, and drench her pillow with her lover's piquant scent.

"Are you ready?" Sebastian glanced at the crescent moon, his muscular shoulders sagging.

No!

Kiss me one last time.

Don't let me forget what we've meant to each other.

But they had to do this.

Being truthful was important to both of them.

No one wanted to live amid a shadow of doubt.

"Will ye go first?" Her throat tightened at the thought of what was at stake. "Remember, ye're supposed to recite the lines with clear intention."

He glanced at the paper in his hand. "I'll recite the words, but I don't believe we're bound by magic." Inhaling deeply, and in a voice devoid of emotion, he continued, *"This spell no longer serves me. With the last wisp of smoke, set my soul free."*

The churning in Ailsa's chest brought bile to her throat.

She looked to the heavens, expecting to hear a violent clap of thunder, witness a blinding flash of light tearing through the night sky. A reckoning. Punishment for the pleasure they'd stolen.

Nothing.

Not a sudden breeze.

Not a crow's caw.

Not an eerie chill chasing down her spine.

"It's your turn to sever our bond," he said, his tone much cooler than it had been of late. "Once you've read your lines, we'll burn the papers together."

Ailsa reached for the folded note but drew the wrong one

by mistake. Silently, she began reading Sebastian's lewd message.

I could scour the shores for a lifetime and never find a pebble perfect enough to honour you.

Shocked, she met his gaze. The words were beautiful, deeply personal. They touched on previous conversations. Showed how their relationship had developed into something meaningful.

She might have stepped forward and pressed a tender kiss to his lips, thanked him and promised to cherish it always. But a distinct air of tension made her swap the notes and recite the recantation.

An emptiness enveloped her when the last word left her lips. As if an invisible force had punched through her chest and stolen her soul.

He must have felt it, too.

With a dazed expression, he set the paper to the lit candle and watched until the flames destroyed their fantasy.

"We should return to Fortune's Den before Gibbs gets frustrated and deserts his post." Sebastian visited the hothouse to fetch their clothes and then led the way back to the house.

Minutes passed while he went upstairs to finish dressing. Minutes where she felt nothing but numb. To busy herself while waiting, she found Michael's grimoire and began flicking through the pages.

The list of spells was strange. A prayer to stop a dog barking at night. A charm to dream of the deceased. A mantra to make a lover confess his secrets.

The last one was of particular interest. But Ailsa had to determine how she felt before questioning Sebastian.

She turned to the first page, keen to examine the rune symbols written at various points in the margins. The markings were similar to the sigils, in that they looked foreign to the untrained eye, but she couldn't shake the feeling they had been strategically placed.

"There's a pattern to the annotations," she said when Sebastian returned, looking handsome in a dark blue coat. She crossed the room to show him the page. "Do ye see the rune that looks like an arrow?"

He stepped closer, his powerful aura invading her space. She feared she would feel nothing, but the stirrings of lust simmered beneath the surface.

"Yes. There are numerous ones throughout the book."

"Aye, but only next to words that begin with the letter T."

Their arms touched as he leaned over her shoulder. "There's one next to the word *trust*. Another by the word *trouble*."

"I suspect it's a code. A secret message. But we will have to sit at length and try to determine what the other runes mean."

"Agreed." He looked at her, his gaze curious. "How strange. Our minds are clearer now we're no longer under the grip of the spell."

Her heart sank like a brick in a well.

Did he not feel desire's potency?

Did he not want to take her in his arms and drink from her lips?

"Aye," she said, swallowing past the painful lump in her throat. "It all seems so obvious now." That said, she had not studied Michael's grimoire before. And the need to protect her heart had her erecting steel defences.

"Are you ready to leave?"

Was he keen to place some distance between them?

She nodded, though dreaded the thought of what tomorrow would bring. She would prefer his irate comments to his cool indifference. "We mustn't forget the grimoire."

"No, nothing is more important than that."

He extinguished the lamps, gathered their outdoor apparel and led her out onto Grosvenor Street.

Another unmarked carriage had pulled alongside Gibbs' vehicle. A man dressed in black stood on the pavement, conversing with Mr Daventry's coachman.

Fear shot through her, but when the fellow saw them and raised his hand, Ailsa realised it was Mr Daventry.

"My wife and I were dining with friends in Upper Brook Street and saw Gibbs waiting." His brow quirked when he noticed the string securing her braid. "I left a note for you at Fortune's Den. The landlord of the Old Crown will speak to you tomorrow at noon. You're to enter via the yard, not the front door."

"With luck, we'll discover the identity of the delivery driver," she said, struggling to hide her embarrassment. Mr Daventry had a second sight when it came to discovering one's secrets.

"May I?" the man said, plucking a white blossom petal from her damp hair. "For a moment, I thought it was snowing in April."

"We were caught in the rain, sir." The memory of their wet bodies moving in unison beneath the cherry tree flooded her mind.

"The rain?"

"I wanted to show Miss MacTavish my mother's hothouse." Sebastian winced as the words left his lips.

"It might have been better to show her the flowers during daylight hours." Mr Daventry cleared his throat. "Well, I shan't keep you. Your mother must have had a variety of plants. Gibbs said he's been waiting for two hours."

Ailsa forced a smile. "Mr Chance said we cannae return to Fortune's Den until midnight. 'Tis easier for Sigmund to sneak me in once the patrons are sotted."

If Mr Daventry doubted her word, he never said. He wished them luck in gathering information from the Old Crown and instructed Gibbs to deliver them back to Aldgate.

Once inside the carriage, shame turned to amusement, and Ailsa couldn't help but chuckle. "I think ye did more than show me the hothouse. My cheeks are still glowing."

Sebastian managed a grin. "After such a thorough education, I pray you remember the names of the plants."

The thread of laughter in his voice roused hope in her heart. "The most notable was the *Prunus avium*, often referred to as the wild cherry tree."

His cobalt eyes glistened in the darkness. "I believe that's a rather accurate description. And what of the *phallus erectus*? Do you recall that with any clarity, madam?"

The sight of his turgid shaft was imprinted in her memory. "Aye. I believe I saw an excellent example. A solid specimen of virility."

Masculine pride brightened his features. "The question is, would you be interested in seeing it again?"

"Would ye be interested in showing it to me?" Did he still feel the burning attraction, or had the flames died? Had their fiery passion been nothing but a magnificent illusion?

He shuffled to the edge of the seat, the curl of his mouth holding the promise of something sinful. "I'm a man who keeps his cards close to his chest. As such, I'm reluctant to declare myself first. Despise feeling the slightest sliver of vulnerability."

She thought to reward his honesty, to ease his torment by

confessing her feelings. But the more time they spent together, the farther she advanced into his secret domain. Every revelation brought them one step closer.

"And yet?" she prompted.

A muscle in his cheek twitched. "From my perspective, nothing has changed." He dragged his hand through his hair. "I want you. More than ever. I'm still locked in the grip of a spell. Your spell."

I want you so badly I can barely sit still, she said silently.

"What I need to know," he began, waves of tension rolling between them, "is if your desire for me has dissipated. Were you swept up in the moment? In the face of this stark reality, has your perception altered?"

She coughed to hide her smile. "Might ye speak plainly?"

"Do you still want me, Ailsa?"

With every beat of my heart.

He threw himself back in the seat, scrubbed his hand over his handsome face and released an agonising sigh. "Tell me now. Put me out of my misery."

A quick glance beneath the blinds said they were ten minutes away from Fortune's Den. She hiked her skirts to her knees, crossed the carriage and came to sit astride him.

No words could explain the myriad of emotions in her chest.

So she brushed the lock of hair from his brow, watched his eyes flicker as she slowly massaged his temples, soothing away his fears.

Their eyes met as she cradled his face between her palms. She saw her own desperation reflected back, an insatiable need that defied comprehension. She saw something else. A tenderness that would remain locked in her heart forever.

She kissed him, time standing still as their breath mingled.

It was unlike the kisses they'd shared in the garden.

Their mouths moved slowly. Gently. A hypnotic melding that tightened every muscle, tugged at the lonely place deep in her chest.

They swallowed each other's moans as their tongues touched. Each stroke was a caress, not a fight for supremacy. Each glide left her core pulsing, a silent call for him to fill the emptiness.

"Free yourself," she uttered against his lips.

He understood her meaning. "We'll soon be at Fortune's Den."

"Are ye nae a man who seeks adventure, who takes risks?"

He smoothed his hands up her bare thighs. "You need time to recover. You'll struggle to take me again. I don't want to hurt you."

Nothing mattered but the need to feel him inside her.

"Are ye struggling to rise to the challenge?" she teased.

He gripped her thighs, pulling her against his solid shaft. "Rest assured, I'm permanently erect in your presence."

"Then ye better hurry if ye mean to have me."

Determined not to waste a second, he freed his manhood. Fumbling amid the mound of skirts, he positioned himself at her entrance.

He pushed slowly, inching his hardness inside her, though the rattle of the carriage on the cobblestones made a gentle coupling impossible.

Knowing he was afraid to hurt her, Ailsa took command, sheathing him fully despite the slight stinging.

"God, yes!" he growled. "You feel so good, love."

Good failed to convey the surge of pleasure flooding her body. Every thrust proved exquisite. The feeling of fullness was divine.

As their bodies moved together, the moist sound of their joining like the sweetest song she'd ever heard, two questions formed in her mind.

Would she always want him this badly?

Was this how it felt to be in love?

Chapter Fifteen

"Don't make me repeat myself, Gibbs." Sebastian glared at the coachman, who insisted on accompanying them into the Old Crown tavern. "I'm quite capable of dealing with an ailing landlord and lusty serving wench."

"Perhaps ye can wait in the yard, Mr Gibbs," Ailsa said, trying to pacify both men. The constant toing and froing left her giddy. "The tavern is closed for customers, and the rear entrance provides the only access."

Mr Gibbs snatched his hat off his head and scratched his temple. "Perhaps you're not understanding me, ma'am. Cutter don't get his nickname 'cause he likes boats. If you insist on going in alone, best keep your eyes peeled for his dagger."

Ailsa's blood ran cold.

Mr Daventry led them to believe it would be a civil conversation. A means of asking a few discreet questions, not a brawl with blades.

Before Sebastian suggested she wait in the carriage, Ailsa said, "'Tis agreed, then. Mr Gibbs will remain in the yard, and we'll shout if we need him."

Ailsa waited until a cart passed before hurrying across the muddy street. Sebastian and Mr Gibbs continued snapping and sniping until they all entered the narrow alley.

The passage stank like the Thames foreshore on a hot summer's day. The smell of rot and filth made it difficult to breathe.

Sebastian placed his hand at the base of her spine and guided her past the row of barrels, stopping at the wooden doors displaying a crude metal sign.

Keen to enter the cobbled yard first, Mr Gibbs darted forward and opened the door. Perhaps he hoped a villain lurked in the shadows and he'd have a chance to flex his fists.

"Dinnae be angry with him," she whispered to Sebastian. "Everyone wants to feel needed. Mr Gibbs is nae different."

His gaze softened as he scanned her face. "Do you want to feel needed, Ailsa? Would it please you to know I find it hard to function without your touch? That I'm counting the minutes until we're alone?"

"It pleases me to know our dependency is mutual." But she couldn't bear to think about how it would end. What these moments of happiness would cost them.

"The yard is clear, milord." Mr Gibbs beckoned them inside, where a woman with skin like cracked leather dunked laundry into a wooden pail. "Mrs White will show you into the tavern. Let's hope your fancy education stands you in good stead."

"I've no doubt it will," Sebastian said confidently. "I've had better beatings at Cambridge than in the White Boar's fighting pit."

The woman dried her gnarled fingers on her dirty apron and beckoned them to follow her inside. "Take a seat, and I'll fetch Mr Jones from the cellar."

They sat at a crude table in a taproom that smelled of stale

ale and burnt wood. The place was dim and dingy, the ceiling and panels to the right stained with soot.

"I wonder how the fire started," she said.

Sebastian reached for her hand beneath the table, and a fire of a different kind ignited. "When men are drunk, arguments often become heated. A candle flame and gin make a volatile combination."

"Still, ye must admit, it's quite a coincidence."

"It ain't no coincidence," came a hoarse voice from the shadows. A scrawny man limped towards them. "Just an accident with a lamp." He scanned their attire as if the garments confirmed his worst suspicions. "Can I get you something to wet your lips, milord?"

"I have refined tastes, Jones." Sebastian glanced at her, his gaze turning darkly intense. "Something sweet from the Highlands is my only pleasure."

"I have whisky from Knockando. My sister wed the son of a distiller in Moray. Will that suit your tastes?"

"I'm sure it will."

"Make that two drams, Mr Jones. I have a cousin in Moray and know the whisky well."

The fellow called to a buxom woman behind the counter and placed his order, then he dragged out a chair and sat at the table.

"I'm told you have questions about a punter who tricked Woodbury into handing over his goods." Mr Jones' eyes were like black marbles in his sockets, hard, cold and glassy. "Know I'll not squeal on my neighbours without good cause."

"So, the man is known to ye, sir, and lives locally." Why else would he make such a direct statement?

Mr Jones shifted. "He's known to me."

"We're here because we're investigating the murder of an

assistant at the auction house." The horrid drawing of the scene flashed into Ailsa's mind. And the blood … heavens … there'd been so much blood. "The villain cracked open Mr Hibbet's ribcage and cut out his heart."

The landlord licked his lips, doubtless wishing he had witnessed the gruesome act firsthand. "Are the Peelers so desperate they seek the help of lords and ladies now?"

"In their eagerness for results, we fear the police force will arrest the wrong man," Sebastian said before gesturing to Ailsa. "We suspect the devil who tricked Woodbury broke into the lady's home. We can identify him," he lied. It was hard to describe a man fleeing in the dark. "But we need his name so we can find him and discuss our suspicions."

The landlord scoffed. "Make sure he hangs, more like."

The serving wench approached, carrying a tray. As she placed three small pewter mugs on the table, Ailsa noted the lock of sable hair poking out of her cap. At a guess, she was no older than thirty and fitted the profile of the woman who had alerted the watchman.

"Perhaps we should tell ye everything we know, Mr Jones," Ailsa said to ease the mounting tension. "Then ye can decide what to do with the information."

"What if I decide to do nothing?" He downed his whisky in an almost savage gulp, hissing at them, though the man could take his liquor. "What if I throw you out onto the street and warn you to stay away?"

Sebastian straightened his broad shoulders. "Then, to protect the lady from future intruders, I shall use every resource at my disposal to find the devil. I'll have the police force trawling these streets, harassing your customers, watching your premises night and day."

In a move as quick as lightning, Mr Jones whipped a blade from his boot and jabbed the tip at Sebastian. "Don't threaten me, boy. I don't care who you are. I could have your eye out with a quick flick of my wrist."

Ailsa's pulse raced.

But Sebastian grinned. "And if I pull the trigger on my pocket pistol, I'll obliterate your ballocks. Shall we begin again without the need for weapons?"

Mr Jones dared to glance under the table, his shock turning into a sigh of surrender. He laid his knife next to his empty mug. "Seems you know how to handle yourself in a fight, milord."

The landlord sounded impressed.

Indeed, Ailsa found Sebastian's ability to beat the man highly arousing.

"When one enters a ring with Madman Murdoch, one learns to prepare for every eventuality." He released the hammer and placed the small pistol on the table. "Now, where were we?"

Ailsa turned to the serving wench whose chin still scraped the floor. "Our job is to find a murderer, nae accuse innocent people of crimes. But ye fit the description of the woman who told the watchman she heard screams at the auction house. And ye kept Mr Woodbury busy so the villain could deliver his tomes."

She expected the woman to thrust out her chest and deny the claim, and almost fell off her chair when the wench started sobbing.

"I swear. I swear on my ma's grave, Cutter, I didn't know anything about no murder." Her hands shook as she dashed tears from her cheeks. "I needed the money, that's all. And Mullings paid me three pounds to deliver the message."

"Mullings!" Mr Jones shot out of his chair, his face as red as hell's furnace. "I want that bastard here, and I want him here now! Do you hear me? Race up them bloody stairs and drag him out of his blasted bed."

"I—I'm sorry, Cutter." Snot tricked from the wench's nostrils. "He said it was just a favour for a friend."

"Fetch him!"

While the woman hurried away, Mr Gibbs came bursting into the taproom. He took one look at the knife and pistol on the table and stopped dead in his tracks. "I heard shouting, milord."

"You may join us, Mr Gibbs." Ailsa beckoned him over. "Mr Jones is assisting us with our enquiries."

Mr Jones cursed. "When a man threatens to blow a hole in your ballocks, you have no choice in the matter." He glanced at the ceiling and cursed. "Though I thank you for bringing the matter to my attention. I'll not have vermin living under my roof."

After a series of bangs and shouts from above stairs, a man raced into the taproom, his lank brown hair framing his face like shabby curtains.

"You want to speak to me, Cutter?" He caught Ailsa's eye as he finished buttoning his trousers. Recognition dawned, and he swallowed like he had a brick lodged in his throat.

Mr Jones grabbed Mullings by the scruff of his shirt and forced him into a seat. "When I gave you that scar on your hand, I said next time you'd lose a finger. Answer these good people, else I'll take two."

With pleading eyes, Mullings willed her to remain silent.

"Ye came to my home, Mr Mullings, to deliver a casket from Chadwick's." It seemed like a lifetime ago. So much had changed since the night Sebastian held her close in the darkness. "Except ye delivered the wrong package. Mr Wood-bury told us everything."

"I suggest you tell us exactly what happened." Sebastian

tossed back his whisky and seemed impressed by the smoky aftertaste. "Convince us you're innocent of murder."

Mr Jones grabbed his knife from the table and firmed his grip on the handle. "Don't lie, lad. There's a thumb at stake."

Beads of sweat coated Mr Mullings' brow. "I sometimes do jobs for people, people what can't do jobs for themselves."

"Someone hired ye to deliver the wrong books?" Hopefully, she would learn what had happened to the rare copy of *Utopia*.

"Yes. The assistant at the auction house."

"Hibbet hired you?" Anger flared in Sebastian's eyes.

Mr Mullings nodded. "He wanted me to get Woodbury drunk and deliver one of the books to Mr Smith in Tavistock Street. A magician's manual, he said. I was to make sure he received it at nine o'clock that night, but I had trouble finding a hackney."

Mr Smith? The sinister fellow dressed in black?

"But ye delivered the grimoire to me." No wonder Mr Smith had been watching her from the shadows. He'd been expecting to receive the spell book.

"Yes, I knew I'd made a mistake when I opened Smith's box to see what the fuss was about and found that *Utopia* book. I came back to swap them, but he gave chase." Mullings pointed at Sebastian.

So, the delivery man was the mysterious intruder.

Still, the toad was lying. He returned empty-handed and meant to steal the casket, not swap it.

"The wooden boxes looked the same," Mr Mullings grumbled. "So I kept my mouth shut and delivered the last box to Mr Smith. I ran before he could check the contents."

The story sounded plausible but what of Mr Hibbet's motive?

"Did Mr Hibbet say why he hired you?" Sebastian asked. Like their impassioned emotions, their thoughts were aligned.

"No. Just that Smith was to get the spell book, and Betsy was to approach the watchman at the bottom of Broad Street and say she heard screams from the auction house."

Ailsa jerked at the revelation. "Mr Hibbet paid ye to inform the watchman?" Good heavens. Did he know someone would murder him in cold blood?

Mr Mullings confirmed the theory by adding, "He said it had to be at nine o'clock as he was expecting a visitor and there might be trouble."

So, the murderer was known to Mr Hibbet, and it all had something to do with delivering the grimoire to Mr Smith and not Professor Mangold. Nothing but a foolish mistake had drawn Ailsa into the fray.

The notion left her limbs heavy. If Mr Mullings had completed the task successfully, Sebastian would have had no reason to call. No reason to believe they were under a spell. No reason to kiss her wildly and make passionate love to her in the garden.

He would always be the man who gave her cold shivers when, in truth, his touch ignited a fire in her blood.

"You have to believe me, Cutter." Mr Mullings' sob broke Ailsa's reverie. "I didn't know someone would murder the man. It was just a simple delivery job. The likes of what I've done before."

"You brought trouble to my door," came the sinister reply.

"I'll pay. I'll give you what I earned."

"Oh, you'll pay." Mr 'Cutter' Jones turned to Sebastian. "You've got what you came for. Happen it's best you bugger off now."

Mr Gibbs jerked his head at the door, urging them to take heed.

They brooked no argument and left promptly with their fingers intact. They'd reached the alley before hearing Mr Mullings' piercing cry.

Ailsa gripped Sebastian's arm. "Mr Daventry will demand we find Mr Smith and take him into custody," she said to drown out the din. "But the fellow stalks the shadows, and I doubt his name is Smith."

"We've the address in Tavistock Street, though that might be a temporary abode."

"Perhaps we might use the grimoire to lure him into a trap," she said. Mr Hibbet had gone to great lengths to give the man the book. He may have even lost his life in the process. "At the least, we should visit Tavistock Street before we report to Mr Daventry."

Sebastian agreed, but his gaze moved along the passage to the closed gate in the iron railings, where a man dressed in black stood watching them.

A chill passed over Ailsa's shoulders. "'Tis hard to know without seeing his face, but I fear that is Mr Smith."

"Then why is he hiding behind the gate?" Evidently struck by an alarming thought, Sebastian moved to shield her with his muscular body. "I want you to move slowly backwards until we reach the street. There's every chance we've learnt too much. Protecting a secret is a classic motive for murder."

Ailsa might have accused him of irrational thinking, but the passage grew that bit darker. A quick glance behind explained why.

"Sebastian," was all Ailsa managed to say as four men dressed in black entered the alley. They were tall and broad and looked keen for a fight. "W-we have company."

Mr Gibbs wasn't the least bit fazed. He shrugged out of his greatcoat and threw it to the ground. "Happen we'll get to see what you're made of, milord. Let's hope you're not like a pair of bellows, full of nothing but air."

Sebastian narrowed his gaze, eyeing the four men before stripping to his shirtsleeves. He handed Ailsa his coat. "You'll find the small pistol in the inside pocket. Don't be afraid to use it."

The men began a slow walk towards them.

"I'll take the two on the left, Gibbs."

"Can you handle two, milord?"

"I could handle three, but I wouldn't want you to feel inadequate." Sebastian cricked his neck and flexed his fists. "Will there be parley, gentlemen?" he said, his prowl predatory as he stepped closer. "Or shall we fight it out first?"

A dark-haired man with a squashed nose spoke up. "Give us the grimoire, and there'll be no trouble."

"Who said I have the book?"

The blackguard glanced at the door to the Old Crown's yard. "The delivery driver said he made a mistake." The devil spoke in the eloquent tone of an educated man, not a thug from the rookeries. "We searched the lady's house last night and know you removed the tome from the premises."

They had been to her house?

All must be well, else Monroe would have sent word.

"I pray my servants were unharmed, sir." She hoped talking might prevent the men from exchanging punches. One could often reason with an intelligent man. "Let me speak plainly. We dinnae have the book in our possession."

"But you do know where we might find the grimoire." He glanced at his counterparts in crime. "One way or another, we mean to get the information, madam."

"What's so important about the grimoire?" Sebastian said with mounting suspicion. "Why do I suspect we'll have our hearts cut from our chests as soon as we reveal the book's whereabouts?"

Had Mr Hibbet been forced to give Mr Smith the book?

Was he dead because he'd failed to deliver on a promise?

"We cannae disclose the location." Ailsa's voice trembled in time with her limbs. She hugged Sebastian's coat, covertly slipping her hand into the pocket. "Nae to strangers. Nae to men who threaten violence."

"Then you leave us no choice."

The attack came quickly, the opposing sides charging into battle as if they carried the pain of an ancient injustice.

When it came to the art of pugilism, Sebastian was as skilled as Mr Gibbs. Both men blocked a series of punches, their own efforts hitting the targets with ease.

"We could earn a tidy sum if we fought together, milord." Mr Gibbs' fist connected with his opponent's nose, a loud crack accompanying the sudden burst of blood.

Sebastian ducked to miss a right hook before thumping one man so hard in the stomach the fellow collapsed into a heap. "You speak of Aaron Chance's monthly competition?"

"Mr Chance is on the hunt for a dangerous duo." Mr Gibbs caught one man with an uppercut to the chin, rendering the villain unconscious.

Ailsa might have given a relieved sigh now the odds were even, but two more black-clad beasts entered the alley.

"Will ye both stop talking and concentrate." Fear ran like icy fingers down her spine. Mr Smith was so determined to get his hands on the old tome he stood at the iron railings, ready to send reinforcements.

Suspecting they would soon be outnumbered, Ailsa gripped the pocket pistol, preparing to draw the weapon and fire.

But another man stepped into the alley.

A golden-haired Adonis whose handsome looks gave him the appearance of an angel. It was a foolish mistake to make. Cold, unforgiving eyes and the cruel twist of his mouth marked him as the devil's spawn.

Christian Chance cracked his knuckles. His gaze turned vicious as if he lived for the prospect of drawing blood. "Who shall I throttle first?" he mused, racing forward and knocking one man out cold.

"Enough!" came the sudden cry from the iron gates.

Pistol fire stopped the brawlers dead in their tracks.

They all turned their attention to Mr Smith, who gripped the railings with pasty white fingers. Aaron Chance stood beside him, a smoking pistol in one hand, the muzzle of another pressed to the blackguard's temple.

Chapter Sixteen

Seconds passed, but no one moved.

Mr Smith's lackeys stood like automatons, unable to speak or think for themselves and merely waiting for their next instruction.

Sebastian examined his red knuckles, pleased to discover the blood wasn't his. He flexed his throbbing fingers, confident none were broken. That didn't stop his heart lurching when he met Ailsa's worried gaze.

Fear slithered through him as various scenarios played out in his mind. What if Smith's men had got the better of him? What if they'd taken Ailsa hostage and tortured her like they had Hibbet? The notion brought bile to his throat.

Was it any wonder he kept his heart locked in a fortress without access to the outside world? It was the only recourse for a man determined to avoid pain. He couldn't cope with losing someone else he loved.

He couldn't cope with losing Ailsa.

The thought squeezed the air from his lungs.

Was he in love with Ailsa MacTavish?

But there was no time to examine his feelings now.

Aaron Chance commanded Smith to open the iron gate. "Turn the blasted key," he shouted upon hearing Smith's refusal. "Don't make me ask you again."

"You won't shoot," Smith said confidently.

"Not in the head," Aaron countered, the threat of violence evident in his tone, "but I'll make sure you lose a leg. Take heed. My brother has fists like mallets and can hit with a force that would make Satan shriek."

When it came to the Chance brothers, brains and brawn made a lethal combination. Men plotted their downfall. None succeeded.

Christian Chance grinned, all glimpses of the studious man superseded by the rogue with a hunger for blood. "Don't force me to pull the blade from my boot. I can hit a mark from fifty yards."

Despite his disgruntled grumbles, Smith opened the gate. "You're making a grave mistake. Search my coat pocket. I have a lawful reason for being here."

Aaron shoved the man in the back, forcing him to walk forward. "Take it up with Denton. I'm here to even the odds and appease my brother's sense of chivalry."

Ailsa came closer. "We need to find a quiet place to question Mr Smith." She touched Sebastian's arm, her hand trembling against his shirtsleeve.

Ignoring the fact they had company, he cupped her cheek, suppressing the need to drink deeply from her lips. "You're shaking," he said for her ears only.

She blinked back tears. "'Tis nothing."

"You don't need to hide the truth from me." God, he was the greatest hypocrite ever to walk the streets of London. "We'll discuss it later when we're alone." And he could soothe her fears.

The flash of heat in her eyes confirmed sating their physical needs would be a priority. "Mr Chance won't allow us a moment's privacy," she whispered.

"We have to report our findings to Daventry and still need to visit old Mr Chadwick. It will afford an opportunity to discuss matters at length."

"Well, do you want to search his pocket, Denton?" Aaron brought Smith to an abrupt halt and prodded him in the back with the muzzle.

Forced to focus on the present problem, Sebastian scowled at the man he had last seen at the auction. "First, I want to hear his feeble excuses. I want to know why his agents would beat innocent men just to get their filthy hands on an ancient spell book."

"I'll never tell you," Smith countered, his gaunt face twisting with barely contained fury. "You'll have to shoot me."

"Don't tempt me," Aaron mocked.

Ailsa glanced nervously at the alley's entrance before stepping forward. "Perhaps we should find a private place to discuss this civilly. 'Tis only a matter of time before we're discovered."

Sebastian decided the plan was too risky. "Smith will find a means to escape if we move from here." The sly devil likely knew a spell to make him vanish.

Christian nodded towards the Old Crown's yard. "Cutter Jones will lend us a room to conduct our business. The devil owes me for services rendered."

Cutter Jones! The wretch longed for a reason to hack off Sebastian's digits. "The landlord is three pennies short of a shilling. As I'm fond of my fingers, I suggest we find some-where else to interrogate the prisoner."

"Do you have a weapon?" Aaron's dark gaze moved to Smith's puppets as he did a brief head count.

"Just a pocket pistol." Ailsa pulled the item from Sebastian's coat pocket and grinned. "'Tis small but effective."

Aaron scoffed. "I said a weapon, not a lady's bauble."

That *bauble* had earned Sebastian a rogue's respect. "It's not the size of the weapon, but how one uses it. I disarmed Cutter by threatening to decimate his ballocks." Sebastian kept a blade in his boot, but he'd had no time to retrieve it.

Christian laughed. "Then we'll have no problem gaining entrance. Cutter admires a man who isn't afraid to take risks."

"Might I make a suggestion?" Aaron motioned to the men who watched their every move. "I'll remain here with Gibbs and keep these devils company. Christian will ensure Cutter is accommodating."

Sebastian considered the plan. He decided to take one of Smith's men. Should Cutter go on a knife-wielding rampage, it paid to have a witness.

"How did you know we'd need reinforcements?" Sebastian asked Aaron Chance. He took the pistol and kept it trained on Smith.

"I didn't until I saw you brawling in the alley. Christian found something of interest in your book. He thought you should know before speaking to Cutter, but an accident on Cornhill meant we had to take a detour."

A faint glimmer of optimism surfaced. Had Christian found a pattern, a means of deciphering the rune markings? "Miss MacTavish suspects it's a coded message." A message from Michael that had sat on a dusty shelf unread for five blasted years.

Smith groaned. "Pursue this line of enquiry at your peril."

So, there was some truth to the claim. "I don't know who you work for, Smith, or why these messages are important to you, but you will pay for the lives lost in pursuit of your goal."

Smith met his gaze, his disdain sharpening his stark features. "I'm not the one facing the noose. You might escape punishment, my lord, but your friends will hang for treason."

Treason!

Sebastian reached into his coat pocket, whipped out Melbourne's letter and waved it under Smith's nose. "Your Home Secretary says otherwise. We act on behalf of the Crown and have permission from the highest authority to investigate the matter."

Smith faltered. "That could be your tailor's bill or a note from your lover."

He thrust the letter into Smith's bony hand. "Read it before you question my integrity!"

The rogue opened the missive, his gaze racing to the seal and signature at the bottom of the page. His shoulders sagged, the fight leaving his body. "Damn and blast. It appears we're on the same side."

What the devil?

Smith worked for the government?

"Then ye won't mind me rifling through yer pockets." Wearing a frown of suspicion, Ailsa came forward. "If ye have a reason for being here, ye have nothing to hide."

Sebastian froze. Every instinct said she should run, far enough no scoundrel could ever hurt her again. But the thought roused visions of her at home in the Highlands. If a few feet felt like a cavernous void, how would he fare when she was miles from reach?

Alerting them of his intention, Smith opened his coat and delved into his pocket. He handed Ailsa a calling card along with a silver insignia.

She studied the items before offering them to Sebastian. "Mr Smith works for the Alien Office in Crown Street and oversees domestic surveillance."

Sebastian examined the card. "You're responsible for deporting French nationals?" To be more precise, Smith hunted spies. "What has chasing revolutionaries got to do with old spell books?"

He knew the answer, of course.

Someone was using runes and symbols to pass secret messages.

To say Sebastian was intrigued was an understatement. But a sick feeling in his gut left him questioning how it related to Michael.

"Spell books?" Smith snapped. "You have more than one?"

Sebastian daren't mention his brother without first knowing the facts. "Forgive me. It was a slip of the tongue. Though I know a grimoire was stolen from Chadwick's Auction House last year."

"Then you know enough to get yourself killed." With his hands raised in surrender, Smith turned slowly. "Might you lower your weapon, so we may compare notes in the hope of finding a traitor?"

"First, call off your men."

With a curt nod from their master, the agents backed out of the alley and congregated at the entrance.

"Ask me a question, and I'll answer honestly." Sebastian released the hammer on the flintlock pistol and handed Aaron the weapon. "In return, you will afford me the same courtesy."

Smith nodded. "Can you confirm you have the grimoire in your possession and that it contains symbols drawn in the margins?"

Sebastian beckoned Ailsa closer. "That's two questions, but I'm sure Miss MacTavish feels generous. As you have her rare copy of *Utopia*, it is only fair she replies."

Smith did not deny having More's book.

"The answer is yes to both questions, sir." Ailsa shot Smith a look of steely determination. "But I'll nae agree to an exchange until we've caught Mr Hibbet's murderer."

Pride filled Sebastian's chest. Most women would swoon at the sight of blood. But Ailsa was courageous, intelligent, a woman who would raise strong sons. Not that he'd ever considered the last quality important until now.

"Why did Mr Hibbet agree to give ye the grimoire?" she continued. "Did he know ye work for the Alien Office?"

The spymaster grumbled under his breath. "Hibbet contacted me after the auction. He never mentioned how he knew me or asked why I wanted the grimoire. He said he wished to prevent it falling into the wrong hands."

The wrong hands?

Then Hibbet must have known about the secret messages. Was that why he owned a book of rune sigils? Had he attempted to decipher the symbols? If so, then in all likelihood, a French spy killed him.

"What did your friend find so interesting about the book?" Smith asked, desperate for more answers to his questions.

Christian waited for Sebastian's nod of approval before continuing. "I may be wrong, but I believe it's a diary of upcoming meetings. The first is in Shadwell Church on the first day in May."

Smith did not seem surprised. "Why race across town to inform Lord Denton?"

"Because every man should know the facts before interviewing a rogue like Cutter Jones."

Keen to ask Smith another question, Ailsa could hardly stand still. "When Mr Hibbet offered to give ye the book, I suspect ye posted a man outside the auction house. The question is, can ye describe the person who entered the building and killed the gentleman?"

Sweet child in heaven. Why hadn't he thought of that?

Ailsa's insightful mind fired his blood.

She held him entranced, bound by her womanly spell.

Indeed, her comments were pure supposition, yet Smith's shoulders slumped like he could no longer bear the weight of this burden. "I did post a man outside the auction house." He motioned to one of his marionettes. "I wanted to know if Hibbet knew I worked for the Alien Office or believed I was interested in the occult."

Sebastian straightened. "You kept a man there all night?"

Smith nodded. "Until the coroner came. But it won't help in your quest to find a murderer, I'm afraid."

"Could your man not see clearly in the dark?"

"No. No one entered the building, and no one left."

Chadwick's imposing house in Finsbury Square confirmed there was money to be made from selling old furniture and rare books. The butler wore a coat embroidered with the auction house crest, an image of two lions bearing a shield.

"I'm afraid Mr Chadwick no longer receives visitors, my lord." The butler returned Sebastian's card. "Mr Murden deals with problems at the auction house. You should refer all enquiries to him."

Sebastian curbed his temper. He explained his call related to murder and presented the letter from the Home Secretary. "A Chadwick employee is dead. I can return with the magistrate and fill the square with constables. Either way, I will speak to Mr Chadwick today."

The butler winced. "Wait in the hall, my lord. I shall see if Miss Chadwick is available to deal with the matter."

While the exterior of the house boasted symmetrical lines and elegant simplicity, the interior was like a hoarder's paradise. Framed pictures filled every wall space. Ten figurines and vases covered the console table in the hall. Sebastian had never seen so many umbrellas wedged into a brass stand.

"It smells rather musty," Ailsa whispered as they waited. "Dust clings to the nostrils and throat. I have to resist the urge to cough."

Sebastian slipped his arm around her waist, drawing her close. They'd spent the entire journey kissing. Still, he could not get enough of her. "Perhaps you'd like to smell something more enticing."

Her coy gaze dipped to his neck. "Don't tempt me."

"I plan to do exactly that once we're finished here."

She covered his heart with her gloved hand, unaware she had the power to make it gallop at a moment's notice. "Then let us pray Miss Chadwick is more accommodating than the butler."

Miss Chadwick was not at all accommodating. She warned them of her impending arrival by stomping along the landing and grumbling about the inconvenience.

She flounced downstairs wearing a pale pink morning robe trimmed with excessive ribbons and other fripperies. "May I help you?"

Though some might consider her a beautiful woman, Miss Chadwick's vacant eyes and pouty scowl made her as dull as a dead rose.

When she failed to address Sebastian suitably, he presented his card. "We're here to speak to Mr Chadwick."

She tossed the card onto the console table without giving

it a glance. "About what? Not that murder at the auction house. My poor father has had nightmares since learning the news."

"Losing a trusted employee must be distressing," Ailsa said with a hint of sympathy. "Losing a beloved son must have been a terrible blow."

Miss Chadwick froze. "I—I beg your pardon?"

"Mr Hibbet was yer half-brother?"

Her eyes widened. "Who told you that?"

"Mr Murden," Sebastian interjected. "When we questioned him about the assistant's murder. And Hibbet told a colleague he had been given the apartment because he was Chadwick's son."

"His son? That's preposterous." Miss Chadwick's shoulders shook. "I'll not hear any more of this nonsense. Good day to you." She shooed them towards the door. "My father is ill and of no mind to speak to you. Be on your way."

A sudden flash of anger forced Sebastian to straighten. "Enough!" he cried. "I am a peer of the realm, madam. A man of noble blood. You will do as I say, or I shall arrest you for conspiracy to pervert the course of justice."

The lady jerked. She snatched the card and studied the script before blanching. "Forgive me, my lord. My nerves are frayed. I've not left the house since hearing about that dreadful murder."

That was a lie.

She had been creeping about Hibbet's apartment.

"We must speak to your father, but perhaps you might answer a few questions first. I don't want to disturb him any more than necessary. Nor do I wish to return with a police entourage."

She offered a watery smile. "Of course. Let us go to the

drawing room, and you may probe me at length. Pickson will have the maid bring tea."

The drawing room was an emporium of gaudy trinkets and useless knick-knacks. They were forced to move cushions, a tapestry and a stuffed stoat to make room on the sofa.

Miss Chadwick sat perched in a wing chair and spent an age straightening her robe and patting her blonde locks.

"I'll get to the matter of Mr Hibbet shortly," Sebastian said as another thought struck him, one he had not considered important before. "But we need a list of people who sold items at auction on the day of the murder."

Who had owned the grimoire?

In light of Smith's revelation, it was of vital importance.

Miss Chadwick shrugged. "How should I know? My father deems women too silly to cope in a man's world. I'm called upon to entertain clients, smile, nod, and discuss the weather."

No wonder she despised Hibbet.

He'd been treated like the prodigal son.

"How long has yer father been ill?" Ailsa said.

"A year or so." The lady sighed like she wished the man would stop breathing.

"What ails him?"

"A weakness of the muscles and bones. His speech is slow, his thoughts often incoherent. His condition confounds the most educated physicians."

A deep mistrust made Sebastian question if Mr Chadwick was ill or being subdued by a drug or poison.

"I'm told you disliked your brother," he said, provoking a reaction. "That you were jealous because he gained your father's attention."

"Jealous?" The lady slammed her hand on the arm of the

chair. "Who told you that? Not Mr Murden. He despised Mr Hibbet and knew him to be a fraud."

"Yes, he said you doubted the man was your brother. When did news of his illegitimate offspring come to light?"

The lady fixed them with an irate glare. "A month after my father became ill. The delirium had taken hold, and Mr Hibbet used it to his advantage."

Perhaps Chadwick panicked at the prospect of leaving this woman in charge of his precious business. Or Hibbet may have invented the tale and fed a sick man a diet of lies.

"We must ask ye a question that's bound to rouse yer temper," Ailsa said in a gentle tone. "Where were ye the night Mr Hibbet died?"

Affronted, the lady's cheeks ballooned. "Where? Why? Surely you don't think I could do something so wicked. Look at these hands." She wiggled her dainty fingers. "Do they look like they could subdue a man in such a horrid fashion?"

She could have brought Hibbet a bottle of brandy laced with laudanum. Waited for the drug to take effect before plunging a knife into his chest. Hibbet suspected someone would kill him but may not have deemed Miss Chadwick a threat.

"Still, we're required to record everyone's alibi," Ailsa said. "Where were ye between the hours of six and nine?"

"Where I always am," Miss Chadwick snapped. "Feeding a frail man his supper and reading a few pages of his favourite book, although I'm usually asleep by eight. Pickson will confirm my whereabouts."

Pickson would agree with whatever this woman said. "Before we speak to your father, I have one more question."

"Yes?"

"If your father believed Hibbet was his son, why did he not let him run the auction house?"

Miss Chadwick gave a nonchalant shrug. "Mr Murden has been the manager for twenty years. He visits weekly with an update, though I am not permitted to attend the meeting. Mr Hibbet visited too, of course, to spin a web of wicked lies."

"Does your father see anyone else?" According to the butler, Chadwick did not have visitors. Or was that a ploy to avoid answering their questions?

"Just that odd fellow Mangold, though the man gives me cold shivers. He's an old friend of my father's. They studied anatomy together at The London Medical College before seeking alternative professions. Neither man had the stomach for dissection."

Sebastian almost slipped from the chair.

Mangold wanted the grimoire and had knowledge of anatomy.

Were they close to solving the case?

He looked at Ailsa, his chest tightening. She might return to the Highlands within days. The profound need for her company had him in a quandary. Would she stay if he asked? But did that not make him as selfish as the fiend who'd torn her gown? The man who'd tried to ruin her for his own gain?

Chasing a distraction, Sebastian stood. "We require five minutes alone with Mr Chadwick. Merely to ask about his relationship with the deceased."

The lady remained seated and gestured to Ailsa. "He'll not let a strange woman enter his chamber."

"He has no choice." Sebastian offered Ailsa his hand. "We're partners, both employed to investigate the case."

She slid her palm over his.

He wanted to entwine fingers, entwine limbs, lose himself in her jade-green eyes and magnificent body.

"Very well." Miss Chadwick stood and led the way. "He

usually sleeps deeply during the day. If he must be disturbed, let him growl at me."

They made their way upstairs to a landing cluttered with French furniture. Miss Chadwick knocked on her father's bedchamber door but didn't wait for a reply.

The room smelled of damp clothes and dirty chamber pots. Dark curtains kept out the sunlight. Dust clung to every surface. The air carried an air of neglect, as if Mr Chadwick was a broken ornament that had served its purpose. An item left in the corner, soon to be discarded.

Propped against a mound of pillows in the four-poster bed, Mr Chadwick opened his eyes and gazed at Sebastian through the gloom. "Joshua? Is that you?"

The man called for Mr Hibbet.

Miss Chadwick rushed forward. "It is Susannah. Joshua has gone abroad, remember. To meet a client who wishes to sell antiques." She sat on the edge of the bed and brushed hair from her father's brow. "Lord Denton has come to say how pleased he is with Joshua's work."

She stood and joined Sebastian. "He won't remember a thing I've said," she whispered. "Whatever you do, don't mention Mr Hibbet is *dead*." She mouthed the last word.

They stepped forward, but Mr Chadwick took one look at Ailsa and cried, "Jezebel! Get that woman out of my house."

"Pay him no mind," Miss Chadwick muttered. "He thinks all women are my mother. She ran away to the Continent when I was twelve."

"'Tis best I stay out of sight." Ailsa shuffled back into the shadows.

Sebastian approached the bed.

It was pointless asking the man questions, so he continued with the fabricated story. "Joshua told me about the rare copy of *Utopia*. I wished to gift it to the university. Are all men not seeking enlightenment?"

Yet Sebastian's awakening hadn't come from the pages of an old tome.

If it means that much to you, you may have the book.

Ailsa's words had unlocked a door he kept barred. It was where he hid his vulnerability, where he stored an inner yearning for companionship, where he kept *hope* prisoner.

"Though I suspect the best form of enlightenment is to look within," Sebastian said, recognising the shift inside him. "The truth lies in the shadowy places one avoids. The mind is often the greatest deceiver when a man is searching for the right path."

A heart that had sat like an immovable stone in his chest now thumped so wildly he could hardly catch his breath. A feeling deep in his bones said he'd been granted a second chance at life.

Mr Chadwick reached out and gripped Sebastian's hand, a sudden youthfulness shimmering in his dark eyes. "You look well. Happy. It's so good to see you home, Joshua."

They were the mutterings of a sick man, yet they resonated deep in Sebastian's chest. Home was a term used to suggest belonging. To some, it was a house, a village or town.

To Sebastian, it was a shared breakfast at Fortune's Den, an embrace in a dark bedchamber, a row at an auction, an erotic coupling in the garden.

Anywhere was home when with the woman he loved.

Chapter Seventeen

Mr Daventry sat in the drawing room, considering the recent developments in the case. He had made notes about Mr Smith and agreed to investigate the matter with the Alien Office.

"I find it hard to believe I wasn't informed of Smith's involvement." A little annoyed, he rubbed his sculpted jaw, though Ailsa wished he would bring the meeting to a swift conclusion.

Pressing business left her restless.

Business that included talking and kissing and any activity that would appease the need to feel close to Sebastian.

"And St Clair has had no luck locating Hibbet's mother?"

"No. The house has been boarded up for a year."

"Sir, I suggest we visit Mrs Murden and confiscate the coded letter sent by Mr Hibbet," she said, hurrying matters along. "It may contain important information."

Sebastian agreed. "Hopefully, Christian Chance can decipher the missive." Equally keen to leave, he shifted in the seat beside her. "Though if the markings in the grimoire are messages from French spies, Smith may use his authority to claim ownership of the evidence."

Ailsa glanced at him, wondering why he had not mentioned Michael's book. Based on what they'd discovered this afternoon, did he fear his brother was a spy?

Mr Daventry drummed his fingers on the arm of the wing chair. "We need to know who sold the grimoire. And if the person is part of a plot to trade secrets."

"We'll visit the auction house before returning to Fortune's Den," Sebastian said. "Murden will have a record of the transaction."

Ailsa contemplated kicking his foot. How were they to have a moment alone if he kept adding to their list of queries?

Since breaking the spell, was it not imperative they examine their feelings? Would their kisses continue to be as passionate? Would their lovemaking be a thoroughly sensual experience? Or would their enthusiasm soon wane?

"Hibbet must have known about the coded message in the grimoire and suspected Mangold was a spy," Mr Daventry mused. "Else, why would he arrange to send the book to Smith?"

"Perhaps that's why he had the book of sigils," Ailsa said. Sensing something was amiss, Mr Hibbet must have studied it secretly. "And it would account for the theft of a similar grimoire last year."

If the markings in Michael's book were any indication, spies had been using the method to share secrets for years. It was a clever plan. Most people were too scared to open spell books. Others thought them a pile of old nonsense.

"But why kill Hibbet in such a ritualistic fashion?" Mr Daventry fell quiet for a moment. "If Mangold wanted rid of him, why not stab Hibbet in the heart and be done with it?"

"How can Professor Mangold be the killer? Mr Smith said

nae one entered the auction house that night." Ailsa wasn't sure they could trust Mr Smith's word. His cronies were likely scouring the streets of London, hunting for the murderer.

"Is there another entrance?" Mr Daventry asked. "One used by delivery persons, perhaps?"

Sebastian shrugged. "We'll add it to our list of enquiries."

Heavens above!

The entire business proved tiresome. Though she shouldn't feel aggrieved. The longer the blackguard roamed free, the longer she spent with Sebastian.

"I'll investigate the Alien Office." Daventry closed his portfolio, much to her relief. "You have a list of tasks. Report back with your findings."

Ailsa noted the time on the mantel clock. If they left now, they would arrive at the auction house at five. And they had assured Aaron Chance they would return to Fortune's Den before seven.

"We'll do what we can today and finish the tasks tomorrow." Guilt sat like a heavy weight in her chest. She would suggest beginning their enquiries at first light. Nothing mattered more than stealing an hour alone with Sebastian.

Mr Daventry stood. His curious gaze moved between them, but he merely smiled and wished them a pleasant evening.

Once outside, Sebastian checked his pocket watch. "I imagine Murden will be working until seven now Hibbet isn't there to secure the premises."

If not, they could visit him at home, question him about the owner of the grimoire and retrieve the coded letter.

"We could deal with the tasks tomorrow," she said, though her conscience begged to differ. Lives were at stake, and she could not spend the hour in Sebastian's arms while there was work to be done. "That said, Broad Street is a few minutes away. Best we deal with the matter today."

"It shouldn't take long."

Was that a veiled way of saying they had time for kissing? "I must visit Pall Mall and check on the servants before we return to Fortune's Den." If Mr Smith's men had caused a disturbance, she needed to know all was well.

"Do you mean to go alone?" Sebastian looked at her lips. "I would have to advise against venturing anywhere without me."

"Ye would?" She bit back a smile.

"Aye," he teased.

"What do ye plan to do when I journey to the wilds of Scotland? Will ye accompany me then?" He would love the Highlands. Love the freedom one found in the heart of the pine forests or wading on the banks of vast lochs.

"Sadly, I have responsibilities here." His deep sigh reflected a boy's shattered dreams. "You know I cannot leave England. My time is best spent between London and Thornborough. People's livelihoods depend on the good management of my estate."

He made duty sound like a burden.

It didn't have to be that way.

"So many titled men idle away their days. The ability to do what is right is an attractive quality." Something she admired. Still, she longed to see him free of his shackles, roaming over hill and glen.

"Yet I'm plagued by thoughts of wickedness."

Butterflies fluttered in her stomach. "Tell me about these sinful thoughts. I might help ye overcome them."

A sensual smile tugged at his lips. "There's only one way to master my addiction."

"Yer addiction to sinful thoughts?"

"My addiction to you."

Her pulse thumped a rapid beat in her throat. Arousal stoked a fire in her blood. "Then let us be on our way. The carriage should afford us a modicum of privacy. A secluded place for an in-depth conversation."

"I share your impatience." He cupped her elbow and led her to where Gibbs sat atop the box of Daventry's carriage. "Gibbs, we need to call at the auction house. Then to Miss MacTavish's home on Pall Mall. In between times, I must collect something from Grosvenor Street."

Did he wish to prolong the journey?

Did he hope she might join him beneath the cherry tree before checking on Monroe and the rest of her staff?

"It's easier to visit Pall Mall first, milord."

"It's easier to drive the carriage myself, but I have no desire to see you out of work, Gibbs."

Gibbs doffed his hat and grinned. "Right you are, milord. Broad Street, Grosvenor Street, then Pall Mall. Who says the life of a coachman is dull?"

Sebastian handed Ailsa into the vehicle. "Is it me, or is he less argumentative?"

The carriage lurched into motion.

"Mr Gibbs has a newfound respect for ye since ye punched those men in the alley."

Sebastian laughed. "If I'd known fighting was the cure for insubordination, I'd have invited him to the White Boar."

The comment reminded her of his need to punish the world for the loss of his brother. "Do ye fight as a way of dealing with grief?"

From his sharp intake of breath, he had not expected the personal question. The usually confident man faltered and struggled to speak.

"Can ye see that ye're just prolonging the agony?"

A darkness passed over his features. "Fighting is a means of releasing aggression. I wouldn't expect you to understand."

"Ye dinnae think I get angry?"

"With all due respect, you've never lost someone close. You don't wake at night in a cold sweat wishing you could trade places. You don't stare at an empty tomb feeling like something is missing."

No, she did not understand the true depth of loss, but she knew how one could punish themselves for something that wasn't their fault.

"While ye fight, I hide," she said, the wave of shame surfacing when she thought of the attack at her come-out ball. "Our way of dealing with emotions may differ, but we've both spent the last five years running."

"Running? From what?"

"Ourselves."

He frowned, though offered no challenge.

"And I do wake in the dead of night, wondering what I did to deserve a stranger's disdain. Wishing I could go back in time and make different choices. I did lose someone close to me. I lost myself."

After a tense silence, he reached across the carriage and held her hand. "I lost myself, too. The anger was all-consuming. It still is to an extent, yet I'm different when I'm with you. Calmer. More at peace."

Her heart swelled. "I never thought I could trust a man besides my father, but I've always had faith in ye, Sebastian."

"You can always trust me to be pedantic," he said.

She smiled. "Aye, ye've never failed me on that score." She paused, not wishing to dredge up the past but needing to reassure him. "Ye're nae to blame for what happened to

Michael. He'd want ye to be happy, nae beating men to a pulp."

His gaze softened. "Thank you."

"What for?"

"For forcing me to discuss a subject I usually avoid."

"Talking makes kissing better. It doesnae have to be the lewd kind."

"I rather like the lewd kind."

She did, too, but discussing the past was just as important. "When we've checked on my servants, ye might dazzle me with yer suggestive repartee."

He winked. "Why wait until then?"

They arrived in Broad Street and alighted. Mr Murden had left early, the clerk confirming he was responsible for locking the doors tonight as the Murdens were dining at Mivart's Hotel.

"Murden is keen to ensure his wife has no reason to stray," Sebastian whispered, giving her a playful nudge.

"Well, Mr Daventry can't accuse us of neglecting our duty." And with luck, the clerk would return from the office with the name of the person who sold the grimoire.

The clerk took so long, Sebastian started pacing the hall.

Ailsa experienced a similar tension when the church bells chimed the half hour. "Where can he be?"

The fellow returned minutes later, offering a profuse apology. "Forgive me. I searched through the cabinets twice, but the records for that particular day have been misplaced."

How convenient!

"You're certain they're not in Murden's office?" Sebastian said.

"Quite certain. All documents are filed at the close of business the same day." The clerk scratched his head. "Unless they were in Mr Hibbet's apartment and somehow got swept up with other evidence."

Sebastian thanked the man and said he would discuss the matter with Mr Murden. They left, reminded Mr Gibbs they were heading for Grosvenor Street and climbed into the vehicle.

"At least we have information to relay to Mr Daventry."

Sebastian sighed. "Yes, but it's obvious what's happened. The murderer took the documents because they somehow incriminate him."

"Or Mr Hibbet disposed of the records."

They continued discussing all possibilities during the short journey to Grosvenor Street, doubts surfacing over Mr Murden's innocence.

"What is it ye need?" she said as the carriage stopped outside Sebastian's abode. "Nae another clean coat."

"Just today's correspondence. I'll be ten minutes." The sudden heat in his gaze made her stomach flip. "Would you care to come inside?"

Her heart skipped a beat. "To wait or to distract ye from the pressing task? Ye know what happens when we're alone together."

He smiled. "I do have something I want to give you."

"What if someone sees me entering the house?"

"We're betrothed and allowed to push the bounds of propriety."

Ailsa laughed. "We're nae pushing them. 'Tis more a stampede." The truth hit her then, like a bolt from the heavens. Although it was a fake betrothal, she would be no one's bride if she did not marry him.

"I'll enter first," he said, alighting. "Join me in five minutes."

She nodded and watched him walk away.

A sensible woman would refuse. But she was already on the road to Ruin. She might arrive at her destination at any moment, shocked at how quickly she had covered the distance.

She could imagine the line in the *Scandal Sheet*.

Scottish lass leaves her morals in the Highlands.

And yet she would rather die than forgo a private hour alone with the man she loved.

A sudden tap on the window made her jump.

A maid opened the door and climbed inside the vehicle.

"Evening, ma'am." She gave a small curtsey before sitting in the seat opposite. "His lordship says I'm to wait with you for five minutes, then show you inside."

"Oh!"

Was this something Sebastian did with all his female guests?

During Ailsa's last visit to the man's home, Cumpson hadn't seemed the slightest bit concerned by her presence. But she had entered under cover of darkness and kept her hood raised.

"Do ye make a habit of playing escort to Lord Denton's friends?"

"Oh, no, ma'am. His lordship never brings ladies home."

"Never?"

The maid shook her head. "His lordship said if I tell a soul about you, he'll cut out my tongue and feed it to the poor." She lowered her voice. "The master said you're betrothed, which accounts for his odd manner."

"His odd manner?"

"He was whistling as he mounted the stairs."

For a gruff man, such behaviour must seem shocking.

The maid sat nodding and moving her lips as if counting the minutes in her head. Eventually, she shuffled forward. "I beg your pardon, ma'am, but I can escort you inside when you're ready. People tend to ask fewer questions when they see a maid."

The girl led Ailsa into the house. "We've all been given leave to clean our rooms. We're below stairs if you need assistance."

And with that, the girl hurried along the hall.

Sebastian was not in the garden or in the study. Ailsa followed the potent smell of his cologne to the first floor.

He must have heard the pad of footsteps because he opened the door to his bedchamber and beckoned her inside with one finger.

Intrigued, she pushed the door open and entered the masculine space.

Lord help her!

The room was dark and smelled of him. A dominant mix of sandalwood and musk and virile male. The man in question stood near the bed wearing nothing but loose trousers hanging low on his lean hips.

Ailsa might have melted into a puddle had he not stepped forward to show her what he'd hidden behind his back.

"I thought ye had important correspondence to deal with."

"Something else took precedence."

"Oh?" She stared at the corded sinew of his shoulders, at the way every muscle in his body clenched as he moved.

He came so close she imagined pressing her mouth to his bronzed skin, drawing her tongue over his small dark nipples. "I want you to have this. It's a gift."

She knew what it was before she gripped the spine. That didn't stop her gasping. "'Tis the Tudor lady's diary."

He raised his hands. "I have a confession to make. I wanted the diary just to give you a reason to rail me. I wanted it because it made me think of you."

Confused, she met his gaze. "Being nice to me might have served ye better." And yet she loved their petty squabbles, the disagreements that now ended with them kissing.

"But it's the fire in your eyes I recall when I'm alone at night." He gestured to the oak canopy bed. "Do you want to know how many times I've come with your name on my lips?"

Her cheeks flamed. If this was lewd banter, she definitely approved. "Aye. Tell me."

"Twice a day since the auction. Fifty times before then."

"I cannae claim to own quite so many."

He hissed a breath. "You've thought of me and touched yourself?"

"Aye. Once or twice."

Maybe a little more, but a lady was always vague.

Raw, masculine heat glowed in his eyes. "You might think this presumptuous," he said, gesturing to his toned physique. "But I wanted you to see me at home in my chamber, stripped of all finery. I wanted you to see the relaxed man, the one unburdened by the mistakes of the past."

"What is a mistake if nae a means of advancement?"

"I'd live with the pain of a thousand mistakes to spend one night with you." He reached up, captured the errant curl brushing her cheek, and let it slip slowly through his fingers. "Come to bed, Ailsa."

From some men, it might sound like a command.

From him, it sounded more like a plea.

They would incur Aaron Chance's wrath if they were late.

"We don't have to make love," he drawled.

Ailsa laughed. Did he not know her friend Lillian had given her a thorough education on the wants and needs of men?

"Is that so?"

Ailsa tucked the book under her arm. She reached for the waistband of his trousers—noting he'd undone the buttons—and tugged the garment down until his erection sprang free.

Heaven help her! He was glorious.

So thick and hard she couldn't help but stare.

She wrapped her gloved hand around his shaft. "Ye're happy to lie next to me and suffer in silence?"

It was the first time she'd touched him like this. The first time she'd felt the true power of possession.

His eyes flickered in their sockets as she drew the skin slowly back and forth, revealing the swollen head. "Remove your gloves."

That *was* a command.

She obeyed, dropping her book and gloves on the floor before continuing her ministrations. "Do ye like me touching ye?"

"You know damn well I do." A creamy tear escaped the slit, but he gripped her hand to stall her. "I'll not rush this. I want you in my bed, Ailsa. I want to worship you properly. I don't care if it takes all night."

Once in his bed, she would never want to leave.

She was lost in a whirlwind of love and lust and couldn't deny him, even if she wanted to. "Then undress me."

His wicked gaze held her rooted to the spot as his fingers moved over the buttons on her pelisse. He slipped one button, his hand skimming her breasts before moving on to the next.

Her greedy sex pulsed when he pushed the garment off her shoulders. Her breasts were so full and heavy they strained against her corset. She was already damp between her thighs, the inner ache almost unbearable.

"I want you naked this time," he drawled, dropping to his knees to remove her shoes and stockings. "I want you writhing beneath me. I mean to wring every last whimper from those delectable lips."

He spoke with a rake's swagger, yet every touch conveyed heartfelt tenderness.

Sebastian stripped her bare. He stepped out of his trousers, his manhood so engorged, thick veins ran from root to tip.

"You're the only woman I've ever wanted," he said, taking her hand and leading her to bed. With primal intensity, he stared at her as she settled back against the pillow. "God, I want you with a passion I can barely contain. But I mean to savour every second."

She touched his cheek, caressed his jaw, tried not to think about the pain she'd endure when their affair ended. *I belong to you*, she wanted to say. *You've possessed me body and soul.* "Make love to me, Sebastian."

He lay on top of her, his skin so hot it chased away her cold fears. He captured her mouth, the kiss a slow, deep exploration, an intense tangling of tongues that sent her pulse racing.

"I need to taste every delightful inch." The fire in his eyes said he meant to do something wicked.

He trailed his tongue down the column of her throat. Lavished her breasts until she was arching off the bed and forcing her nipple into his mouth.

Suck, suck hard, she urged him silently.

The whisper of a kiss against her thigh made her breath hitch. "Open your legs, love. Let me worship you. You'll enjoy it, I swear." He nudged her thighs apart and buried his head between them.

The first stroke of his tongue dragged a moan from her lips. "Sebastian!" She tried to raise a protest, but by all that was holy, she had never felt anything so divine.

No One's Bride

Her legs trembled with every flick of his tongue on her bud. Like a wicked wanton, she sank her fingers into his hair and ground her hips against the pleasurable onslaught.

The rising tension in her body reached fever pitch. Her release was so close she gave her lewd thoughts a voice. "Hurry. I need ye filling me, pushing deep. Take me now, Sebastian. I want to come with ye inside me."

The man growled as he mounted her, entering her with one long, possessive stroke. His groan echoed through the room. They clung to each other, their sweat-soaked bodies moving in unison.

But her climax was already upon her, her inner muscles clamping around his thrusting manhood. She gripped his buttocks, sinking her fingers into his flesh.

"Hell!" He rode her through the violent shudders. "I'm going to spend." He withdrew and pumped his shaft, his seed spurting over her abdomen, his chest heaving.

Ailsa watched in awe.

His blue eyes shone. His mouth curled into a satisfied grin. "Love, you're so magnificent I can barely catch my breath. I could spend a lifetime making love to you."

A surge of emotion stole her breath. Naively, she'd thought one kiss would be enough. One night of lovemaking would satisfy her desires.

It only made the fear of loss greater.

She would never stop wanting him.

She would never stop yearning for more.

She would never stop loving this man.

Chapter Eighteen

Fortune's Den
Aldgate Street

Even when sleeping, thoughts of Sebastian consumed her. The potent scent of his cologne teased her senses. She could feel the soft brush of his fingers against her cheek, the gentle stroke of his lips over hers.

"Ailsa. Wake up, love." The seductive timbre of his voice stirred her from slumber. "We're needed downstairs."

She opened her eyes to find Sebastian sitting on the bed. He took her hand, lacing their fingers and pressing a lingering kiss on her knuckles.

"I find shaking a woman by the shoulders does the trick," came Aaron Chance's stern comment from the doorway. "Kissing only encourages a woman to remain in bed."

Sebastian released her and stood. "I'd tell you to mind your own business, but as this is your house, I shall keep my opinions to myself."

"I'll not afford you the same courtesy. I expect to see you downstairs in a few minutes. Daventry will be here shortly, and I'd like to see my bed before dawn. This isn't a damned hotel. People can't come and go as they please."

Mr Chance marched away, complaining under his breath about the dratted inconvenience.

Ailsa glanced around the small bedchamber. It was dark, and the rowdy din from the gaming rooms had ceased.

Sebastian had dressed but not shaved. The gold shadow of stubble made him appear rugged, enhancing his masculine appeal.

"What time is it?"

"Three o'clock in the morning."

"Three?" She sat up, aware his gaze journeyed over her plain nightgown as if it were gossamer. "What could Mr Daventry want at this godforsaken hour? Do ye suppose there's been another murder?"

"What else could it be? He sent a note with his agent Evan Sloane, informing us to dress and await his arrival."

Ailsa threw back the sheets and climbed out of bed. "Is it safe for me to walk the hallways? What about the men who hire rooms?" She had not heard so much as a groan or creak the past few days.

Sebastian brushed a copper curl behind her ear and smiled. "Aaron was testing your mettle. He stopped hiring out the rooms a month ago and is having them refurbished."

A veil of sadness fell over her whenever she thought about Mr Chance. He was ruthless in business. The most dangerous man ever to make her acquaintance. The patriarch who took care of his family.

But who took care of him?

A sudden thought dragged her from her musings. "What if

Mr Daventry has solved the case? Perhaps he visited the Alien Office and assisted Mr Smith in catching the culprit."

The mere mention of the spymaster gave her chills. He would have let his men beat Sebastian and Mr Gibbs just to get his hands on the grimoire. In all fairness, when the security of a nation was at stake, one had to be merciless.

"It wouldn't surprise me if Smith knew the killer's identity and has spent the day laying a trap." Sebastian's gaze journeyed slowly over her nightgown. "Do you require help dressing?"

The warm glow of happiness spread through her chest. "And risk the wrath of our host? I shall find a way to manage."

He glanced at the door. "And you think I'm gruff."

Ailsa laughed. "Let's pray Mr Chance meets a Scottish lass who's willing to take him on a wild adventure."

A secretive smile softened his lips. Was he imagining their scandalous interlude in the garden? Did he recall sliding deep into her body last night?

"Ailsa." He paused. "Whatever happens with Daventry, don't think it's the end of us. It is only the beginning."

She didn't question what that meant.

A woman in love invented romantic fantasies. But what future was there with a man who refused to marry? How long would a love affair last? Weeks? Months? Every day she risked ruin.

"Denton!" Aaron Chance's call echoed from the landing.

"We'll discuss the matter later." Sebastian closed the gap between them and kissed her quickly before striding from the room.

Ailsa dressed and tried to keep her thoughts on the case, not the haze of uncertainty that was her future.

Mr Daventry arrived within minutes of her entering the plush drawing room Mr Chance used as an office.

He wasn't alone.

Mr and Mrs Murden came scurrying behind him, smudges of soot on their pale faces. Both looked like corpses risen from the grave, their gait unsteady, their eyes wide with confusion.

"What the devil is this?" Mr Chance straightened to an intimidating height. He firmed his jaw and glared through eyes as black as Satan's soul. "This isn't Bow Street. You can't bring your waifs and strays here in the dead of night. I'm warning you, Daventry, this is more than a sane man can tolerate."

"I had no choice," Mr Daventry countered. "I need your brother to examine the coded letter. And I'll not have Smith getting his hands on it first."

"Smith? Who the hell is Smith?"

"The man from the Alien Office," Ailsa said. "Sir, might I fetch Mr and Mrs Murden refreshment? They look in desperate need of brandy." The pair were trembling and somewhat bewildered.

Mr Chance threw his hands up in exasperation. "By all means. Let me rouse Cook. I'll have her prepare a light repast and fetch my best bottle of claret from the cellar. Perhaps Smith will join us shortly. It must be his man camped in Golden Fleece Alley watching these premises."

Ignoring the man's sarcasm, Ailsa poured brandy into two glasses and gave them to the shaken couple. "We called at the auction house yesterday but were told ye had left early to dine with Mrs Murden at Mivart's Hotel."

Mr Murden nodded as he cleaned his spectacles with his handkerchief. "I wanted to broach the subject of Hibbet's letter. Luckily, I took it with me, or it would have perished in the house fire."

"We suspect arson, a deliberate act to destroy vital evidence," Mr Daventry said. "Murden sent word to Hart Street, fearing the incident might be connected to the murder. I arrived at the Great Marlborough Street office while they were waiting to answer the magistrate's questions."

Sebastian drew the obvious conclusion. "So, Hibbet arranged to send the grimoire to Smith in the hope of catching a spy. Perhaps the coded letter is further evidence, and he trusted Mrs Murden with the truth."

Or Mrs Murden was a spy.

Judging by the woman's feeble countenance, it was doubtful.

"Is Christian here?" Mr Daventry scrubbed his hand down his face and looked exhausted. "We have desperate need of his services."

Mr Chance gave a curt nod. "Unlike some of us, he retired at a decent hour. Doubtless you want me to wake him." He tugged the bell pull like a hangman testing the rope. "I'll drag him from bed myself if it means getting rid of you."

Sigmund appeared, received his orders and stomped upstairs to rouse the other Mr Chance.

While waiting, Ailsa thought to probe Mrs Murden further. She guided the woman to a seat. "Is there a reason Mr Hibbet would send ye the coded letter?"

The lady's legs quivered as she sat in the chair. "We're all friends and have known each other for years. I can only think Joshua trusted me to keep a secret."

"When did ye receive the missive?"

"The night poor Joshua died. A penny boy delivered it at nine o'clock, and I gave him our leftover supper."

Did she know her husband suspected her of having relations with Mr Hibbet? It was a sensitive subject that couldn't be ignored.

"Are ye aware of the auction house gossip? Do ye know people believe Mr Hibbet was more than yer friend?" Ailsa winced as the words left her lips. "Do ye know who started the rumours?"

Mrs Murden's cheeks turned cherry red. Her nervous gaze flitted to her husband in a look of desperation, not guilt. "I have my suspicions, but without proof, it's not right to mention names."

"Ye suspect Miss Chadwick," Ailsa stated. She had the most to gain from sullying Mr Hibbet's name. Her father would not take kindly to his illegitimate son dallying with a jezebel.

Mrs Murden nodded. "To say so aloud would see my husband out of work. And he's dedicated his life to making the business a success."

Sebastian asked the next pressing question. "Other than Miss Chadwick, who knows about the coded letter?"

"Miss Chadwick?" Mrs Murden frowned. "No one knows about the letter. We've not mentioned it to a soul. Not until tonight. We assumed Mr Daventry knew because Joshua had left a clue."

Oh, dear!

Now they would have to explain why Mr Murden was rummaging through the drawers in the apartment.

"I—I mentioned the letter to Miss Chadwick," Mr Murden suddenly blurted. "It was a slip of the tongue, but she's the only person I told."

From his fireside chair, Aaron Chance snorted. "It seems you've found your arsonist. Now, would you all kindly sod off?"

"Miss Chadwick seems the likely culprit, sir," Ailsa said,

"but we still need to find a motive, and she lacks the strength to break a man's sternum."

"You speak like I should care, madam," Mr Chance countered.

Sigmund returned, but to everyone's dismay brought bad news. "Christian isn't here, sir. His bed is still made. Shall I visit Dawkins in the stable yard and make enquiries?"

Mr Chance's eyes turned as black as the portal to hell. "No. I'll deal with the matter myself." He rose from the chair like a demigod. The offspring of Odin. A deity of war. "You've an hour to deal with the matter, Daventry."

"I'll need the grimoire."

Mr Chance nodded to Sigmund. "Give him what he wants. When the hour is up, see them all out." His gaze shifted to Ailsa. "Miss MacTavish may stay if she's nowhere safe to go." And then he strode from the room as if preparing to slay demons.

Mr Daventry wasted no time. "We've an hour to decipher the code. Denton, Christian spoke to you about the symbols. I'll need you to make sense of those on the letter."

"Miss MacTavish has a theory." Sebastian looked at her, admiration swimming in his eyes. "Together, we should be able to identify some of the markings."

Five minutes later, they were seated around the dining table. Ailsa had the letter spread out in front of her, while Sebastian had the old grimoire. Daventry paced back and forth, his impatience stretched as tight as a bow.

Mr and Mrs Murden sat watching, whispering between themselves, confused why Mr Hibbet would write in code.

Ailsa studied the symbols beneath the light of two silver candelabras, though deciphering them posed a problem. She glanced at the grimoire before meeting Sebastian's gaze. "In the grimoire, the symbols appear beside words. In Mr Hibbet's missive, one symbol replaces one letter."

Mrs Murden gave a discreet cough. "There was a note with the letter, but I threw it in the fire. It said to look for a book hidden in Joshua's bedchamber and all would become clear. My husband looked but couldn't find one."

"Christian said they're using the symbols like an alphabet." Pushing out of his chair, Sebastian added, "Wait a moment. I'll be back shortly."

"Be quick, Denton."

Sebastian left the room and returned with his brother's grimoire and the book of sigils found in Mr Hibbet's apartment.

Mr Daventry noticed these new additions but said nothing.

"Let's assume you're right," Sebastian pointed to the symbol on the paper, "and the strange arrow represents the letter T."

Ailsa snatched the pencil from the table and wrote T under every arrow. "Now we need to find the other twenty-five letters."

Sebastian studied the sigils, comparing them to those drawn in the grimoire. "The sigil for courage is drawn next to the words beginning with C in the book."

"That's it!" She scrawled C next to the corresponding symbol. "'Tis as simple as finding the pattern and looking for the first letter of each word."

They continued their task in earnest, the incessant ticking of the mantel clock reminding them they had less than an hour before Sigmund carried out his master's orders.

Despite Mr Daventry being a heavy presence over their shoulder, the words on the coded letter became clear.

Ailsa wasn't sure what she had expected to find. Perhaps

the name of a murderer or secret information that might prove invaluable to Mr Smith.

"What does it say?" came Mrs Murden's anxious question. Perhaps she *was* having relations with the assistant and feared it might be a confession.

It was a confession.

One with greater implications than that of a romantic entanglement.

Mr Daventry tutted. "Now it makes sense."

"What makes sense?" Panic flared in Mr Murden's eyes.

Ailsa took a deep breath. "Mr Hibbet confessed to spying for the French. He was part of an elaborate network that's been operating since the end of the Napoleonic Wars."

"Hibbet!" Mr Murden looked like he'd been slapped in the face with a fish. "A spy! But I've known the man for years. He never leaves London. His work at the auction house is dull. How could he have acquired the information?"

"He acted as a broker," Mr Daventry said. "Passing secrets between two parties. We might assume Mangold arranges the meetings. Why else would Hibbet risk his life to prevent the professor getting his hands on the grimoire?"

"Mr Hibbet's contact must have discovered his plan to turn traitor, and that's why he killed him," Ailsa said, her suspicions shifting to Mr Murden.

Mr Smith said no one entered the building. Had the killer been waiting in the shadows for hours to avoid detection?

She folded the letter, ensuring Mr Murden couldn't read the last line. Hidden in the apartment was a document naming all conspirators. They needed to find it without drawing the attention of Mr Smith's men. Else they might never learn the truth.

It was then she noticed Sebastian underscoring words in his brother's grimoire. The words explained how one should perform the incantations, yet the secret message surely told a different story.

The story seemed to tear the soul from the man beside her. Sebastian dashed his hand across his eyes, stood so abruptly the chair legs scraped the boards and almost toppled over.

He stormed from the room.

She heard the trudge of heavy footsteps as he mounted the stairs.

"The past is like a tired babe," Mr Daventry said in the tone of a wise seer. "It continues to taunt us until we put it to bed."

Ailsa noted Michael's grimoire left open on the table. Dare she read the message? Would it be a terrible breach of a man's privacy?

Mr Daventry ran a finger over the foxed page. "One would almost think Denton left it open on purpose. Strong men give the impression they don't need help. But the clues are often less than subtle."

It was a cue to read Michael's private missive.

"Lord Denton's welfare is my only concern," she whispered, hesitating before picking up the small spell book. "I'm in love with him."

"I know." He spoke like she had every reason to worry.

She began reading.

The message wasn't as coherent as Mr Hibbet's letter.

Stolen from a sailor in a foreign land.
Kept hidden.
They're passing secrets in spell books.
Sickness prevails.
A fever.
Trouble afoot.

Trust you to act.

Good Lord! It was a plea for help. A request that had gone unanswered for years. No wonder Sebastian had left so abruptly.

"Michael knew something but struggled to convey the message without alerting anyone to the truth." If he'd survived, he might have spoken to the authorities.

Mr Daventry read the message. "Denton shouldn't be too hard on himself. Even to the trained eye, the markings look like sorcerers' symbols. I found a similar book once but dismissed it as nonsense."

Yet she felt the problem was far more complicated.

"I should go to him." Soon Mr Chance would return and demand they leave the premises. "I'll be but a moment."

She left Mr Daventry questioning the Murdens and climbed the stairs to Sebastian's temporary bedchamber. All was quiet. He wasn't throwing clothes into a valise. He wasn't stomping about the room in a vile temper. Wasn't cursing every man to the devil.

Ailsa found him sitting in a chair in the dark room, his head buried in his hands, every breath laboured.

"Sebastian." The door creaked as she pushed it open, but he did not raise his head and meet her gaze. With tentative steps, she entered the room. "Sebastian. Whatever ye think ye've done, it's nae yer fault."

She knew why he blamed himself.

Grief had stolen upon him like a thief in the night. Guilt gnawed away at his conscience, punishing him for not tackling the matter sooner.

Seconds passed.

The heaviness of his burden hung in her chest.

The need to soothe him, to take away his pain, forced her forward.

"Sebastian." She laid a hand on his shoulder, but he didn't recoil. Then she could not stop touching him, stroking his hair, his broad back. "I've read Michael's message."

As slow as a man in his dotage, he raised his head. His tortured gaze found hers. "Do you know how long that book has sat on my shelf gathering dust?" He didn't wait for a reply. "Five years. Five bloody years."

"And ye had nae reason to think it was anything but a silly spell book. Aye, ye might have questioned why Michael would read such a thing, but ye couldnae have known it contained a hidden message."

If she had received *Utopia* instead of the grimoire, he wouldn't have been prompted to examine his brother's copy.

"Michael reached out to me. He trusted me to act."

"And ye would have if the message had been clear."

He released a sad sigh. "But I've failed him."

"How, when ye didnae have the knowledge needed to deal with the problem?" He had failed someone, but it was not Michael. "Be angry at yerself but nae because ye couldnae decipher the symbols."

He frowned. "What should I be angry about?"

"For hiding a kind, loving man behind a wealth of bravado. For tricking people into thinking ye're an obstinate oaf."

The faint flicker of a smile played on his lips. "So, I'm obstinate and gruff. How on earth do you tolerate me?"

"It hasnae been easy."

"No, those sweet moans you make scream of hardship."

She fought to suppress a chuckle. "'Tis lucky I'm a Scotswoman. We're made to withstand intolerable situations."

"Intolerable?" He stood, towering over her, edging her backwards until she hit the wall. "Are you saying you found my touch unbearable?"

She closed her eyes against the gentle stroke of his fingers across her cheek. "'Tis more than a lady can endure."

With a desperate urgency, he reached under her skirts and caressed her bare buttock. "I suppose you shiver from sheer revulsion."

Desire turned her body molten. "Aye."

He braced his arm against the wall, trapping her against his hard body. "Then this must be loathsome," he whispered against her ear as his fingers slid over her sex.

On the contrary, it was heavenly. Divine.

His nearness left her body weak.

"I've the tolerance of a saint," she panted.

"Good." His hot breath tickled her neck, and he nipped her gently. "Then you're no stranger to punishment." Those devil fingers moved back and forth in a tantalising rhythm. "You'll bear it with good grace."

She gripped his coat as his fingers plunged inside her.

Sweet mercy!

The need to strip off their clothes, to feel his hot skin pressed against hers, was too much to bear.

"Your body betrays you, love." He was raining kisses along her jaw, sucking her earlobe. "You're so wet, I might be forced to question your word."

The man played her like a maestro, curling his fingers inside her channel while stimulating her sex. The pressure inside her built, tightening every muscle.

"Tell me you hate me," he growled, his hand stilling.

"Oh! Don't stop. I'm so close, Sebastian." She was about to shatter into a million pieces. "Touch me."

"Tell me you despise me." He pushed deeper, punishing

her with every stroke. "Tell me it's laughable that I can't get enough of you."

"I dinnae despise ye—" The words were lost to a keen cry.

"Good, because I'm madly in love with you."

Waves of ecstasy rippled through her body. Such was the depth of her euphoria, she wasn't sure she heard him correctly.

"I'm in love with you, Ailsa," he repeated, a chuckle bursting from him. "Damn, it feels so good to say that aloud."

She blinked in shock, though her body hummed with pleasure.

"We were made for each other," he whispered.

Had he not just pushed her to the glittering heights of a climax, she might have had more faith in his word. "Are ye sure it's nae lust talking?"

He kissed away her doubts. "It's as if I've always known. As if our lives have been a journey across stepping stones just to arrive at this moment."

Ailsa looked into his compelling blue eyes, wondering why she had ever doubted his capacity for romantic gestures. "That's the second most beautiful thing ye've ever said to me."

"What's the first?"

"That lewd note I keep with me always."

He scanned the bodice of her dress. "Perhaps I should write you another. One to stimulate the senses."

Panic set in as she heard the pad of footsteps on the stairs.

Sebastian straightened her skirts and was about to step away, but she cupped his cheek, stared into his eyes and made a confession.

"I love ye with every fibre of my being."

Chapter Nineteen

After spending the day helping Mr Daventry construct a plan, Ailsa's first task was complete. She left the Chadwick residence and pulled her cloak tightly across her body. Fog crept through the dark streets like a supernatural being, but this investigation had taught her the living were more terrifying than the dead. Keen to return to the safety of Mr Daventry's carriage, she stepped onto the pavement and peered through the murk.

The coach was a hulking black shadow amid the gloom. Still, the sight brought little comfort. Feeding information to Miss Chadwick had been the easy part of the plan. At some point in the next hour or two, Ailsa would confront a murderer.

With the thud of her heartbeat masking the sound of her hurried footsteps, she reached the vehicle and climbed inside.

"Well?" Mr Daventry shuffled right, making room for her on the seat. "Did Miss Chadwick take the bait, or was she suspicious?"

Ailsa found the woman's reaction odd. She had stared at the stuffed stoat, the life draining from her face, her mouth gaping. "I told her we have the letter Mr Hibbet sent to Mrs Murden. That he confessed to spying for the French. She seemed dazed by the news."

"Trust me," Aaron Chance said from the seat opposite, "don't presume to know a woman's thoughts. All are born for the stage." He glanced at Ailsa and inclined his head. "Originals excepted."

Mr Daventry rapped on the roof. The carriage rolled forward and picked up speed. "It's a shame Miss MacTavish is in love with Lord Denton. Is it not time you considered taking a wife?"

"A wife?" Mr Chance scoffed like he would prefer to eat his own arm. "I'd rather take a dose of poison. I trusted a woman once. Look where it got me. A mere boy left to raise four children on the streets."

"You can't live in the past forever."

"I'm master of my own domain and can do whatever I please."

Mr Daventry smiled. "Love is all that matters. I'm certain Miss MacTavish will agree."

"Love doesn't warm cold limbs," Mr Chance snapped, his tone full of contempt. "Love doesn't fill a grumbling belly."

Keen to bring the conversation back to the case, Ailsa said, "I mentioned Mr Hibbet left a list of associates hidden in his apartment. That the search for the document will begin tomorrow."

"Good. And the grimoire?"

"I said we suspect the symbols are a secret language, and Lord Denton has taken the book home to study."

The thought chilled her to the bone. Fear pricked her heart like the sharp point of a blade. She pictured a gruesome scene. The man she loved shackled to his desk, the heart that had so recently thawed, ripped from his chest.

Love was beautiful.

The loss of it proved frightening.

Hence why her emotions wavered between pleasure and pain.

"Mangold will have received a letter stating the same," Mr Daventry said, "but explaining the grimoire will be given to the Alien Office tomorrow." He pulled his watch from his pocket, inspecting the time beneath the lamplight. "I've a man watching Mivart's Hotel in case Mr Murden leaves. Another following Kirkwood."

Might Mr Kirkwood be involved in espionage?

Would he not have come looking for Michael's grimoire sooner?

"Why would a spy sell the book at auction?" Mr Chance said. "Why not just meet in a secluded place and trade secrets?"

Mr Daventry shrugged. "I suspect Hibbet had the book and sold it as part of his plan to expose his colleagues."

That explained why there was no record of the seller.

Mr Hibbet had secretly included it in the auction.

Mr Murden had contacted Professor Mangold and told him of the sale, as he always did when any unusual curiosities arrived for auction.

Did that not mean both men were innocent?

Was it foolish to make assumptions?

After taking a detour to waste time, they arrived in Broad Street. They entered Chadwick's Auction House and left the door unlocked.

"Smith has a man watching the premises. Let's pray we catch the murderer before the spymaster seizes the evidence."

They mounted the stone staircase and entered the apartment.

Impatient to get the job done, Mr Chance pulled a book

from the shelf and flicked through the pages. "How are we supposed to conduct a thorough search in the dark?"

"We'll search the apartment once the murderer is in custody. We won't have long to wait."

"You'll owe me for this," Mr Chance warned.

"And I plan to repay you in ways you can't begin to imagine." The thread of amusement in Mr Daventry's voice was unmistakable. "Trust me. You'll thank me for taking the time to include you."

While the men wandered around the apartment, Ailsa crept to the hall and listened for the clip of footsteps on the stairs.

Many minutes passed.

Long excruciating minutes where all she could think about was Sebastian being tortured by a spy. That said, he was not alone. Christian Chance and Mr Gibbs were hiding in the wings, ready to confront the devil who came for the grimoire. And if he came for the list first, they would apprehend him before he visited Grosvenor Street.

What could go wrong?

There wasn't time to consider the matter further.

The slam of a door downstairs preceded the swift patter of footsteps.

Ailsa hurried to the drawing room and warned both men they had company.

Mr Chance disappeared into the bedchamber while Mr Daventry pulled the chair from the desk and made himself comfortable.

"Are ye nae going to hide?" came her panicked whisper.

"I can't control events from the cupboard, and I'd rather the villain think he has a chance of escaping." Mr Daventry gestured to the window near the desk and told her to draw the curtains. "Hurry. If need be, you can shoot from there."

Shoot!

She'd never fired a pistol in her life.

Seconds after she hid and closed the curtains, the door to the apartment creaked open. Despite trembling from head to toe, she peered through the small gap, but it was almost impossible to see with any clarity.

A tall, slender figure moved into the drawing room but failed to notice Mr Daventry sitting in the shadows. Unlike Professor Mangold, the person moved with a confident gait but stopped to remove something from his pocket.

Ailsa's heart thundered in her chest.

Was it a weapon?

Her thoughts turned to Sybil Daventry, a woman whose love for her husband shone like a bright beacon. Ailsa would rather shoot a spy than see Mrs Daventry in widow's weeds. And so, with an element of calm, she slowly drew the pistol from her pocket and waited.

The strike of a match on sandpaper produced a small amber flame. The man—for he wore a surtout and top hat— lit the candle on the console table nearest the door.

The devil stood amid the golden glow, the light dancing across his hooked nose and prominent cheekbones. Ailsa could not see his eyes but caught a familiar whiff of damp clothes.

Countless thoughts flooded her mind.

But Mr Daventry spoke, a deep sinister voice in the gloom. "Mr Chadwick. Miracles do occur. Lame men can walk."

Mr Chadwick?

But this man looked younger and nowhere near as frail as the poor fellow in the bed. Did Mr Daventry know him or had he made an intuitive guess?

"Who are you? What are you doing in my apartment?"

Mr Chadwick didn't spout gibberish. He spoke in a stern voice, though one could not mistake the rattle of nerves.

"I'm here to arrest the man who slaughtered his employee. The savage who ripped out Hibbet's heart to make an example of him. Heaven forbid other spies turn traitor."

With surprising arrogance, Mr Chadwick stepped forward. "Have you been on the brandy, constable? I own this establishment and merely came to inspect the premises."

"I'm not a constable."

"Then who are you?"

"Your worst nightmare."

A heavy silence lingered.

Ailsa fought to keep her shaking hands still in case she dropped her weapon. The knot of fear in her throat made breathing hard, but it gave way to a sudden wave of relief. If this man murdered Mr Hibbet, then Sebastian was safe.

"I shall give you until the count of five to leave," Mr Chadwick said. Clearly, he did not know Mr Daventry. "Or I shall have you arrested for trespassing."

"The magistrate gave me the key. This apartment is a crime scene, a place under investigation until the villain is apprehended."

Mr Chadwick took a moment to consider his position. His frantic gaze darted around the room as if the answer to his troubles was in plain sight.

"You've come for the list." Mr Daventry tapped his coat pocket.

"Give it to me." Mr Chadwick's firm reply was a blatant admission of guilt. "Name your price, and I shall ensure you receive suitable recompense."

"I cannot be bought."

Mr Chadwick scoffed. "Nonsense. All men can be bought."

"You mean bribed." Mr Daventry relaxed back in the chair. "You gave Hibbet this apartment when you persuaded him to work for you. Doubtless Mangold's interest in the occult gave you the idea of using a grimoire to deliver your coded messages."

A sly smile darkened Mr Chadwick's features. "Hibbet convinced me he was my son. That's why he had the apartment."

"That's not what he wrote in his confession." With languid grace, Mr Daventry pulled his watch from his pocket and glanced at the time. "By now, your daughter and butler will be under arrest for high treason. When faced with the gallows, you'd be surprised how quickly a knot of secrets unravels."

The lie had a marked effect on Mr Chadwick. With a growl of frustration, he pulled a pistol from his surtout pocket and cocked the hammer.

"They won't find my butler at home. My daughter will have taken her nightly dose of laudanum and won't hear a thing." He took aim. "Other than a spy's confession, you've no proof I've committed a crime. All I need do is shoot you, steal your gold watch and throw you into the alley."

Mr Daventry didn't even flinch. "Then before you pull the trigger, explain what made an upstanding citizen betray his country."

Believing he had the upper hand, Mr Chadwick gave an arrogant shrug. "Money. What else? I've no loyalties to the Crown."

"And you killed Hibbet because he developed a conscience."

"I killed Hibbet because he took my money while stabbing me in the back," he snapped, his anger rising like a tempest. "He's been planning my downfall for months. There's nothing as contemptible as a deceitful friend."

Had Mr Hibbet been prepared to die?

Why did he not write a confession and flee to America?

Perhaps because the police force had to investigate a murder.

"Why feign illness?" Mr Daventry seemed eager for answers but was struck by a moment of clarity. "Ah, I understand your reasoning. Murden manages the auction house. He's the one who sold the grimoire. How could you have known about it while delirious and confined to your bed?"

Mr Chadwick snorted. "Murden's a fool. He's auctioned four grimoires this year and never questioned where they came from or why Mangold purchased every copy. And then Mangold holds meetings with his sorcerer's apprentices, not knowing a French spy is amongst them analysing the text."

Mr Daventry laughed. "You're the fool. You'll leave this room dead or in shackles. When the authorities have the list, they'll arrest your colleagues."

Mr Chadwick appeared confused. "How do you plan to achieve this impressive feat when I'm aiming a pistol at your head? With magic?"

"With logic. Only a fool would presume I'm here alone."

Mr Chadwick jerked and stepped back while scanning the shadows. His gaze came to a crashing halt at the closed curtain, sending Ailsa's heartbeat skittering.

"Then perhaps I'll shoot your colleague."

Before the villain came closer, Ailsa slipped out from behind the curtain, her pocket pistol raised. "Put yer pistol down, sir, or I will shoot."

Mr Chadwick took one look at the small pistol and laughed. "You couldn't kill a cat with that thing." His tone turned sinister. "You will give me the list and let me leave, or I will shoot her."

Events took a sudden turn.

Everything happened simultaneously.

A book came hurtling through the air, catching Mr Chadwick by surprise. He instinctively fired, the lead ball blowing a hole in the ceiling. Mr Daventry threw a dagger, the blade hitting the devil in the leg. Ailsa fired, the small lead ball striking Mr Chadwick in the upper arm, causing him to drop his weapon.

Like a panther in the darkness, Mr Chance came charging out of the bedchamber. He leapt onto the desk and launched himself at the blackguard, one punch knocking Mr Chadwick out cold.

Ailsa expected a moment of calm to catch her breath, but an agitated Mr Daventry raced to the window and stared out onto Broad Street.

"What is it, sir?"

Was he looking for the watchman?

Having the power of second sight, had he arranged for the magistrate to arrive with ten blue-coated constables in tow?

"We need to leave. We need to leave now." The panic in his voice made her blood run cold. "We'll bring Chadwick with us."

The man was still unconscious on the floor.

Blood seeped from the wounds to his arm and leg.

"But what about the list?" Did they not need to hand the names to Mr Smith and have the spies arrested?

"There's something wrong." Mr Chance sounded more angry than unnerved. "Chadwick came for the list, confident it was the only evidence against him, yet he knows about the grimoire."

One did not need a great mind to understand his meaning.

"Good grief! You think an accomplice has gone to steal the book?"

Sebastian!

Would he be prepared?

Would his over-confidence be his downfall?

"Not just one accomplice," Mr Daventry said, his grave tone sending a shock of fear to her heart. "I fear Denton is about to be ambushed."

"So, Michael didn't mention the grimoire? He didn't tell you how he came to own the book?" Sebastian studied Kirkwood over the rim of his glass. He took a sip of brandy while looking for signs of deceit, but struggled to concentrate when thoughts of Ailsa filled his head.

He should never have agreed to the damn plan.

Was Daventry capable of protecting her?

Hopefully, the murderer would come for the grimoire, and Ailsa would be safe. His only focus should be deciding if Kirkwood was somehow involved.

"No. But I suspect your brother stole it from one of the crew." Kirkwood shifted uncomfortably in the chair. He seemed reluctant to speak, but after exhaling a weary sigh said, "There was talk of a traitor aboard ship. That naval secrets learned in Simon's Town were being passed to spies when we docked in France."

"But you're not suggesting Michael was involved?" Since deciphering his brother's message, Sebastian accepted Michael had died from a fever. The rest was a plea for help, not a spy's secret machinations.

Besides, love filled Sebastian's heart, not hatred.

The powerful emotion rode roughshod over self-loathing.

"If he was, his intention would have been to infiltrate the ranks and bring the men to justice." Kirkwood tossed back his drink and placed the empty glass on the side table. "I suggest you raise the matter with the Admiralty. The grimoire came from Simon's Town. They were being sold by the dozen, although it would be impossible to know who bought them."

With luck, the names of the spies were on Hibbet's list, though he kept that information to himself.

"Well, it's late." Kirkwood took the spell book from his lap and stood. He held it firmly before finally handing Sebastian the volume. "This one merely contains the message from your brother. He obviously meant for the Admiralty to search for other copies but didn't know who to trust."

He'd trusted me, and I failed him.

But then he wouldn't be in this predicament.

He wouldn't be in love with Ailsa.

"I shall take the matter up with the appropriate authorities." Sebastian had given his servants leave to remain at the Bell and Crown until closing, so he escorted Kirkwood out.

They said good night, though a sudden wave of apprehension kept Sebastian at the door. He held his breath until Kirkwood climbed into the waiting hackney.

As the vehicle rattled away, the cause of his discomfort became apparent. Smith came striding across the street like a vicar on a mission to eradicate sinners. His men lingered in the background, the ever-faithful congregation.

"What the devil do you want, Smith?" The man was an itch one couldn't scratch. "Should you not be out combing spy haunts?"

Smith opened the flap of his leather satchel and gestured to the rare copy of More's *Utopia*. "I'm here to trade books. I have a letter from the magistrate permitting me to take the grimoire as evidence."

Sebastian wouldn't give Smith the grimoire if the King ordered it.

"Show me the letter." He wasn't sure why he asked, but a niggling in his gut said something was amiss. "After downing a bottle of claret, Sir Oswald would sign his own death warrant."

And there it was. A slight flicker of alarm in the man's beady eyes. "Might I come inside? I'll not discuss a matter of national security on the doorstep."

Sebastian's pulse jolted. Daventry said the murderer might come for the spell book tonight. Had Smith killed Hibbet? Had he come to destroy the grimoire or submit it as evidence at the Alien Office?

"By all means, come in, but your cronies must remain outside." Gibbs and Christian Chance were waiting in the drawing room, but he would not risk them being outnumbered.

Smith agreed.

Surely he didn't think Sebastian would give him the book without a fight. Still, he welcomed the man over the threshold and locked the door.

Smith followed him to the drawing room.

Tension clawed at Sebastian's shoulders. Every instinct said Smith had a secret. "Will you take brandy?" He gestured to the empty chair before crossing the room to the console table. "There's a chill in the air tonight."

Smith's steps faltered when he saw Christian and Gibbs on the sofa. "Not during working hours." He clutched his satchel, his gaze flitting around the room like a startled hare.

Sebastian pulled the crystal stopper from the brandy

decanter, poured himself a drink and drained the glass. "You may as well have a drink. I won't give you the grimoire."

"But I have a letter—"

"I don't give a damn about the letter. In the morning, I shall consult the King on the matter myself." Did Smith think him a petty crook afraid of swinging from the gallows? "I'm a viscount, Smith. A title affords a man a certain influence with the Crown."

He sensed Smith's growing frustration.

Christian and Gibbs felt it too. Both men straightened and shuffled forward in their seats. Sebastian caught their gazes. One look was enough to suggest they suspected treachery, too.

"Perhaps you should tell me what this is really about." Sebastian faced the scrawny fellow. From the possessive way Smith clutched his satchel, he had something to hide. "Why are you so desperate to take the book tonight?" What game was he playing?

Smith decided to reveal a card from his guarded hand. "We've reason to believe spies have infiltrated the higher echelons of society."

Sebastian laughed. "Are you accusing me of being a spy?"

"No, my lord. We believe Miss MacTavish is a spy. The question remains as to whether you had knowledge of her disloyalty."

"Miss MacTavish!" He might have laughed again, but panic rioted through him. Was this a conspiracy to shift the blame or the ramblings of an incompetent agent? "I assure you, Miss MacTavish is not a spy."

Smith shuffled his feet. "W-we have her in custody. She confessed to knowing about the coded messages."

Ailsa!

By God, he'd throttle anyone who hurt her.

"In custody?" Sebastian repeated.

Smith could have stabbed him through the heart and it wouldn't have been as painful. He clenched his jaw, keen to charge across the room and rip this fool's head from his shoulders. Instead, he took a calming breath.

"We arrested her an hour ago." Smith pulled More's book from his satchel and dropped it on the chair. "You'll give me the grimoire or face a charge of treason. My agents are waiting and will act on my command."

Sebastian looked at the men Daventry had sent to offer protection, realising some fights were not won by those with the hardest punch.

"Before I give you the book, answer me this. How much did they pay you? How much did it take for you to turn your back on your country? Five hundred pounds? Five thousand?"

Smith remained silent.

Sebastian searched his mind for logical explanations to his mounting questions. Why would Hibbet send Smith the book when he'd hidden a document containing the conspirators' names in his apartment? It made no sense. Unless Hibbet didn't know Smith was involved.

"I knew of your guilt before I welcomed you over the threshold." Sebastian would tie Smith up in knots until he didn't know his arse from his elbow. "Hibbet realised you were involved after he'd agreed to give you the book. But he had time to send a letter to Mrs Murden. We deciphered it this morning. The purpose of this evening was to lure you into a trap."

Smith's shoulders shook, but he did not deny the accusation.

Gibbs cleared his throat. "Sometimes a man works long

hours, sheds blood, sweat and tears, and gets little reward for his efforts."

"Such a man might peer into a treasure chest and find fool's gold tempting," Christian added. "When facing the daily grind, money is the only means of salvation."

And the Chance brothers knew that better than most.

Amid the brief silence, a growl rumbled in Smith's chest. "I've sacrificed everything for this country," he spat, "risked life and limb. Yet now they say there's no longer a threat to security. They mean to close the office and disband the army who've fought to stop the trade of secrets."

"And so you thought to switch sides. You—"

A sudden thought stopped Sebastian in his tracks. Smith wasn't working alone. A spy had hired him. Was it someone with the power to frame Ailsa? Someone entrenched in the heart of government? A person capable of seeing an innocent woman hang?

His life flashed before his eyes.

A long and lonely existence.

One of torment and torture. Nothing but pain.

"In times of crisis, a man must fend for himself." Smith's irate voice dragged Sebastian from his reverie. Without warning, he reached into his satchel and pulled out a pistol. "Now give me the damn grimoire."

Sebastian froze.

Smith's finger shook as it rested on the trigger.

One mistake, and it would all be over.

"Doubtless you get paid upon delivery." *Or bludgeoned to death to ensure his silence*, Sebastian thought while trying to settle his rising pulse. "The book is in my study. You'll find it on the desk."

It was Michael's book.

Hopefully, Smith didn't know the difference.

"Fetch it!" The fool waved the pistol at Christian Chance.

A sudden knock on the front door left Smith jittery. "That will be my men. They know to arrest you for treason. All three of you. Fetch the book, and I shall explain I was mistaken."

So, his men didn't know of his duplicity.

"What of Miss MacTavish?" Sebastian didn't give a damn about himself. "What assurances do I have she will go free?"

One of Smith's agents had taken to hammering his fist on the door. Rather than reassuring the rogue, it left him trembling.

"I lied about Miss MacTavish. I presume she's at home. Now get me that book, and I'll leave you in peace. Don't make me shoot you."

Sebastian almost dropped to his knees in relief. Ailsa was safe. He nodded for Christian to obey the villain's orders, knowing the Chance brothers never did what they were told.

Christian stood and moved slowly towards the door. As he passed, he turned quickly, grabbing Smith around the throat.

A struggle ensued.

Sebastian rushed forward.

But the deafening crack of pistol fire stopped him dead in his tracks.

Chapter Twenty

Mr Daventry hammered on Sebastian's door with his clenched fist. He didn't call out for fear of frightening Mr Smith into doing something foolish.

Almost choking in panic, Ailsa swung around to face the group of agents from the Alien Office. "Did Mr Smith say what he wanted with Lord Denton? Has he come for the grimoire?" Or did he mean to silence anyone who'd deciphered the code?

The fellow, who'd had his nose broken by Mr Gibbs in the alley, shrugged and shifted uncomfortably. "We were just following orders, ma'am. We were told to wait outside while Mr Smith discussed the exchange."

The exchange?

So, he had come for the spell book.

Mr Chance growled his frustration. "Step aside. Let me kick down the door. If that blackguard has hurt my brother, he'll hang from the balustrade."

Perhaps their concerns were irrational, and Mr Smith's reason for visiting was genuine. But the short sharp crack of pistol fire penetrated the night air, sending them all stumbling back in shock.

Mr Daventry kicked the door hard.

The wood splintered.

They all charged inside, following the howl of a man in pain.

Mr Gibbs' strained voice reached her ears. "Hurry. Find something to stem the bleeding."

"Sebastian!" Ailsa dashed along the hall, not knowing how her weak knees kept her upright. She burst into the drawing room behind Mr Smith's men, their broad shoulders blocking her view. "Sebastian!"

Tears welled as she came up on her tiptoes.

"Don't move him," Mr Daventry growled. "The lead may have penetrated a major artery. We need to pack the wound and apply a tourniquet."

"Sebastian!" Ailsa tried to push through the crowd of men and managed to glimpse Mr Chance. He looked calm and unruffled, which meant it wasn't Christian Chance bleeding to death on the floor.

Dinnae let it be Sebastian.

The room started spinning.

Her vision grew hazy.

She was falling, a slow slide into oblivion.

But strong arms encircled her waist, scooping her up and carrying her across the hall to the study. She didn't need to open her eyes to know it was Sebastian. His potent scent filled her head. The heat of his body turned her blood molten.

She dared to look at him. The first glimpse of his face amid the candlelight failed to soothe her spirit. "Tell me ye're well." He looked pale, weary. "Tell me ye're unhurt."

He tucked a lock of hair behind her ear. "My heart almost stopped beating when Smith said he'd arrested you. Now you're here, I can release the breath I've been holding for hours." He held her tightly to his chest, kissing her lips, nose, and brow. "If I'd lost you tonight, Ailsa, I'd have—"

"I know." Too scared to think about what might have happened, she said, "Were ye forced to shoot Mr Smith?"

"He shot himself in the leg during the tussle."

Tears of relief trickled down her cheeks, though her stomach still roiled at the thought of losing Sebastian.

"Smith came for the grimoire." Sebastian dashed her tears away with the pad of his thumb. "Someone offered him money in exchange for the book. I'm just thankful he came here first and wasn't compelled to find the list."

She explained what happened with Mr Chadwick. "He persuaded Mr Hibbet to join the cause and feigned illness to avoid detection."

He didn't care about Mr Chadwick's motive. "Why the devil did you step out from behind the curtain? Chadwick might have shot you."

"I couldnae let him shoot Mr Daventry." She knew fear had caused his sudden outburst. A fear of losing those close to him. "But we're both here to tell the tale. That's all that matters. Oh, and the fact yer arms must be aching from holding me for so long."

A smile tugged at his mouth. "You're a master of distraction and know how to drag a man out of a sullen mood."

Sebastian dropped into the wing chair, pulling her onto his lap. The panicked shouts from the drawing room spilled into the hall, the din and the thud of footsteps receding.

A light knock on the door brought Mr Daventry.

"We're taking Smith and Chadwick to the Infirmary. I'll alert the magistrate and Home Secretary and arrange for my agents to search for the list." Before they could offer their services, he added. "I must thank you for your excellent work, but I shall deal with everything from hereon in."

"You will keep us informed?" Sebastian said.

"Yes, and you'll need someone to fix your front door, Denton. I trust you'll see Miss MacTavish safely home."

"Indeed."

With that, he bid them good night and closed the study door.

All grew quiet.

They were alone.

For a heartbeat or more, they locked gazes.

Any pain associated with losing him subsided, leaving the warm feeling of contentment, the pleasurable waves of utter bliss.

She cupped his cheek tenderly. "I love ye so desperately, I can hardly breathe." He'd been the first to declare himself last night, although confessing his feelings must have been difficult. "I'm nae sure how it happened, but it's the most marvellous thing in the world."

"I'm deeply in love with you, Ailsa." His smile proved blinding. "And I know exactly how it happened. You have me enchanted."

"Ye believe it's magic?"

"I know it's magic. The kind of magic I never expected to find in this lifetime. The kind that has a man searching for the perfect pebble."

She smiled, her heart swelling. "Are ye saying ye're a penguin and nae a gruff bear? I quite like dealing with yer tantrums."

He took her hand and laced their fingers. "I'll always be gruff and stubborn, but you're patient, tolerant and kind, and somehow we fit together as perfectly as our fingers."

Ailsa glanced at their joined hands. What if she had never

made the wager at the auction house, never touched him, never known how beautiful love could be?

"Ye do realise Scotswomen have fiery tempers?" she teased.

"When it comes to you, I'm happy to get burned." He released her fingers to delve into his coat pocket. "We've been so busy of late, I couldn't find a pebble but did manage to locate a stone. I'm not sure it's perfect, but you can be the judge of that."

She had a vision of him searching the garden at night, cursing when he stubbed his toe, complaining when the rain came. "If ye found it under the cherry tree, I'll treasure it forever."

"Ah, the cherry tree." His cobalt eyes roved over her seductively. "That has to be one of the most memorable nights of my life."

"Aye." Whenever she saw the blooms, she would relive those sensual moments. She'd felt a soul-deep connection even then. And yet the future was still a haze of uncertainty.

Sebastian must have read her mind. "There's a wonderful weeping willow on the banks of the Ouse at my estate in Buckinghamshire. We might take a picnic and make love there."

Logic quickly overruled the flurry of excitement. "'Tis sixty miles. Too far to sneak away for a secret rendezvous."

"It won't be a secret. Not if you like my stone." He clasped her hand and placed a tiny velvet box in her palm. "Open it, Ailsa. If it's not what you want, if I'm not what you want, be honest with me."

Tears gathered behind her eyes. A rush of emotion choked her throat. "Ye're everything I want." She didn't care what was in the box. She would love it with the same passion she loved him.

She lifted the lid with shaky fingers and stared at the pretty garnet and diamond ring. It was so beautiful she could cry.

"It belonged to my great-grandmother, yet I only think of you when I look upon the gems. The red garnet reminds me of your passionate spirit, your immense courage, your delectable lips and fiery hair. The diamonds are the raindrops glistening against your pale skin, the sparkle in your eyes when we make love."

She ran her finger over the diamonds set into tiny silver leaves on the shoulders. "For a grumpy man, ye have such an eloquent way with words."

"Do you like it, Ailsa?"

She swallowed hard. "I love it."

He breathed a relieved sigh. "Will you marry me? Will you do me the honour of becoming my wife? Say you'll have me."

It took effort not to throw herself into his arms and sob uncontrollably. Her heart was so full it might burst. "Aye. Being yer wife would be a dream come true."

He held her chin and kissed her in the slow, hypnotic way she loved. "We may need to get the band adjusted," he said, pulling the ring from the box and slipping it slowly onto her finger. "Though I have a strange suspicion it will fit."

It was a perfect fit.

Just as they were perfect for each other.

Ailsa held up her hand, noting how the stones glistened in the candlelight. "That makes three gifts ye've given me. I feel I need to make a gesture."

Sebastian slid his hands under her cloak, settling his palms on her buttocks. "I can think of a way you might thank me. And I need a reason to get rid of the clutter on my desk."

She glanced at the pile of neatly stacked books, at the

hard walnut surface, an erotic scene filling her head. "Ye do? Then perhaps ye should lock the door in case the servants return. Tidying is tiring work."

"So tiring, you'll be forced to stay the night."

He stood, lifting her into his strong arms as if he couldn't bear to be parted for a second. They kissed as soon as he locked the door. They were already panting when he pushed the inkstand aside and lowered her onto his desk.

The need to forget the terrifying events this evening, and the way he tugged at his trouser buttons, said this would be a wild and desperate coupling.

"I shall worship you at length later," he said, shoving her skirts up to her thighs, encouraging her to wrap her legs around his hips.

Then he was halfway inside her, easing himself deeper.

His manhood thickened, stretching her wide.

She gripped him tightly, meeting his measured thrusts.

"We need to marry quickly," he breathed, his hand slipping between their bodies to stroke her sex. "I want you here every night, dining with me, reading beside me, coming around my cock, sleeping in my bed."

A groan of ecstasy escaped her. "Are ye sure that's what ye want? Marrying me means ye'll lose the wager. I shall own all the books on these shelves."

"You're supposed to be looking at your betrothed, not admiring my collection. And we both lost the wager. It means I own the rare copy of *Utopia*."

"Ye can keep the book, though ye owe Mrs Daventry eight hundred and seventy pounds." She arched her back, rising to meet every deep plunge. "Oh! Dinnae stop! I have my own version of heaven." And this was as close as it came.

A sinful smile touched his lips. "There's nothing Thomas More can teach me." He slowed as she came apart around him, her climax making her moan and shudder. "This is my idea of paradise."

Home of the St Clairs
Three weeks later

"Aaron never attends social events and cannot abide dancing," Christian said, apologising for his brother's absence. "He rarely leaves the club and sneers at wedding celebrations."

Sebastian heard him, but his gaze kept flitting to Ailsa waltzing with Devon Masters. She looked so beautiful in sapphire-blue silk. Her skin glowed. Her hair shone like a halo of fire, and he couldn't wait to see it draped over his pillow.

"I understand. My sister insisted we have a wedding ball, but I shall snatch my wife at the first opportunity and make a quick escape." Sebastian patted Christian's solid upper arm. "Thank Aaron for his assistance in solving the case. And without your help, we might still be examining the rune symbols."

Keen to steal Ailsa away from Masters, Sebastian moved to leave, but Christian gripped his arm to stall him.

"Daventry has asked for my help solving a problem at the British Museum. He believes my knowledge of rare artefacts will be invaluable."

Christian's ability to fight three men would prove useful.

"It sounds interesting, yet I sense there's a problem."

"I suspect Daventry has an ulterior motive." Christian ignored the two ladies who'd stopped a few feet away to ogle his fine physique. "But he insists he needs my expertise."

Sebastian bit back a chuckle. Whatever Daventry's game, those who worked for him soon found themselves married. "My advice is, be firm. Tell him you can spare a few hours. Besides, I can't see Aaron giving you leave from the club for any length of time."

Christian nodded. "Daventry can be damn persistent."

The music ended, prompting Sebastian to take action. "Please excuse me. If I fail to capture my wife before the orchestra flexes their bows again, I'll be forced to watch her dance the night away with other men."

He pushed through the crowd, stopping to accept a guest's felicitations before grasping his wife's hand as she left the dance floor. "There's only so much a gruff lord can take," he teased. "If I see another man's hand on your waist tonight, I might throttle him."

Ailsa laughed and batted him on the arm. "We're supposed to dance with the guests. Be grateful we're nae in Scotland. The clan chiefs line up to steal a kiss."

They'd be in Scotland soon enough. Then Sebastian would need to explain to her father why they'd married without seeking his blessing.

"I don't mind kissing shaven men but draw the line at kissing those with wiry beards." He pulled her closer and lowered his voice to a husky whisper. "I want a moment alone with my wife. There's a secluded spot in the garden. Let's escape through the terrace doors."

She needed no coaxing.

She held his hand as they descended the stone steps into the garden. The moon was full, the lightest breeze stroking their hair. Being with her felt so magical he could think of nothing but seduction.

"Did ye ask Mr Daventry about the case?"

"Yes, they arrested the last spy yesterday. All those mentioned on Hibbet's list are now in custody. Chadwick will hang. He admitted to starting the fire at the Murdens' house."

"Miss Chadwick must have told him about the coded letter."

"They can't prove she was involved, though the Crown seized all Chadwick's assets. The lady fled with jewels and a stuffed stoat and was last seen on a ship heading for the Continent."

Ailsa sighed. "Poor Mr Murden. He's lost his home and his position at the Auction House."

Daventry would not let an innocent man suffer. "On the contrary, Lucius Daventry owns the auction house." The man was as rich as Croesus, and the King had been keen to show his gratitude. "Mr Murden is now the manager and lives in the upstairs apartment."

She gripped his hand and gave a beaming smile. "That is a relief. At least it all ends on a happy note. And for all his oddities, it's good to know Professor Mangold is innocent."

"He's innocent but still a damn fool." Not wishing to touch on Mr Smith's passing again, Sebastian led her along the path, away from the lit braziers, deep into the shadows. "There's a bench tucked away in a topiary alcove. We can sit there."

"Only sit?" she teased.

"I have a list of all the ways I mean to please you tonight." A list as long as his arm. "Let's begin by talking. When you hear what I have to say, it's guaranteed to make kissing better."

Desperate to begin at once, he brought her to an abrupt

halt, ready to haul her against his chest and whisper sweet nothings. But a masculine voice reached his ears, one he knew to be Lucius Daventry.

"Hush." Sebastian pressed his finger to Ailsa's lips and lowered his voice. "I heard Daventry mention your name." He pointed to where the path forked left, leading to the secluded bench.

Keeping tight to the dense foliage, they crept closer.

A quick peek around the hedge confirmed Daventry stood amid the shadows while Lady Perthshore sat on the bench.

"But you distinctly said there'd be no more meddling."

"Sometimes people need a gentle coaxing to see what is glaringly obvious," Daventry said. "Anyone would think I'm asking you to commit a crime."

"Interfering is a crime. I enjoy good gossip like the rest of us, particularly when presenting a certain Scottish lady with options. Still, I'm tired of writing titbits for the *Scandal Sheet*."

Ailsa nudged him and mouthed, *Lady Perthshore writes for the Scandal Sheet!*

Sebastian was more interested in what the matron meant by giving a Scottish lady options. Perhaps it explained the influx of gentlemen interested in dancing with Ailsa.

"All I'm asking is that you mention certain topics amongst your circle of friends. All information you relay will be factual. Consider it akin to sharpening Cupid's arrow."

After a brief silence, the lady huffed. "Who is it this time? Don't say Pilkington. The man is a consummate bore and dribbles into his soup."

Daventry cleared his throat. "The Chance brothers."

Good Lord!

Aaron Chance would be livid if he knew.

"Those rogues at Fortune's Den? You go too far, Daventry, too far. What lady in her right mind would seek an alliance with those unprincipled brutes?"

"They're rogues by circumstance, not birth."

"Yes, their grandfather might have been an earl, but no amount of blue blood can change the fact they had Ignatius Delmont for a father."

Sebastian peered around the hedge to see Daventry opening his arms wide. "Am I not proof every scoundrel can redeem himself?"

"Piffle! Your father was a scoundrel. You've always had morals."

"I believe the same is true of the men at Fortune's Den."

Sensing the conversation was drawing to a close—and not wanting to be caught snooping—Sebastian drew Ailsa along the path and back to the main garden.

"What shall we do?" Ailsa said once they'd locked themselves inside the small orangery. "Should we mention it to Christian?"

Sebastian laughed. "If Daventry thinks he can get Aaron Chance to marry, good luck to him. The man would rather rot in hell than walk down the aisle."

Ailsa took hold of his hands, pulling him away from the window and into the verdure. "Mr Daventry played a part in seeing our relationship blossom. Are ye nae worried we've been tricked by a master?"

"Tricked?" Sebastian laughed. They'd not been misled. He'd always had the greatest respect for her, and had simply stopped himself from feeling anything more profound. "All Daventry did was encourage us to spend time together. I love you. I knew the moment I touched you, my life would never be the same."

She nibbled her bottom lip. "Are ye sure?"

This glimpse of vulnerability touched him deeply. She

wouldn't be saying such things had they not overheard Daventry's conversation. "Love, I've never been more certain of anything."

"Perhaps we never broke the spell. Ye lacked heart when repeating the ritual."

"Yes, because it's all nonsense. And on the slim chance I was wrong, I didn't want to stop loving you. It had nothing to do with Daventry or his machinations."

To prove his point, he captured her chin and kissed her.

She responded with the same feverish intensity, her tongue sliding desperately over his. Heat chased through his veins, pooling hot and heavy in his loins. The need to have her left him breathless.

"We'll not spend our wedding night here," he said, dragging his mouth from hers with a growl of reluctance.

"Then take me home to bed." Her hand slid seductively down his waistcoat to stroke his throbbing erection. "We start the long journey to Scotland tomorrow, and I'm keen to know what's on yer list."

He hissed a breath. "It's a very long list."

"Tell me."

He stilled her wandering fingers before he lost control and took her on the cold floor. "I have a gift for you first. I know you can barely keep your hands off me, but a man must make a romantic gesture on his wedding day."

Excitement glistened in eyes that looked emerald-green in the darkness.

His gift would be perfect.

He reached into his coat pocket and handed her the square box. "I know you miss the Highlands and probably wish you'd married a Scotsman, but I wanted to give you something to remind you of home."

"I'd be nae one's bride had we nae married." Thankfully,

she removed her hand from his throbbing cock to cup his cheek. "My home is here now."

She opened the box, her eyes widening as she gazed at the gold brooch and the oval emerald between two entwined hearts. "'Tis a Luckenbooth, though I've never seen one this beautiful."

"I'm told it's a Scottish love token."

"Aye." Her smile faded. "But now I feel terrible. I should have bought ye something special. When ye open my gift, ye'll think all I want is yer mastery in bed."

Intrigued, he probed her further. "What did you buy? You may as well tell me now. You know what will happen once we're home."

She hesitated briefly. "A first edition of Crawshaw's book of British trees." A pretty pink blush stained her cheeks. "I thought we could make another list, make it our mission to find those in secluded places."

Sebastian's breath caught in his throat. He didn't think he could love her more than he did in that moment. It wasn't that he found the idea arousing. It was that someone cared enough to plan a future with him.

"Do ye know how many species of trees there are in England?"

Sebastian kissed her tenderly on the lips. "No, but I shall have immense pleasure finding out."

Thank you!

I hope you enjoyed reading *No One's Bride.*

What does Mr Daventry have planned for Christian Chance?
What does it have to do with artefacts at the museum? And
can a man who puts family first ever hope to fall in love?

Find out in …

A Little Bit Dangerous
Rogues of Fortune's Den - Book 1

Made in United States
Orlando, FL
26 June 2023

34538899R00178